AZ Murder Goes . . . Artful

This book is lovingly dedicated to

Louis Henry Silverstein
May 17, 1938-July 5, 2001

Beloved bookman and bibliographer
who with his usual wicked wit
preferred the title "Literary Anthropologist"

AZ Murder Goes ... Artful

Edited by
Barbara Peters with Susan Malling-Foster

Poisoned Pen Press

Poisoned Pen Press
6962 E. First Ave. Ste. 103
Scottsdale, AZ 85251
www.poisonedpenpress.com
info@poisonedpenpress.com

Printed in the United States of America

Table of Contents

Introduction

To many of us in the mystery world, the month of February brings to mind beautiful Scottsdale, Arizona and the *AZ Murder Goes...*conference sponsored by the indefatigable Barbara Peters and The Poisoned Pen. In 1996, the inaugural theme was the classic crime novel, followed in 1997 by *AZ Murder Goes...Artful.*

I was there in 1996, and I should have been there in 1997. I had my airline ticket in my pocket, but a last-minute family emergency kept me away. So, together with you, I've looked forward to the vicarious pleasure of enjoying the conference through the witty, informative, inspiring lectures now gathered in this volume.

It's a particular joy for me to write this introduction, as I've had the honor of publishing Philip Craig, Aaron Elkins, and Sharyn McCrumb on the Scribner list, and I live "just down the road a piece," as we say in the South, from Nevada Barr. They, and the other contributors, are among our finest examples of the way in which art and mystery form a splendid partnership, and they and their writing typify why I, personally, love art mysteries and will continue to publish them whenever I can.

The juxtaposition of art and crime fiction is, of course, nothing new.

Looking back to the revered Golden Age, we see art playing a recurring role in the novels of Ngaio Marsh, Dorothy L. Sayers, Michael Innes, and many others. The trend continues today, perhaps even stronger, with writers such as Jonathan Gash, John Malcolm, Iain Pears, Jane Langton, Marcia Muller. The list could go on and on.

Why do we crave mysteries about art, and what, exactly do we mean by art? Art, in the context of this book, can be found in museums, in architecture, in ancient monuments, in the folk customs of Appalachia, and even in the natural beauty of our national parks and vacations retreats. I, for one, have always wished I had taken Art 101 in college, but rumor had it that there were just too many slides to remember. Now, through the world of mystery, I, like others, can catch up on some of the magical essence of art that my 18-year-old self missed decades ago.

It's easy to see the appeal of the traditional art setting for the mystery novelist. Museum-quality art means big money, and where there's money, there's often greed and envy, and maybe even forgery and murder. Interesting characters and deliciously devious plots abound.

But character and a plot idea are only the beginning. All of the writers represented here share a passion for research. For Nevada as she penetrates deep into virtually uncharted caves, for Sharyn as she wanders the hills of western North Carolina and discovers previously unknown facts about her own family history, for Elizabeth as she crawls into ancient tombs along the Nile, for Aaron as he explores the great museums of Italy, for Keith as he ponders Frank Lloyd Wright in an unlikely landscape, for Phil as he delights for the first time in the island paradise that is to become his home and inspiration, for Nicholas as he uncovers wonderful secrets—could they be true?—among the art-world powerful, and for Roy, who shows us an unsuspected side of London, it's the research that lights the fire. It takes on a life of its own, leading in thrilling and unexpected directions.

In these pages you'll encounter some of the most gifted of contemporary mystery writers, you'll appreciate their quiet humor, their imagination, their attention to nuance. You'll learn something about the process but even more about the art of mystery writing. *AZ Murder Goes...* provides a magnificent opportunity for writers and readers to meet, in person or through the printed page, to reflect on the enduring power and pleasure of mystery fiction.

I haven't yet asked for a refund on that unused plane ticket of mine. I plan to head for Scottsdale again soon for another unique and stimulating encounter with mystery in the Arizona desert.

Susanne Kirk
Executive Editor, Scribner

Arts

Aaron Elkins

◇

The Mystery of Art
(and Vice-Versa)

The Mystery of Art
(and Vice-Versa)

In 1985, when I turned in my third novel about the "skeleton detective," Gideon Oliver, I concluded with regret that that particular series was just about played out. How many things, after all, can you say about bones? (I'm glad to report that I was premature; Gideon Oliver is alive and thriving, currently in the south of France working on his tenth adventure.) What I needed, I thought, was another protagonist, another voice, and—above all—another subject with enough substance to keep me involved through book after book, enough innate interest to appeal to readers, and enough credible possibilities for skullduggery to make it a plausible setting for foul play. Given those requirements, it wasn't exactly rocket science to come up with art.

If ever a milieu was a natural for the murder mystery, it is the art world, the world of collectors and museums. It has everything a mystery-writer could dream of: objects worth millions, clever forgers, wacky eccentrics, pretentious stuffed shirts, slick wheeler-dealers, and more ingenious scams than anyone will ever know—all set in a burnished context of wealth, avarice, naked greed, and simmering envy.

Happily, there are also plenty of fascinating intellectual byways to take one's characters down, and it's these I'd like to consider for a while. In each of the books I've put him in,

Chris Norgren, a curator of Renaissance and Baroque art, has gotten himself deeply involved in a case of art forgery—which, knock on wood, he has always managed to solve. At the same time, he has yet to resolve satisfactorily, even for himself, the question of just what a forgery *is*.

It's trickier than it seems at first glance. Say Peter Paul Rubens paints a picture and signs it; that's an authentic work of art, right? On the other hand, if I carefully paint a picture in Rubens' style and sign Rubens' name to it, that's just as obviously a forgery, right?[1] Easy enough, but those are only the extremes, and there are lots of in-betweens. Rubens, like a lot of other Old Masters, had a studio full of apprentice painters whose shoulders he leaned over and whose pictures he corrected, sometimes extensively. So what would you call a picture in which the finishing touches on the important parts—the faces and hands—were largely applied by Rubens, but the rest—bodies, background, etc.—was painted by an unknown apprentice? Is it a Rubens? Say he painted a full ninety percent of it, does that make it a Rubens? What about eighty percent? Forty percent? Ten percent? What if, regardless of the percentage that he painted, he signed it with his own name, as he often did? Does *that* make it a Rubens?

What if he *did* paint most of it, but *didn't* sign it, but some enterprising nineteenth-century or twentieth-century dealer, recognizing it for what it was, added a discreet little "PP Rubens" in the lower right corner just to give it a little oomph…and increase its selling price by a cool 10,000 percent, from $20,000 to $2,000,000?

These questions are important because there are hundreds, maybe thousands, of these things still floating around, every one of them a potential source of fraud and other assorted

---

1. Well, actually it isn't. There's no law against doing that, or artificially aging the canvas, or even going so far as to put phony Flemish inscriptions in faded brown ink on the back, or even claiming to anyone who will listen that it is a genuine Rubens. Technically, it becomes a forgery only when I try to *sell* it as one.

villainies. Of course, when you have students and apprentices like Van Dyck and Jordaens, which Rubens did, the level of art is likely to be pretty high, but that doesn't change the potential for hanky-panky.

The same applies to Rembrandt and his even more gigantic workshop—or factory, as it has been called. One of the tasks that Rembrandt would set out for his students was for them to make exact copies of his paintings. They would be richly praised by the master himself for making copies indistinguishable from his paintings. You may rest assured that there are plenty of these still around, a good many with Rembrandt's signature having been applied, shall we say, posthumously. And one of his last—and best—apprentices, Aert de Gelder, continued working in Rembrandt's style for fifty years after Rembrandt's death, so just imagine how many Rembrandt-like paintings have been floating around for the last 350 years, practically begging for someone to scrawl a single word—"Rembrandt"—across the bottom.

And bear in mind, on paintings like these, scientific analysis is virtually useless—the wood panels or canvases are the same ones used by Rembrandt himself, the pigments are the same ones that were in use at the time, the techniques are the same. So how do you "prove" something like that is or isn't by Rembrandt?

On top of all this, both Rubens and Rembrandt—and their workshop-factories—executed copies to order by the wagon-load. These factors, and a great many similar ones, make life hairy and full of risk in the art world, and make for terrific, twisty mystery plots.

Do you know the famous Gilbert Stuart portrait of George Washington? Chances are, you think you've seen the original in a museum in your part of the country, and you're right— sort of. There's one in the Met, one in the National Gallery... and approximately forty others out there, all the same, and all painted by Stuart in 1795. And the very next year he painted Washington from life again—the so-called "Athenaeum" version, the one on the dollar bill—and then made approximately seventy-five copies of *that* one on commission. Are they all "authentic," or is the first one *more* "authentic" than the others?

Perhaps you know John Singleton Copley's huge painting of a seafaring disaster, called *Watson and the Shark*, a thrilling and beautiful scene showing a man being rescued from the sea with a monstrous shark trying to get at him. You may have seen it at the National Gallery in Washington—or at the Boston Museum of Fine Arts. The National Gallery one came first—commissioned by the fortunate Mr. Watson himself, but the Boston one—an exact replica—was painted in the same year, 1778. Is one the "original" and therefore far more desirable and worth much more money? Or are they both equally original? If you say the second is a copy and only the first is an original, then what would you say if the first had been accidentally burnt up in a fire in Copley's studio before he sent it off, so he sat down and did another—now the only one. Is it still just a copy, or is it the original? Might you feel differently about it, depending on whether you were trying to sell it or trying to buy it?

And what do you do with a Michelangelo that is an exact copy of a painting by an earlier, lesser artist, and was even artificially aged by the young Michelangelo to make it look more like the real thing? Is it a fake? A fake what? A *real* what?

For that matter, getting down to the basics now, just what exactly is wrong with a fake? That is, if somebody named John Jones paints a picture completely in the manner of Henri Matisse—not a copy of a Matisse, but a picture in Matisse's style—with such competence and flair that it is every bit as beautiful as a fine Matisse, and in fact totally indistinguishable from a genuine Matisse (except, possibly, with the aid of electron microscopy, spectroscopic analysis, and so on), why should we value it any less than a real Matisse? A case in point is Rembrandt's *Man with a Golden Helmet*, one of the world's most revered and beloved works of art—until a decade or so ago when along came a nasty new technique called neutron photography, which smugly managed to prove that it hadn't been painted by Rembrandt at all, but by some unknown—talented but unknown—contemporary. At which point the art world went into one of its periodic blue funks and the offending painting was hustled off to the basement of its Berlin Museum in disgrace.

Well, why? Had a beautiful object ceased to exist? No, it was still right there. Was it any less beautiful than before? Of course not, it was the same painting. Did discrediting it mean it was any less masterfully painted? Not at all. Did it make people love the picture itself any less than before?

You better believe it.

Why, exactly? That's the question, and I don't know any completely satisfactory answer. Art philosophers and art historians have been arguing happily, or at least vigorously, about it for centuries. But what I do know is that questions, ambiguities, and disagreements like these make for wonderful plots, motives, and red herrings around which to weave the nasty business of murder, thievery, and the other elements that are at the heart of a mystery novel.

There are other aspects too. Recently, I've gotten more and more interested in the ethics of cultural property, primarily the question of: Who Owns Art? This is a much more current issue than the old controversies about whether or not England should give the Elgin marbles back to Greece or if the Benin bronzes in American museums should be returned to Africa. Say, for example, that your parents lived in Poland, or France, or somewhere else in occupied Europe during the Second World War and that their prize possession was a small Turner watercolor, bought years before for the equivalent of $1,000. The painting was then confiscated by the Nazis to go into Hitler's or Goering's collection, but disappeared from sight at the war's end. You and your family have done what you can to hunt for it, but to no avail.

Now you open up the *New York Times* and see a photograph of it on the front page of the Arts section. It has just sold at Christie's for $1,200,000. You get on the phone immediately. You explain that it was originally stolen from your family and that it is your property. Let's say that you even have the papers to prove it beyond a doubt (which is hardly ever the case in a situation like this). What happens? Does the person who bought it have to turn it over to you because it's stolen property? Why should he? He's not a Nazi, he didn't steal anything. He paid his own good money for it (just as your family did originally), buying it from a legitimate auction house, which bought it from a legitimate collector, who bought it from a legitimate dealer, who bought it from…etc., etc., back through the mists of time to 1945 and beyond. And if he *does* turn it over to you, what about that million-plus dollars that he's out? Will Christie's give it back to him? If so, will the collector who sold it through the auction house reimburse Christie's for the loss? Why should she? Why should any of them? They all bought the painting on good faith. And what do the courts have to say about this? They haven't worked it out either, although American courts in general have leaned in favor of the original owner in such cases, while European courts tend to favor the good-faith purchaser. Either way, somebody is going to wind up feeling extremely unhappy and ill-used—with considerable justification. As you can see, there are wonderfully complex legal and moral issues involved—more than enough to kill for.

Sometimes it seems to me that Chris spends half his time arguing and thinking about this kind of thing, and if I'm going to be frank, I have to admit it's the half that I have the most fun with. Happily, I don't expect to run out of material any time soon.

Photo Credit: John Dawson

Aaron Elkins

Biography

Ex-professor Aaron Elkins has been writing mysteries since 1982, winning an Edgar in 1988, an Agatha (with his wife Charlotte) in 1992, and a Nero Wolfe Award in 1993. His two series feature anthropologist-detective Gideon Oliver and art curator-sleuth Chris Norgren. His nonseries mystery, *Loot*, replaces Chris with another, and remarkably similar, art curator named Ben Revere. In addition, he and Charlotte co-author a mystery series about struggling female golfer Lee Ofsted. Aaron's work has been (roughly) translated into a major TV series and has been published in seven languages. Gideon Oliver's case, *Twenty Blue Devils*, was a selection of the Mystery Guild and the Readers Digest Condensed Mystery

Series. Aaron has served on the Mystery Writers of America's national board of directors. The Elkinses live on Bainbridge Island in Washington State, their marriage having survived (more or less intact) a series of moves coast to coast and their continuing collaboration on novels and short stories.

Aaron has a special tie with Arizona, having received an M.A. from the University of Arizona in Tucson.

Bibliography

The Gideon Oliver Novels:
> *Fellowship of Fear*, 1982
> *The Dark Place*, 1983
> *Murder at the Queen's Armes*, 1985
> *Old Bones*, 1987
> *Curses!*, 1989
> *Icy Clutches*, 1990
> *Make No Bones*, 1991
> *Dead Men's Hearts*, 1994
> *Twenty Blue Devils*, 1997
> *Skeleton Dance*, 2000

The Chris Norgren Novels:
> *A Deceptive Clarity*, 1987
> *A Glancing Light*, 1991
> *Old Scores*, 1993

The Ben Revere Novel:
> *Loot*, 1999

With Charlotte Elkins, The Lee Ofsted Novels:
> *A Wicked Slice,* 1989
> *Rotten Lies*, 1995
> *Nasty Breaks*, 1997

Nicholas Kilmer

◇

*Your Secret is Safe
with Us*

Your Secret is Safe with Us

I want to stay in business, so I'm stuck with fiction.

I was actually party to one art crime I can mention—but merely to prevent it. As agent for a person who owned a great deal of inherited southwestern oil money, I had executed the purchase (at an auction that took place at the Opéra Comique in Paris—a romantic occasion if it hadn't been so hot), of a painting by an associate of Gauguin's, for which we had spent a lot of my client's money. After the purchase was made, over string beans and champagne at a sidewalk café, my client revealed that he or she preferred the right half of the picture. "Now I own it, I'll cut it down the middle and throw away the left half," he or she announced.

I persuaded my client that since the painting was destined to go over the mantle in a house that was not yet completed, the architect might build a trick wall to conceal the offending portion of the picture. Then, should they wish one day to put the work back into circulation....

Before going into the art business, I'd been an academic for many years, finishing up as dean of a small art college that crashed and burned just as I was thinking that I had better start to seek my fortune. I began buying and selling used paintings and did all right during the dizzy and irresponsible inflation of the art market during the eighties until the bottom of the S & L economy started leaking and threatened to fall out the bottom of the paper sack it—and we—are all in together.

A friend and client, who had exited publishing, suggested that people who'd lost their shirts in commodities and real estate were heading for jail and so couldn't buy art any longer, but still must be entertained. There was still sure to be a market of a sort for books. Why didn't I write about the art business until times got better. "Art crime," he enthused. "Forgery, skullduggery, smuggling, theft—you know all about the art market."

As his slip acknowledged, in the art world it is not always easy to distinguish between crime and normal business, since the trade is burdened with even less regulation than the S & L's had carried. The possibilities blossomed before me. The art trade was filled with entertaining characters, far more able and interesting than myself, who shake off stories like dogs coming out of a pond. So I started writing. Since I did not want to step out of the business forever, I counseled caution to myself. Keep it fiction.

Because the art world is a small world, it would hardly be prudent to offend my clients, friends, colleagues, and enemies, most of whom can read, and all of whom (like me) prefer to breast their cards forever.

But when I maneuvered fiction into my sights, the romance of the real kept getting in the way, striving to lure me into the have-your-cake-and-eat-it trap of the *roman à clef*. There were stories already so well known in the art business that I could not be accused of revealing confidences if I were to retail them under my own covers, such as that of the museum director who, having been caused by his or her board of trustees to purchase a Renaissance painting in Italy and smuggle it out, was fired when caught in the act. He or she was not reinstated even after the painting, returned to its native haunts, was discovered to be a fake. A fun story when fleshed out, but how could I demean it into pretended fantasy without reopening old wounds in individuals and institutions on whose good sides it was better to be. In the above instance, three of the ex-director's children are now respected members of the art establishment, with whom I do, or did, or may wish to do business now and then.

But supposing there was a market for crime stories. I recalled the time many years ago when I first met A, now a good friend: an art dealer. Let us say A and I met in Utah. A had been responsible for the sale of a painting to another colleague, B—which painting I happened to be in the position to unmask as a fraud. In age and quality the picture was not far distant from what it purported to be. The problem was that a signature had recently been added to it. Though the painting was honest, its signature was forged. Forgery is a crime, of which neither A nor B was guilty, and of which, in fact, both were victims in this case. But although neither of them was at fault, I could not recount the story without embarrassing A and B, one of whom had purchased, and the other sold, a fraud. And I would wish to encourage them to be equally discreet with stories they both have at their fingertips that would embarrass me.

I decided that since truth was not an option, given how small the art world was, I must not fictionalize by starting with the people and events I knew, and altering them. I reasoned that if I made fictional characters of those with whom I did, or wanted to do, business, people would point fingers at each other, look sly and knowing, and refuse to understand that I meant to be innocent of all innuendo. (In fact, in spite of my best efforts, my colleague A recently telephoned me and said, "I have to get a copy of your *Man with a Squirrel*, because I just heard from X (a Boston dealer) that there's a character in it who is a great parody of Y (a conservator)." I can deny this all I want. The half-life of such rumors will outlast my protests.

But between us, my own experience is out. I swear it. I will not invent and publish a character who delivers the remark (while contemplating a luscious nude): "A million dollars is too much to spend on a picture we'd have to keep on the second floor." Or another just to drop this conversational grace note, "Then I went back to my hotel...sorry, not *my* hotel, I mean the hotel where I was *staying.*"

The art world's too small and everyone in it knows each other far better than I do. They'd find the person I had in mind. If not, they'll make one up.

But there are moments I've lived through that are begging to be used. For instance, picture me, at 6:17 a.m. on a December morning in 1988, for example, standing at the bank of urinals in a men's room in an airport outside Houston, or Atlanta, between planes. There swaggers up to the other end of the bank of urinals a man or woman I recognize although he or she is in a pilot's uniform this time, gold braid and all. I haven't seen the pilot for six months. He or she still owes me a hundred dollars to reimburse me for the hotel room in which I had arranged to show pictures a colleague of mine had asked me to offer the pilot and a mystery client the pilot was to bring—which client was said to be shy of buying in a gallery, he or she being a wealthy and eccentric collector. While we waited in the hotel room for the client to join us, the pilot, who was with one of the large commercial airlines which has since gone the way of the college I'd been dean of (i.e. out the bottom of the sack), boasted that he or she had been the agent who had put together the Ferdinand Marcos collection. (This had proved to be as prudent an investment for the strongman as the emperor's new suit, if barely less transparent—and many dealers in the world's capitals had been delighted to assist in its acquisition. Once the dictator was on the skids, the Marcos group of "old master" pictures had been hastily refused by every dealer, and any auction house in civilization, that hoped to remain in business for another generation. It was finally de-accessioned at questionable auction on Long Island for something like ten cents on the dollar.)

My chance encounter with the pilot at the urinal was simply one reminder of how small the art world is.

In this December of 1988 the art market was running fast and strong, fed mostly by the promise of profits in everything. That morning at the urinal I had under my arm a picture I had picked up from a client in, for instance, Arizona, which I hoped to sell in Florida or Michigan or Seattle later that day. In its cardboard and brown paper, it represented a small fortune to my client, who wanted the transaction speedy since the tax laws might be changing in a month.

In December of 1988 the art market was so inflated—or "healthy," as we preferred to say—that a single Jasper Johns had sold for seventeen million dollars. Goaded by the Japanese, the French Impressionists were up to as much as thirty five million a pop for a good one, and things were moving fast. For example, in that same month a New York dealer bought at auction in London, for close to half a million dollars, an eighteenth century American painting that not many months before had sold a few blocks away from their own show rooms, at the downscale New York branch of the same house, for around a thousand dollars. The painting had not changed between New York and London: only its provenance and attribution (and maybe its frame). This happened a week or so after the moment we have been contemplating, at the urinals, while I happened to be in Paris again for talks with a curator for a French museum. We were discussing a couple of paintings which the museum was considering for purchase. On account of their value and their importance, their owner felt there might be some difficulty bringing the paintings out of France officially, and they were too large for clandestine transport. As to the romance of this particular Paris trip—the sun rose at ten and set at four. The city of light was bleak and dark and mean and polluted, and somewhat silly. In honor of impending Christmas, the naked trees on the

Avenue Montaigne had been done up in enormous golden plastic bows. The curator I met with was reserved, moving about my friends' apartment, where I was showing the pictures, in an almost furtive way, and letting me do most of the talking. That was a busy week for the curator, I learned during the flight home, since he or she had just been indicted as a *receleur*, or receiver of stolen goods, on account of his or her role in the acquisition (as the museum's agent) of a major Old Master painting, which he or she had spotted in London (being offered at public auction) and recognized as having been illegally exported from France. The painting's putative owner, a barmaid from the south of France, was the former employee of an elderly heiress with whom the curator had corresponded about the painting in question before the heiress starved to death, locked into a bedroom of her villa, surrounded by a dwindling art collection—and cared for by the barmaid.

So when it seemed I must try writing for my living, the recollection of the encounter with the curator, like the moment at the airport urinal, retained some of that *frisson* of experience it seemed to me the author should impart in fiction. The sense of events coming together, also, was suggestive of that unreasonable logic that makes a story seem to have a structure, or at least a purpose.

My earlier encounter with the pilot had been abortive. The pilot's client, the supposedly wealthy and eccentric private collector, proved on arrival to be the well-known director of a well-known gallery, who was best known at the moment on account of being sued on account of his or her prevailing work ethic of taking paintings on consignment, selling them, and refusing to pay the owners.

Some images stay with you. A few months ago I came upon the reproduction of a painting that looked so similar in manner and subject to the one I had once torpedoed as a fraud in Utah, I thought—bingo! Maybe I know who actually painted the Utah picture. If I was right, and if I could demonstrate it, there might be value in that object after all— if I could find it after so long. So I called B, the colleague who had purchased the picture, and learned in confidence that once it had been discredited, B had sold it, along with a job lot of duds, to C, a notorious east coast painter/dealer/ forger. I called A, the dealer who had sold it to B, and learned, in confidence, the name of the notorious *other* east coast dealer in forged pictures—D—who had sold the thing to A initially.

In the convention of the trade these identities of buyers, sellers, and owners are normally not passed on, since like an auction house one of the art dealer's primary functions in the economy is to launder works of art. The dealer's principal stock in trade must be the ability to maintain a confidence: the ultimate reason why I must stick to fiction. But A and B and I had done business enough together over the years that we could trust each other; and B was grateful also since I had not very long ago been in the position to protect B from the disastrous purchase of another fraud. This was a painting I had known both before, and after, C had worked on it— again, by subtracting one signature in favor of a new one that would excite more enthusiasm in the market.

Since I believed I might have come upon the true identity of the Utah painting to which the fraudulent signature had been attached, and since the notorious forger/dealer C was the last person known to have the picture, I needed a practical approach to C, with whom I had never dealt directly. Presumably the picture had speedily sailed off again to auction, with a different signature on it, in Detroit or St. Louis or Spokane. But C might still have it kicking around, or might know where it was. A friend of mine, a scholar, had recently mentioned to me that he or she intended a cautious visit to C. On the principle that one must salt the mine, C did have good things sometimes, it was rumored, mixed in amongst the stock. Although we dealers do not usually show our hands in such matters, I had nothing to lose, and I told my friend the entire story of the Utah picture; sent photographs, clippings—whatever was necessary. I invited my friend to look into the history of the picture after it came into C's hands (as well as its earlier history if he or she could get that far, since I suspected that the picture in question had probably also been in C's hands *before* it was sold, by D, to A).

Now all this, if I were to add the substance of fiction, might serve as the armature for a good story. But if I were to tell it to everyone, my hope of making any money on the Utah picture would be lost.

We have for some reason lost sight of me about my business at the airport urinal.

The most fictitious thing about fiction is that it offers closure. In the art business, by contrast, only about six percent of all activity leads to any conclusion—and only six percent of that six percent is the conclusion one had wanted or intended.

Aside from a passing physical satisfaction, how might I take the fleeting moment at the urinal and let it flow toward a resolution that suggests that the various strains at issue have come together and are moving gracefully and inevitably toward sea level? The inconclusive and unresolving fact is, the pilot and I both allowed our moment of mutual recognition to remain existential, and neither acknowledged knowing the other. Whatever else may have been on his mind, the pilot recognized that it was worth a hundred bucks to him not to say hello. My own instinct was that for a hundred dollars I'd gotten off easy by not causing a scene, and by allowing confirmation of my identity to remain moot. My principal purpose was better served if it were not too broadly known that I had been in Houston or Atlanta that morning, between planes, with that particular painting under my arm.

As it turned out (and/or, let us say), I was to sell the painting later that day to a colleague who would sell it later that day to a colleague who would sell it later that day to a collector, a wealthy and eccentric individual who preferred not to do business with me directly.

The French curator has become director of the museum to whom I did not sell the paintings; which are now, however, no longer in France. I haven't seen the pilot again, not to talk to; and as to my friend the scholar—I never heard from him or her again about my project after the visit to C, the artist/ forger.

Because I hope to find another way to get my hands on the Utah picture, I will rely on you to keep this matter confidential.

Photo Credit: Ross Harris

Nicholas Kilmer

Biography

Formerly Dean of the Swain School of Design, Nicholas Kilmer presently makes his living as an art dealer. He is the author of an art mystery series and divides his time between Normandy and Boston with his wife Julia.

Bibliography

The Fred Taylor Novels:

Harmony in Flesh and Black, 1995
Man with a Squirrel, 1996
O Sacred Head!, 1997
Dirty Linen, 1999
Lazarus Arise, 2001

Other:

A Place in Normandy, 1997

Architecture

Keith Miles

Also known as Edward Marston

‹›

Building a Good Mystery

Building a Good Mystery

I begin this paper in the most appropriate place to initiate any discussion of Architecture—with Robert Mitchum.

When the great movie actor starred in a Western, the director explained to him in detail how he would make his initial appearance on screen. "Bob," he said. "You've been away from your wife and family a long time. You ride up over the brow of a hill and take a first look at your ranch, only to confront a disaster. Indians have attacked. The house is a smoking ruin, your wife has been raped and killed, your children have been murdered, and all your cattle have been rustled. As the camera comes in on your face for a close-up, the full horror of your tragedy must register in your face. Okay, Bob?"

Robert Mitchum shook his head. "Listen," he said. "I got three expressions. I look at the camera. I look to the right. I look to the left. Which one d'you want?"

That reply can be summed up in one word, and it is a reply which defines architecture.

Perspective. It all depends where you stand.

Perspective. It all depends what you see.

Perspective. It all depends what the architect wants to show.

Robert Mitchum was himself one of Hollywood's most enduring pieces of architecture, a man whose sculptured face had less expression and movement than those sculptures carved on Mount Rushmore.

Architects.

What is an architect?

A man—or a woman, of course—who designs and supervises the construction of a building.

The similarities between architects and mystery writers are obvious. They work in allied professions.

Both rely on their creative imagination to produce something out of nothing, to build a small monument to their talent.

Both choose their location with great care, select the best materials, and try hard to satisfy their clients.

Both strive to reconcile art with function, to create something which has both intrinsic aesthetic value and practical use.

Both deal with the relationship between form and content.

Like architects, mystery writers may be influenced by their predecessors, responsive to the work of their contemporaries, and affected by current fads and fashions.

Those of you who attended last year's pioneering conference, *AZ Murder Goes…Classic,* will remember the many surface affinities between the writers we discussed and architects.

In their different ways, Raymond Chandler and Dashiell Hammett built menacing urban landscapes, concrete jungles intersected by mean streets and unforgiving highways. They constructed their novels to block out light and create the dark shadows in which their heroes and villains alike live their lives. Only tough and uncompromising individuals like Philip Marlowe and Sam Spade can resist the suffocating effects of the Big City.

Erle Stanley Gardner was more of a jerry-builder, working at enormous speed to construct a serviceable story without too much attention to solid foundations. His most ingenious design was for the all-purpose courthouse which looms over the extraordinary career of Perry Mason, and in which he has some equally extraordinary legal triumphs.

Dorothy L. Sayers was a more stylish architect. Her novels have the symmetry and harmony of a Renaissance church with an occasional touch of Gothic excess thrown in, plus a mysterious crypt. At its best, Sayers' prose is finely-chiselled, like a slab of stone dressed to order before being winched up to take its appointed place in a grand edifice.

But it's with John Dickson Carr that the architectural analogy is most obvious. No mystery writer took such care over the structure and perspective of his novels. His work has more impossible-to-enter locked rooms than San Quentin Prison. In his most famous Gideon Fell mystery, *Three Coffins*, he gives us a sketch plan of the locked room. When he wanted to work on a larger scale, as in *The Mad Hatter Mystery*, he set the action in the Tower of London and prefaced the story with a detailed ground plan of that famous London landmark.

I'll abandon these parallels between architecture and mystery writing before I stub my toe against the many huge differences between the two callings.

◇ ◇ ◇

Let me now focus on a man whose career had a truly profound influence on twentieth century architecture and whose life had enough drama, romance, and tragedy to fill a hundred mysteries.

Frank Lloyd Wright.

Frank Lloyd Wright was born in 1867. Andrew Johnson was President. More than half of all working people in the United States were employed on farms. Prehistoric canals in Arizona Territory were cleared by the John Swirling Company to bring water from the Salt River to the fertile lands of the valley. The town of Phoenix began to grow. But the Poisoned Pen Mystery Bookstore was only a large cactus with literary inclinations.

1867 was also the year when Strauss's *Blue Danube Waltz* was performed for the first time. And when Anthony Trollope published *The Last Chronicle of Barset*.

When Wright died in 1959 here in Arizona, he was almost ninety-two. Eisenhower was President. Most Americans lived and worked in cities. The micro chip had been invented. Space travel was possible. Norman Mailer, John Updike, William Burroughs, and Saul Bellow all published major novels in that year. Buddy Holly died in a plane crash.

The Guggenheim Museum—designed by Wright—opens in New York.

Those outline facts tell us that we are dealing with a remarkable man whose life spans the most intense period of change in history and yet who constantly adapted himself to each new revolution.

Wright was a survivor. A man with an unparalleled record of over seventy years as a working architect. A man who lived life to the full in every way and who did not know the meaning of the word "retirement."

He was ninety when he designed the Grady Gammage Memorial Auditorium in Tempe, Arizona.

Life.

Wright was born in Richland Center, Wisconsin. His father was William Wright. William had studied law at Amherst College but made a living as a peripatetic music teacher. When his first wife died, he met Anna Lloyd-Jones at a music festival. Though seventeen years younger, she fell in love and married him.

For a while they lived in Weymouth, Massachusetts, where William Wright was the Baptist Minister. They then moved to Madison, Wisconsin. Frank Lloyd Wright and his sisters went to the local school and spent their vacations on the Lloyd-Jones farm in Spring Green.

Wright inherited from his parents a deep love of music and a creative instinct. Something of his father's religious streak ran through him beside a fierce pride in his Welsh heritage on his mother's side. Happy times spent in physical exercise on the farm gave him his lifelong preference for the country over the city.

1885. Catastrophe. William Wright deserted his wife and family, never to return. It was a shattering blow to his son. Frank Lloyd Wright's schooling came to an end. He had to work.

What happened next is best described by John Dos Passos in *Big Money*, the final part of his USA trilogy. This strange, rambling, Marxist view of the American way of life is studded with biographies of real people whom the author admired. One such man was Frank Lloyd Wright—Architect.

A muggy day in late spring in 1888, a tall youngster with fine eyes and a handsome, arrogant way of carrying his head, arrived in Chicago with seven dollars left in his pocket from buying his ticket from Madison with some cash he'd got pawning *Plutarch's Lives*, a Gibbon's *Decline and Fall of the Roman Empire* and an old, fur-collared coat.

Before leaving home to make himself a career in an architect's office (there was no architecture course at Wisconsin to clutter his mind with stale Beaux-Arts drawings), the youngster had seen the dome of the State Capitol in Madison collapse on account of the bad rubblework in the piers, some thieving contractors' skimping materials to save the politicians their rake-off, and perhaps a trifling but deadly error in the architect's plans.

He never forgot the burst of raw masonry, the flying plaster, the soaring dustcloud, the mashed bodies of the dead and dying being carried out, set faces livid with plasterdust.

Walking round downtown Chicago, crossing and recrossing the bridges over the Chicago River in the jingle and clatter of the traffic, the rattle of vans and loaded wagons, and the stamping of big dray horses and the hooting of towboats with barges and the rumbling whistle of lake steamers waiting for the draw.

He thought of the great continent stretching a thousand miles east and south and north, three thousand miles west, and everywhere, at mineheads, on the shores of newly-dredged harbours, along watercourses, at the intersections of railroads sprouting shacks, roundhouses, tipples, grain elevators, stores, warehouses, tenements, great houses for the wealthy set in broad tree-shaded lawns, domed statehouses on hills, hotels, churches, opera houses and auditoria.

He walked with long eager steps toward the untrammeled future opening in every direction for a young man who'd kept his hands to his work and his wits sharp to invent.

The same day he landed a job in an architect's office.

If that description sounds too romanticised, it is very much in keeping with the lyrical style of Frank Lloyd Wright's own autobiography. Wright did not take the same collectivist approach to life and art that Dos Passos took, but he was equally clever at mythologising himself.

"The same day he landed a job in an architect's office."

The architect was Joseph Lyman Silsbee, but Wright stayed less than a year before moving on to the man who became his mentor.

Louis Sullivan, partner in the firm of Adler and Sullivan, was one of the city's most progressive architects at a time when Chicago was setting the pace in design and construction for the rest of America. Wright could not have had a better employer or teacher.

He learned quickly and made such an impact at the firm that the following year—1889—they advanced him money to enable him to get married and to build his home and studio at Oak Park, Illinois. Over a century later, this is still a stunning building that is replete with features quintessentially the work of Frank Lloyd Wright.

Always short of money, Wright found it a real struggle when children came along. He took on bootleg commissions, designing houses for wealthy clients but passing someone else off as the architect of record. Louis Sullivan knew nothing of this second career of his employee until he happened to drive past one of these new houses. He recognised Wright's architectural signature at once, confronted him, then fired him.

That was in 1893. From that point on, Frank Lloyd Wright was on his own. Before 1900, he produced at least seventy designs and forty-nine of them were built. The most significant of them was the Winslow House in 1894. William Winslow was president of a company of architectural ironmongers. He commissioned the new house in River Forest, a suburb to the west of Oak Park.

It is a low, elongated structure with a hipped roof and wide eaves which gave it a Japanese flavour. Its clean lines and individuality brought in a number of other commissions.

But it was in the new century that Wright really blossomed. He wrote many speeches and articles to propound his philosophy and he was the subject of a feature in *Architectural Review*. In 1901, his first Prairie House appeared. For the next seven to eight years, he developed and refined the Prairie Style.

Initially inspired by Sullivan, the Prairie School was characterised by horizontality, open plans, and an emphasis on the natural qualities of materials. With a simple basic idea, Wright achieved the most amazing variety of styles. Look at the key residential buildings of this period: The Willit House, The Heurtley House, Dana House, Cheney House, Glasner House, Robie House, Coonley House. Each is a typical Prairie House and yet quite different from the others.

The finest example is the Dana House in Springfield, Illinois. It is T-shaped with the longest arm extended by the addition of a pergola, containing the family's art collection. It is roofed with low, broad gables.

The buff-coloured exterior bricks and the bronze lustered roof tiles are reflected inside the house in its brown, russet, and gold furnishing. Wright did not just design the house. He designed the carpets, drapery, light fixtures, and furniture. The Dana House was a piece of total architecture, a fully-realised vision of Frank Lloyd Wright.

He was famous, prosperous, and in demand. As well as houses, he built the Hillside Home School in Spring Green, Wisconsin; the Larkin Administration Building in Buffalo, New York (over the entrance of which he inscribed the dictum, *Honest Labor Needs No Master, Simple Justice Needs No Slaves*); and the celebrated Unity Temple in Oak Park, Illinois.

In 1909, he turned his back on it all. He left his wife and children, went to Germany to write and produce a portfolio, and lived in sin with Mamah Borthwick Cheney, wife of client Edwin Cheney. The scandal made Wright *persona non grata* in Chicago. He stayed in Germany, then Italy, with the so-called scarlet woman, then came back to a storm of disapproval and professional neglect.

The next couple of years living with Mamah were the least productive of his career. They lived in isolation at Taliesin in Spring Green until tragedy struck in 1914. While Wright was away on business, a crazed employee set fire to Taliesin. Seven people died in the blaze, including Mamah and her two children.

Wright lost his house, his lover, his second family. Most men would have gone under. He responded by building Taliesin II. He met the new love of his life, Miriam Noel, and they lived intermittently in Japan while he worked on designs for the Imperial Hotel. When Tokyo was hit by a major earthquake, the building survived intact and Wright's reputation was enhanced.

Happiness turned sour when he divorced his first wife and married Miriam Noel. Within six months, she left him, but hounded him unmercifully. When he met and fell in love with the exotic Olgivanna Milanoff, the vengeful Miriam began legal action. She set private detectives on to the couple and had them arrested under the Mann Act at one point. She also tried to have Olgivanna, who came from Montenegro, deported.

Yet it was during this period—the 1920s—that Frank Lloyd Wright produced some of his most interesting work despite being beset by a series of difficulties. He was afflicted by domestic upheaval, a second fire at Taliesin, severe financial difficulties involving hostile moves from the bank, a bad press in Wisconsin, and an additional responsibility in the shape of his new child, Iovanna, born in 1926.

His most interesting work was not with huge projects like the Imperial Hotel. Nor with the massive skyscrapers with which other architects were making their names. Nor even with the industrial architecture into which millions of dollars were being poured. Frank Lloyd Wright specialised in domestic construction and designed houses for rich Californians. It was in this period that the Concrete Block System was developed.

It was yet another startling change of direction for Wright and showed once again his ability to reinvent himself in order to pursue new ideas and meet altered situations. Change was an accepted part of his life. As he later wrote in *The Future of Architecture* (1939):

> Architecture...proceeds, persists, creates according to the nature of man and his circumstances as they both change...The law of organic change is the only thing that mankind can know as beneficent or actual!

And what was the fruit of these Californian ventures?

> Barnsdall House, Beverly Hills
> Millard House, La Miniatura, Pasadena
> The Storer House, L.A.
> The Freeman House, L.A.
> The Ennis House, L.A.

Each building was a further improvement in the use of concrete blocks as the basic material for construction. To his rivals, who were busy absorbing international influences and creating massive architectural statements in major cities, it must have seemed odd that the great Frank Lloyd Wright was working on such a small canvas.

It was not just a case of simple necessity. Californian clients wanted him in ways that others did not. Wright was seriously committed to a faith in the virtues of the Concrete Block System. At its finest, it produced extraordinary results.

And it led to his involvement in the Arizona Biltmore Hotel.

Wright did not invent the system but he saw its potential and exploited it to the full. He took the most humble, unexciting, workaday building material—concrete—and turned it into a visual delight. Decorated concrete blocks, artfully assembled in large numbers, could produce the most spectacular results. The Californian houses are residential Xanadus, stately pleasure domes in miniature for the discerning eye and the wealthy client.

The clients had to be wealthy because, although the concrete blocks were relatively cheap to make, there was a degree of wastage in the process. Also, Wright was unable to keep within budget. Louis Sullivan coined the phrase "Form Follows Function." Wright's unspoken dictum was "Cost Follows Art."

It was not only the intricate patterned exteriors of the Californian houses which were celebrated. His treatment of interior space and design was equally startling. Furniture, fittings, drapery, carpets, and everything else was designed by Wright as part of a complete package.

The astonishing variety and (apparent) low cost of the Concrete Block System led to an article by A.N. Rebori in the December 1927 issue of *Architectural Record, Frank Lloyd Wright's Textile Block Construction: Experiments in California.* After reading the article, Albert Chase McArthur wrote to Wright, with whom he had worked as an apprentice, asking for permission to use the system—and for practical advice.

The request could not have come at a better time for Wright. Short of work and money, he was under several other pressures as well. Snatching at opportunity, he sent what turned out to be a fatal telegram from Spring Green.

"Dear Albert, Congratulations. Textile block ideal for your purpose. Should come out to help you start perhaps. FLW."

In seeking help from his old master, Albert Chase McArthur instead finished up with a design partner. The sorcerer came down to Arizona to work with his apprentice and it was this relationship which inspired *Murder in Perspective.* Where did Frank Lloyd Wright's vision end and Albert Chase McArthur's design start? Who was the real architect behind the hotel? That was the basic mystery with which I started.

Frank Lloyd Wright's architectural legacy is incomparable. As a human being, he was a flawed diamond: brilliant and many-faceted but containing a fissure of human fallibility. His life is compounded of domestic instability, wild romantic gestures, sexual peccadilloes, financial irresponsibility, and recurring tragedy.

He showed amazing resilience to overcome the endless setbacks, professional betrayals, and long periods of unemployment which he faced. It was a case of survival with honour.

Frank Lloyd Wright was America's greatest optician. He taught his country to see, to look at the way people lived through new and more critical eyes. He made them appreciate the concept of organic architecture. Buildings had to be extensions of nature and not brick or concrete denials of it.

Taliesin West in Arizona embodies the four architectural principles which dominated his work for seventy years: the Nature of the Site; Methods and Materials; Destruction of the Box; and Building for Democracy, letting architecture reflect and reinforce the basic freedoms and values of democracy.

From every perspective, Frank Lloyd Wright is one of the greatest creative artists of the twentieth century. Thanks to him, America has learned to look at its architecture in a very different way.

Recommended Books:
  Finis Farr: *Frank Lloyd Wright: A Biography*, 1961
  Ayn Rand: *The Fountainhead*, 1971
  Bruce Brooks Pfeiffer (ed): *Frank Lloyd Wright: Collected Writings, Vol. 2* (1930-32), 1992
  Brendan Gill: *Many Masks: A Life of Frank Lloyd Wright*, 1987
  Meryle Secrest: *Frank Lloyd Wright: A Biography*, 1992
  Robert L. Sweeney: *Wright in Hollywood: Visions of a New Architecture*, 1994

Keith Miles

Biography

Keith Miles, aka Edward Marston, Conrad Allen, and Martin Inigo, came from Wales to read Modern History at Oxford. He has been a university lecturer, radio, television, and theatre dramatist, and in addition to writing has worked as an actor and theatre director. He is the author of several mystery series, one Elizabethan in background, another revolving around the Domesday census of 1086 A.D., another set in the Restoration era, another brought forward to the early 20th Century under the name Conrad Allen, and yet another focusing on Frank Lloyd Wright under Keith Miles. As Miles and Inigo, he has also written mysteries with golf and sports backgrounds. His Elizabethan novel, *The Roaring Boy*, was a 1996 Edgar Allan Poe Award nominee for Best Novel.

The author is a well known host and raconteur at mystery events and served as the 1997 Chairman of the Crime Writers Association. When not travelling or fulfilling speaking engagements, he lives in rural isolation in Kent.

Bibliography

The Nicholas Bracewell Novels (as Edward Marston)
>   *The Queen's Head,* 1988
>   *The Merry Devils,* 1989
>   *The Trip to Jerusalem,* 1990
>   *The Nine Giants,* 1991
>   *The Mad Courtesan,* 1992
>   *The Silent Woman,* 1994
>   *The Roaring Boy,* 1995
>   *The Laughing Hangman,* 1996
>   *The Fair Maid of Bohemia,* 1997
>   *The Wanton Angel,* 1999
>   *The Devil's Apprentice,* 2001

The Domesday Books (as Edward Marston)
>   *The Wolves of Savernake,* 1993
>   *The Ravens of Blackwater,* 1994
>   *The Dragons of Archenfield,* 1995
>   *The Lions of the North,* 1996
>   *The Serpents of Harbledon,* 1996
>   *The Stallions of Woodstock,* 1998
>   *The Hawks of Delamere,* 1998
>   *The Wildcats of Exeter,* 1998
>   *The Foxes of Warwick,* 1999
>   *The Owls of Gloucester,* 1999
>   *The Elephants of Norwich,* 2000

The Christopher Redmayne Series (as Edward Marston)
>   *The King's Evil,* 1999
>   *The Amorous Nightingale,* 2000
>   *The Repentant Rake,* 2001

The Merlin Richards Series (as Keith Miles)
>*Murder in Perspective,* 1997
>*Saint's Rest,* 1999

The George Porter Dillman Series (as Conrad Allen)
>*Murder on the Lusitania,* 1999
>*Murder on the Mauretania,* 2000
>*Murder on the Minnesota,* 2002

The Alan Saxon Mysteries (as Keith Miles)
>*Bullet Hole,* 1986
>*Double Murder,* 1987
>*Green Murder,* 1990
>*Flagstick,* 1991
>*Bermuda Grass,* 2002

Other:
>*Stone Dead,* 1991
>*Touch Play,* 1991

Numerous Sports Books, Screen, Stage, and Television Plays, Children's Books, and Non-Fiction.

Roy Berkeley

>

Behind the Scenes in London

Behind the Scenes in London

I have just written an opinionated book that features my photos of 136 buildings in London.

No, I am not an architecture critic. I am a historian.

My book is called *A Spy's London*.

It all began when the British government began permitting people who served in SOE (Special Operations Executive, Britain's WWII sabotage-and-subversion outfit) to publish their carefully-edited memoirs. I had known that SOE's offices and safe-houses were located primarily in the Baker Street area (the organization was euphemized as "Baker Street") and several of the memoirs identified specific addresses. The next time my wife and I went to London I took with me a scribbled list of these addresses, intending to see whether the buildings were still there and whether any plaques would tell the passerby just what he or she was passing by. Well, yes and no. Yes, the buildings *were* still there, having survived the best efforts of the *Luftwaffe* and the real-estate developers, and no, there were no plaques or other indications of the momentous events and unique personalities associated with these very ordinary-looking buildings. I thought of doing a travel article about the secret history of this stretch of Baker Street. And then it occurred to me that there were other places in London where spies and spycatchers plied their separate trades—or merely *lived*—and that I had just invented a new kind of travel book.

◇◇◇

A Spy's London (like my current project, *A Spy's New York*) is, of course, not about the buildings themselves, but about what happened inside them. It is a look into the secret history of an otherwise well-known city. And it reminds the reader that events of great moment can be planned or executed in quite ordinary surroundings by people who may not be ordinary but are doing their best to seem so. It's also a kick to discover the secret histories of high-profile places like Harrods, Brown's Hotel, and Buckingham Palace, all of which made it into my book.

Since the London streetscape has changed very little in recent decades, it is possible, for example, to stand on the very stepstone with one's hand on the very doorknob that Soviet mole Guy Burgess turned when he walked out of his flat into New Bond Street for the last time. (Burgess thought he would just accompany fellow-mole Donald Maclean to France and hand him over to Soviet intelligence officers. The Soviets had other plans.)

And just as a work of fiction becomes more real, more enjoyable, more memorable when the author describes physical settings, so history can become more real, more enjoyable, more memorable when the reader has a strong sense of the physical settings of historic (and sometimes even Historic) events. The actual physical settings can either confirm one's mental picture of events and personalities or jar one into a better and deeper understanding of those events and personalities.

I didn't start with the *sites* and then try to find stories about them; in most cases I started with the *stories* and then found the sites. As an ex-newspaperman, I had expected to go through a newspaper's clips-file and get addresses. I quickly found out that British newspapers did not report the addresses of suspects or victims. But I did find a stash of London telephone directories dating back to the Thirties, Forties, and Fifties in a library in the old part of London known as The

Site 3

City. With them I was able to locate most of the people I was writing about, and tell their stories. (There was one person whose stranger-than-fiction story I *had* to tell—his real life was the stuff of spy fiction—but he had no phone. I spent an entire day going through the voter-registration records at Westminster City Hall for the last year I knew him to be alive, and I found him in the shabby rooming house where he had settled after coming in from the cold.)

And now let me tell you a few of the stories from *A Spy's London*. The sites, after all, are only pretexts to tell some interesting stories.

Site 3: 21 Queen Anne's Gate, SW1 (my Westminster Walk). This row of charming townhouses dates from 1704; the intricately-carved canopies over each doorway were executed by the same men who carved the figureheads of contemporary sailing ships. In 1919, the house at #21 became the office and official residence of the first chief of MI6 (aka Secret

Intelligence Service or SIS), Britain's CIA. Here the legendary Mansfield Smith-Cumming launched the more pretentious traditions of the Secret Intelligence Service: the chief is called "C" whatever his real name; he is (until quite recently) unknown to the public, even if fully known to adversarial intelligence services; he alone may use green ink for written communication. (Reinhard Heydrich was so impressed with SIS, I understand, that when he headed Hitler's *Sicherheitsdienst* he too insisted on being called "C" and he too established a green-ink monopoly.)

Any novelist inventing a Mansfield Smith-Cumming would be hooted out of town by the reviewers. The man fancied disguises and swordsticks. He built a secret passage connecting the rear of this building and the rear of 54 Broadway, around the corner. And after an automobile accident in France, it was probably he who spread the story that he had freed himself from the wreckage by hacking off his own leg. (The limb was surgically amputated the next day.) Smith-Cumming used even his wooden leg to promote his bizarre image, often stabbing the prosthesis with his letter-opener during conversation.

In 1966, SIS moved to modern Century House, south of the Thames, two miles away geographically but light-years away in its style of architecture and in the style of operations within.

Site 4: The Broadway Buildings, 54 Broadway, SW1 (my Westminster Walk). Novelist Ian Fleming had James Bond's unnamed service masquerading as Universal Export in a large office building near Regent's Park. (And he called the Chief of Service "M".) From friends who worked for SIS (as Fleming did not) he knew (as the general public did not) that SIS masqueraded as the Minimax Fire Extinguisher Company in this large office building near St. James's Park Tube Station. But Fleming accurately described the colored lights over the

Site 4

door to C's fourth-floor office here, which told his secretary whether or not he was to be disturbed.

The James Bond films encourage us to imagine SIS headquarters as glossy, glamorous, and high-tech. The reality here was otherwise. Kim Philby, who had no reason to dissemble in *this* matter, described 54 Broadway as "a dingy building, a warren of wooden partitions and frosted glass windows," served by "an ancient lift." The building itself is quite solid. Its steel frame probably prevented its collapse in 1944 when a V-1 flying bomb demolished a nearby chapel. Only by accident was the bomb deflected from slamming a ton of high explosives into the fourth-floor executive offices of MI6.

Imagine with me how the building must have looked in, say, 1942. The windows are taped (or boarded over) to protect against flying glass. In the lobby is a commissionaire, one of the many retired soldiers and sailors working all over London as doormen or messengers. Passersby often take shelter in the lobby from air-raids or weather; the commissionaire only interferes when anyone tries to go beyond the lobby. Few try. The roof has a thicket of radio antennae: odd for a fire extinguisher company. The roof also has a pigeon loft. Sir

Stewart Menzies (pronounced "Mengiss" for reasons I don't begin to understand) was "C" from 1939 to 1952 and he mistrusted radio communications for his operatives in France; he may have been the intelligence chief of a nuclear power, but he had been a horse-cavalry man in WWI and he remained in many ways a nineteenth-century man.

And, like his predecessors and successors, he was a secretive man. A well-known story, possibly even true, has George VI and Menzies conversing over dinner.

> The King: "Menzies, who is our man in Berlin?"
> Menzies: "Sire, if my service has a man in Berlin, I may not divulge his name."
> The King: "Menzies, what would you say if I said, 'Give me the name of our man in Berlin' or 'off with your head'?"
> Menzies: "Sire, were you to give such an order, and were that order to be carried out, my head would roll with my lips still sealed."

The undisclosing mindset, which for years denied the very existence of MI6, persisted even after Radio Berlin announced 54 Broadway as MI6 headquarters! (The *Sicherheitsdienst* had kidnapped two SIS officers in the still-neutral Netherlands and interrogated them quite thoroughly; the story is elsewhere in my book.) Why, even then, did SIS persist in masquerading as The Minimax Fire Extinguisher Company? Malcolm Muggeridge, who served in SIS during WWII explains: "Secrecy is as essential to Intelligence as vestments and incense to a mass or darkness to a spiritualist seance and must at all costs be maintained, quite irrespective of whether or not it serves any purpose."

I agree. A secret service *should* be secret.

Site 15

Site 15: 16 Victoria Square, SW1 (my Belgravia Walk). From 1953 through 1964, when he died at age 56, Ian Fleming lived here with his wife Anne and their young son, Caspar. The first of the Bond books, *Casino Royale*, was published a month after his move here. More than 20 million Bond books were sold during Fleming's time at Victoria Square.

But Fleming's years here were not entirely happy. He was often depressed. Anne was witty and charming, but unsupportive ("those dreadful Bond books," she called them). In this house she gave frequent dinner parties for people with possibly more literary pretensions, and certainly more literary achievements, than Fleming. He often spent those evenings hiding out at his club. One biographer of Fleming describes an evening when Fleming came home and found Cyril Connolly reading the page proofs of *Casino Royale* to Anne's guests "with heavily theatrical emphasis which the guests evidently found amusing." Malcolm Muggeridge wrote that he often joined Fleming in "a sort of private apartment at the top of the house" where Fleming kept his "masculine bric-a-brac," there to exchange Fleet Street gossip and sip highballs "like climbers taking a breather above a mountain torrent whose roar could still faintly be heard in the ravine below."

Fleming's was a flawed personality. Reviewers have noted the strong connection, in his books, between sex and cruelty. (Andrew Lyett's 1995 biography of Fleming confirms that Fleming was a lifelong sexual sadist.) His attitudes may have been formed at Eton; the British public school atmosphere is said to consist equally of sadism, snobbery, and sodomy. For all that, Fleming seems to have grown up enthusiastically heterosexual—not always the case among fellow alumni. (He attended Sandhurst too, graduating from neither institution, although encouraging people to believe otherwise.)

Fleming was very skilled at self-dramatization generally. When WWII came, he used his connections to get himself a commission in the Royal Navy and a safe job as aide (actually little more than gofer) to Admiral Godfrey, chief of Naval Intelligence. Then while working safely behind a desk in London, Fleming carried a teargas pen and a commando dagger to suggest that he was involved in matters of great secrecy and danger. (At another site in *A Spy's London*, I give the details of one of Fleming's gaudier attempts to Do Something for the war effort.)

Fleming came into his own, however, when he began writing the Bond books. He was a magnificent storyteller, despite his ignorance about much of the subject matter he dealt with. Whenever he wrote about *anything* I know something about, he got it wrong. Like most British writers he was abysmally ignorant about firearms. He was also wildly ignorant about American speech. And I have been told by people who know something of MI6 that he got most of *that* wrong as well. One can only admire the self-confidence that enabled Fleming to write so blithely those compellingly well-written stories that are no less well-written for being chock-full of howlers. My favorite of his short stories is "For Your Eyes Only" (which has nothing to do with the film of the same

Site 35

name), probably because it is set in Vermont and because Bond uses a Savage 99, for years my primary deer-hunting rifle. Fleming acquired his knowledge of Vermont by visiting the Vermont home of his friend Ivar Bryce, just over the hill from where I live. But Fleming knew nothing about Vermont in late autumn, just before deer season, and he seems never to have fired (or even tried to load) a Savage 99, especially with a scope in place.

Site 35: 18 Carlyle Square, SW3 (my Chelsea Walk). Coldly and steadily climbing to power in MI6, Soviet mole Harold Adrian Russell "Kim" Philby moved here in 1944. The house was supposedly bought for the Philbys by his mother-in-law, but observers have speculated that at least some of the money must have come from Soviet sources. In *A Spy's London* I tell parts of Philby's story at several sites, partly because I think it's interesting to look at the place where events happened, and partly because his is such a big story.

In the later days of WWII, when the British realized that Stalin would replace Hitler as the main threat to the West, MI6 was instructed to set up a new section to gather intelligence on the Soviet Union. Philby skillfully edged out the

competition to become head of this section. That's right—
*the head of anti-Soviet operations for Britain's CIA was a Soviet
agent.* (Makes Aldrich Ames look like an amateur, doesn't
it?) But there's worse—Philby was being groomed to suc-
ceed Sir Stewart Menzies as "C"!

Philby began his career with British Intelligence by working for SOE at the start of the war (he had been working for
Soviet Intelligence since the mid-Thirties); he got into MI6
with the help of fellow-mole Guy Burgess. Later in the war
he worked in MI6's counterintelligence section, along with
a group of young American OSS officers, one of whom (James
Jesus Angleton) would later become Deputy Director for
Counterintelligence for the newly-formed CIA. When
Philby's disloyalty became apparent, Angleton's anger at having been snookered drove his suspicious attitude (normally a
good thing in a counterintelligence officer) almost to the
point of paranoia—and some would exclude the word
"almost." Angleton's molehunts within CIA badly damaged
the agency's morale and efficiency and, insofar as they were
caused by Angleton's reaction to Philby's perfidy, are seen by
some as Philby's greatest achievement as a Soviet agent.

By the 1950s there was enough suspicion of Philby—
because of his close association with Burgess and Maclean,
who had fled to the Soviet Union—for MI6 to fire him,
despite its belief in his innocence. He was given a hugely
generous cash settlement and within a few years he was again
working for MI6 in Beirut.

But late in 1961, a high KGB officer defected and, *inter
alia*, convinced even Philby's friends in MI6 that good old
Kim had been a Soviet mole all along. Wanting to avoid any
more bad publicity, MI6 practically encouraged Philby to
flee to the Soviet Union, which he promptly did.

Philby worked for the KGB in Moscow whenever they
asked him to. He died in 1988, regrettably of natural causes.

Site 81

Site 81: 47 Gloucester Place, W1 (my Edgware Walk). This is an absolutely unremarkable building made interesting only by the event that occurred here on the morning of 20 May, 1940. The second-floor (or as we Americans would say, the *third*-floor) flat of Tyler Kent, a code clerk at the nearby American Embassy, was raided by officers from the Embassy and from Britain's Special Branch who found in the flat no fewer than 1929 documents stolen from the Embassy. Included were six top-secret messages between Churchill (not yet Prime Minister) and President Roosevelt.

Tyler Kent was a presentable young man (twenty-nine at the time of his arrest), well-born and well-educated. Convinced that the Jews, whom he hated, were pushing the world into war, Kent wanted to use the secret correspondence between Churchill and FDR to show that the two were conspiring to replace Chamberlain and bring America into the war. Even the full correspondence, made public in 1985, could not have supported such a conspiracy theory. But in 1940, the correspondence could only have aided Hitler. Britain stood alone and was desperately weak, torn between those who would fight Hitler and those who would appease him. In America, FDR was seeking an unprecedented third term, promising voters that American boys would not be sent to intervene in Europe's war.

Kent had begun stealing documents almost immediately after his arrival in London in October, 1939. He soon met Anna Volkov, an emigrée who was passionately pro-Hitler; she took two of the documents to a photographer and gave the prints to an Italian diplomat to pass on to Berlin (Italy was not yet in the war and still maintained an embassy in London). Kent also met Captain Archibald Ramsay, a Member of Parliament who was violently pro-fascist; Ramsay planned to bring Kent's material to the floor of Parliament.

By then, however, British cryptologists had broken into some German cypher systems, and when intercepted German radio traffic revealed that the Germans had an intelligence source inside America's London Embassy, the hunt was on. Ambassador Joseph P. Kennedy, JFK's father, was among the suspects; his Anglophobia and Judeophobia (not to mention his eagerness to "do business with Hitler") made him a strong candidate for suspicion and his every move was carefully monitored. But attention soon focused on Kent. When the connection was made between Kent and his new friends Volkov and Ramsay, Kennedy gladly withdrew Kent's diplomatic immunity and Kent was arrested.

Kent's trial was held *in camera* in October, 1940, thus keeping the content of the stolen documents from American voters just before they returned FDR to the White House. Kent was found guilty of giving documents to a foreign agent (Volkov) and sentenced to seven years. He served five years of the sentence; with the end of the war he was released and deported to the US. He soon married an American divorcee thirteen years his senior and spent the next four decades running through her substantial fortune (from Carter's Little Liver Pills) in pursuit of his two hobbies: yachting, and publishing diatribes against Jews, Blacks, and Franklin Roosevelt.

But there is more to this story. Even before the end of WWII the FBI had analyzed Kent's activities and reclassified him as a *Soviet* agent. Why? He was known to have supplied classified documents to Soviet Intelligence during his previous posting to the US Embassy in Moscow. It was reasonable to assume, therefore, that the Soviets had a hold on him, since they could "out" him at any time. And keeping America out of the war in 1940 was as much in Stalin's interest as in Hitler's, since the two dictators were at the time closely allied against the capitalist democracies. So Kent could have been working for the Soviets without at all going against his pro-Hitler beliefs. Within a few years, MI5 and then the newly-formed CIA also examined the Tyler Kent matter and concurred.

My take on Tyler Kent is that he probably was genuinely anti-Soviet, his views a consequence of his experiences in Moscow (including possibly having been blackmailed into working for the Cheka, Stalin's intelligence and counterintelligence agency). When he left the Moscow embassy, his first choice for a new posting was to *Berlin*, where he would have been more useful to the Soviets than to the Nazis. And of the almost two thousand documents Kent stole from the London embassy, only six originated in Moscow; there was little of interest to Berlin in his stash, but much of interest to Moscow.

Tyler Kent's full story may never be known, but this unremarkable building on Gloucester Place is where he lived, an important part of his strange double life. He was (fortunately) a very minor character in the history of his times. He died in 1988, his last home a trailer park in Kerrville, Texas.

Site 45

Site 45: The Russian Tea Room and Restaurant, 50 Harrington Road, SW7 (my South Kensington Walk). The

last naval attaché at the Imperial Russian Embassy in London was Admiral Nikolai Volkov. When the Tsar fell, the Volkov family stayed on in London and opened this special place; it served the best caviar in London, and vodka too, long before the drink became fashionable in England. In the flat above, the pro-fascist Right Club held committee meetings. Active in all this was the Admiral's daughter, Anna, helping her parents run the tea room, helping Captain Ramsay run his clandestine Right Club and helping Tyler Kent get his stolen documents out where they could assist the Axis.

MI5 had already infiltrated two women agents into the Right Club, and when one of them reported that the club was eager to recruit someone from the War Office, MI5's choice for the job was young Joan Miller, previously employed in the display department of the cosmetics firm Elizabeth Arden and freshly assigned to MI5's counter-subversion section from its transportation section. She was very pretty, very daring, and very taken with MI5's charming and brilliant Maxwell Knight, whose story I tell at two other sites in the book. She began frequenting the Russian Tea Room and befriending the wary Anna Volkov, to whom she mentioned casually that she worked at the War Office. She invented a prewar romance with a Nazi officer to explain her fascist sympathies. Before long she was invited upstairs, where her performance before a dozen members of the Right Club earned her an immediate invitation to join.

"I had to keep reminding myself that I'd seriously wanted to be an actress," Miller writes in her memoir *One Girl's War*. Club members soon trusted her completely, even consulting her as to which Britons should be hanged on *Der Tag* when fascism arrived. By now she was looking for more than a list of club members; MI5's surveillance had identified Anna Volkov as the link between Tyler Kent and the attaché at the Italian Embassy who was passing Kent's material to Berlin via Mussolini's intelligence service.

The eleven year-old Len Deighton witnessed Anna Volkov's arrest here in May 1940; his mother was the tea room's cook.

For two violations of the Official Secrets Act, Volkov received a ten-year sentence. If she hadn't been a woman, says one historian, she'd have gone to the gallows.

She returned here briefly after her release in 1947, but the tea room soon closed when her father died. (When I photographed the place it housed a beauty parlor and nobody on the premises knew anything about the tea room.) At the risk of being accused of indulging in the cheapest pop psychology, I think Anna Volkov had a classic Elektra complex. Early in life she took on all her father's attitudes and values; given his class and upbringing these would have included a vehement Judeophobia. Then came the revolution. Until Stalin killed off most of the key revolutionaries, Bolshevism was readily identifiable with Jews. Anna Volkov would have been furious that her father had been toppled from his position by what she considered a lowly pack of Jews. As to why she wanted to aid Germany during its partnership with the Soviet Union, only a better pop psychologist

Site 136

than I might be able to explain. Perhaps, like any true fanatic, she had room in her mind for only a few ideas at any one time.

Until her death in 1969, she eked out a living from her dressmaking, saw only a few old friends, and clung bitterly to her hatred of Jews and Bolsheviks. She never harmed Joan Miller, despite her courtroom threats to do so. Miller found it all "pretty harrowing"; she had not even disliked the woman. Afterward she threw away the dress that Anna had given her—but saved the buttons for her "memory box."

Site 136: 70 Grosvenor Street/Bourdon Alley, W1 (my Mayfair Walk). OSS (Office of Strategic Services, America's first intelligence-and-subversion agency) needed nine London buildings for its offices. This building housed the headquarters of OSS Europe and its branch chief, the patrician David K.E. Bruce. OSS was often derided as being "Oh So Social"; its officers were recruited from Ivy League and Little Three colleges and from the more prestigious Wall Street law firms. This policy mirrored the elitism of the British services and also the background of OSS founder William J. Donovan, himself an alumnus of Columbia College, Columbia Law School (where he had been FDR's classmate), and Wall Street.

The story of OSS is too big to tell at just this one site; in *A Spy's London* I used *eight* sites to tell of some of the exploits of this legendary organization—these were the people who operated behind enemy lines, spying on the enemy, leading guerrilla bands, and blowing up bridges, factories and trains. I'll just tell you a bit about OSS now and urge you to read *A Spy's London* for the rest of the story.

Working as a special assistant to Bruce here at Grosvenor Street was a young lawyer named William Casey. Not an Ivy Leaguer himself, Casey had asked a friend in Donovan's New York law firm to arrange something (the friend had once parked cars with Casey at Jones Beach). Casey made himself valuable to the new organization by dint of sheer brains and a capacity for endless hard work. As historian M.R.D. Foot tells us, Casey moved in a matter of months from being a senior clerk for Bruce to being "…a force that could help decide the fate of nations." Casey was then only thirty-one years old. (Casey later became Director of the CIA under Reagan. I have no doubt that his policy of arming and supporting any enemies of the Soviets anywhere in the world was rooted in his time at Grosvenor Street, when OSS armed and supported any enemies of the Axis, some of them quite unsavory.)

Behind the elegant headquarters building in Grosvenor Street (in a mews house in the Grosvenor Hill alleyway, reached via the Bourdon Street alley), the OSS printshop produced documents needed by operatives in enemy territory. Legitimate artists and engravers from the US were commandeered for the work—the OSS was not interested in convicted forgers (who were failures, after all). Newly counterfeited documents were aged by being worn under the armpit for a while or being strewn about the floor and walked on for several days. (During the high-tech Cold War, documents were typically aged by being tumbled in a clothes washer with a little dirt and an old tennis shoe, but no water.)

Printshop workers always had cigarettes; they printed their own ration stamps. OSS was a resourceful bunch altogether ("those Wall Street bankers and corporation lawyers make wonderful second-story men," Donovan had joked) and some of them didn't mind who knew it, when the time for secrecy was over. One OSS veteran applied for a job at *Time-Life* after the war and, when the application asked which civilian occupations his wartime service had trained him for, he bemusedly listed forgery, kidnapping, blackmail, counterfeiting, arson, and murder. Someone in the personnel department scrawled across his application, "Hire him before *Newsweek* gets him."

These are but a few of the fascinating stories from London's secret history. What I've been pleased to do is to show the reader the readily visible places and then (literally) entice the reader inside for the "inside story." For me, and I suspect for many others, to see these places where things happened— where real people lived and schemed and worried and despaired and rejoiced—is to see history made real. And to see what happened at the 136 sites in *A Spy's London* is to suspect that such things could happen *anywhere*. And probably did. And probably do.

Roy Berkeley

Biography

Roy Berkeley earned his B.A. at Columbia College in New York City and did graduate work in American History at Columbia and at The New School For Social Research. He taught at The New School and at the graduate school at Wesleyan University in Middletown, Connecticut.

In his life, he has been a freelance adventure-story writer (writing westerns, private-eye, and spy stories under fourteen different pseudonyms) and a photojournalist whose work appeared in publications ranging from *L 'Architecture d'Aujourd 'hui* to *Mechanix Illustrated* and the Coloroto Section of *The New York Sunday News*.

He was Assistant to the News Editor of *The New York Post* and was Editor of *The Long Island Post*.

Since 1984 he has been a Deputy Sheriff with the Bennington County (Vermont) Sheriff's Department. In addition to his regular duties he serves as a State-Certified Firearms Instructor.

He and his wife, Ellen, have lived in Shaftsbury, Vermont for 25 years.

Bibliography

A Spy's London: A Walk Book of 136 Sites in Central London Relating to Spies, Spycatchers & Subversives, 1994
A Spy's New York, TBA

Antiquities

Nevada Barr

‹ ›

Hidden Treasures of Our National Parks

Hidden Treasures of Our National Parks

Whenever I am asked to speak before a group I feel the need to provide answers. All of us—even the dullest and laziest—are students at heart. On some level, however mundane, we wish to learn, to broaden our horizons, and to extend the boundaries of our lives.

This gathering carried with it the added bonus of being patterned along academic lines.

Academic.

Now there's a scary word. A word that implies a number of things. The first and foremost of which is that one knows something. Or, perhaps, that one is at least conversant enough with language to convince others she knows something.

Answers. Or a reasonable facsimile thereof.

In one sense I do qualify for the fringes of academia. I have a masters degree. I started off with the best of intentions. I was going to be an architect. Then I arrived at the University and discovered I could obtain an advanced degree in goofing off. This was the answer to a childhood prayer. Seven years later I matriculated with a Bachelor of Arts in Speech and a Masters Degree in acting. At pretending to be someone I am not and foisting off on an unsuspecting public things that are not true, I am a trained professional.

Now that we have discussed my *curriculum vitae* and you are cognizant of my qualifications we shall begin.

Answers.

In the realm of fiction I can and do provide answers. That's because in the realm of fiction I am allowed to make them up. In real life all I can give you are questions. Today I am here to talk about the national parks, their ancient treasures, and their connection to mystery literature. I have brought with me a *soupçon* of knowledge and a cart load of questions to share with you. Dorothy Parker is reputed to have said when asked to use the word "horticulture" in a sentence: "You can lead a whore to culture but you can't make her think." I am here not to lead you to culture or to knowledge. But, hopefully, I'll make you think.

One of the first questions to occur in a writer's life is: "What should I write about?" I was told: "Write what you know." This stymied me for years. I didn't know anything. I didn't have the discipline to become a specialist in any one area. I'm a dilettante. I like to learn the interesting fun bits, then move on.

Another possibility was forwarded: Write what other people would like to know.

This made terrific sense. This could translate into sales. Commercial success.

All important.

Again I suffered a serious obstacle. I have never been able to figure out what it is others want to know. I have grave difficulty finding out what they want for Christmas. The beat of the different drummer drowned out the music of the commercial spheres.

However, lest you think I gave up too easily, you should know I actually gave this theory a shot.

Romance.

Anybody can write a romance, right? You must understand that I held this belief long ago, before I discovered mystery fiction, and was a "real" writer of "real" books. My snobbery knows no bounds.

So, in a desperate attempt to get published, I lowered myself and began writing a pot- boiler. Give the masses what they want. Bread and circuses. Breasts and cutlasses.

Ah, Prostitution!

You will be relieved to know my sojourn as a shady lady of fiction was short-lived. I was no good at it. Had I been, you might even now be reading the trials and tribulations of the lovely Annabelle Pigeonique.

Like any other genre, romance has its own requirements, skills, insights. Not being a reader of romances, I didn't have the slightest idea why they were so popular. What it is that does the trick, fires the imagination of the reader, makes the heart pound and the bosom heave? I was completely out of my depth.

The sixty pages do still exist on a five and a half inch floppy in my sister's garage. Occasionally, when I get uppity, she threatens to send it to my editor. I have offered to buy the original back at a greatly inflated price but I suspect she has a copy in a safe deposit box somewhere.

> > >

I was back to square one. What to write about. Expertise was out. I didn't know anything. The oldest profession was closed to me.

Then while watching late night TV, I stumbled upon the answer to my dilemma. Moss Hart, who is one of my favorite playwrights, was discussing this very subject in an interview. Moss Hart grew up poor—ugly sordid poor. He'd never been to a garden party, never had cocktails on the verandah nor tea on the terrace. He struggled with play after play depicting poverty, degradation, gloom.

All of them failed.

In a fit of rebellion, he wrote what he really, deep down, wanted to write: light, fluffy, delightful, drawing room comedies about the foibles of the very rich. He became a huge success.

I realized then that, all along, in my heart of hearts, I'd known what I wanted to write about. I have a girlfriend named Debby. When I was little my parents, thinking "Nevada" too weighty for a small girl, nicknamed me Nevie. We always had it in the back of our minds to write a book entitled *The World According to Debby and Nevie*. She grew up to be a visual artist. Now she draws the world according to Debby, but I have inherited the original mantle: writing the world according to Nevie.

Write as you would paint: What you see in your mind's eye. What you hear with your heart. What ever tickles your fancy.

My fancy is tickled by murder, mystery, strong women, beautiful places, acts of derring-do and physical courage. Sort of "Errol Flynn meets Gloria Steinem" in the back county of Yellowstone.

This combination was not realized in a day. I wrote a number of books—most of which still molder unpublished in my garage—before I came up with the Anna Pigeon series. Anna Pigeon, murder, and the national parks created a palette with which I could paint my fancies, live out my fantasies, grind my axes, tell my stories, and, not to underplay the obvious, make a living.

Aha, did I recant, change horses in mid stream, deviate from the way? Become a specialist? No indeed. Even now, as I work on book number six, and occasionally wander the country masquerading as an expert on the national parks, I don't know much.

In my dilettante fashion, I have picked up some information. Not through diligently applying myself, or from a genuine love of knowledge, but because I needed it to make the story work.

Necessity is the professor of invention.

Curiosity comes first. Something triggers my imagination. A story idea creeps up on me. Then necessity arises: In order to make the plot work I've got to learn something. Often this spurs creativity. Avenues for the characters or the action open up that had not occurred to me before.

Still, I cling steadfastly to my ignorance. I seldom learn more than I have to and I forget most of what I learn before the book ever hits the shelves. I like to think of myself as a follower in the classic tradition of Sherlock Holmes who, upon finding the world was round and not flat, informed Watson he intended to promptly forget it again to make room in his brain for more pertinent data. There's plenty of room in my brain.

Okay. So. The parks set the scene, action is born of education, and life presents me with characters. Now, for a first rate murder mystery all that's lacking is a body and a motive. As near as I can tell there are only two motives in all detective fiction: Somebody wants to get something or somebody wants to keep something they've already got. Love, Money, Power, Prestige, Honor, Land, Art, Sex.

I did consider revenge as a possible third motive, but concluded that one only requires revenge on someone who has foiled you in the acts of getting or keeping. Consequently I was forced to abandon it as derivative. It's filed in a subcategory under "Keeping Things You've Already Got."

In The World According to Nevie, America's national parks are the greatest treasure we have. I look upon them as a sort of Fort Knox but without the security system. Hundreds of thousands of acres of terrific stuff with no fences, no burglar alarms, no motion detectors—nothing but a handful of rangers to protect them.

Our National Parks.

This sounds rather uplifting and esoteric, not the stuff of greed and death. But many of these treasures can be converted into cold, hard cash. In Yellowstone, professional poachers take big game for big money. In the Smokey Mountains, bears are hunted for their gall bladders. Considered a cure-all in a lot of Asian countries, they bring in huge revenues. The same with ginseng, a root that grows in most of our eastern parks. The southwest is a treasure trove, mined not only by felons but, metaphorically speaking, quite magnificently by our own Tony Hillerman: potsherds, bones, arrowheads, artifacts. In Organ Pipe National Monument in Arizona they've arrested dozens of reptile poachers creeping about the park taking live Gila Monsters, snakes, lizards, tarantulas to sell to specialty pet stores. There's gold and silver in the hills of Colorado, gas and oil under the lands in New Mexico. In the caves there are stalactites and formations sawed off and hauled out by the ton for trinkets, headstones, faux marble floors. The Caribbean and the great lakes have shipwrecks—sunken treasure—not all of which is gold doubloons. In Lake Superior a cache of submerged trees has been discovered, the wood preserved by the cold, still water. A fortune in raw timber just waiting to be hauled up. With the new seizure laws the drug enforcement agencies have instituted, a marijuana grower can lose all his property if he's caught. So they're growing it on public lands. Nothing for the government to confiscate. Fields of high priced sinsemilla weed in among the trees, waters from your public lakes and streams.

Lots of Stuff to want to get. Lots of stuff to want to keep.

The parks provide me with motive and setting but they also bring me an ingredient I find necessary, not only as a writer of mystery novels, but as a writer period: Magic. Authors find their magic in various places: history, cities, wars, outer space, inner space. For me the magic is in the wilderness, both internal and external.

I have always maintained a somewhat adversarial relationship with science. I accept that it's the god of this century. Like most gods, it's fashioned in our own image. People have come to believe that, through science, all our prayers will be answered, all our sins forgiven, eternal life achieved. We can smoke. If not today, then tomorrow, a cure will be found for cancer. We can drive big cars. A new energy source will be discovered to replace the oil we burn. We can destroy the forests and with them the organisms that produce our medicines. New chemicals will be manufactured to replace what we destroy. We can dump in our oceans. New cleansers will be found to purge the land and water of toxins. We can work on our tans. Surgical procedures will miraculously wipe the years from our faces.

This belief in the omniscience of science has replaced not only the old gods, but replaced elves, fairies, sprites—all the creatures we used to express our respect for and awe of the natural world.

It's my contention that our ignorance is merely scratched by our science, that science has become hubris allowing us to behave as if we created the world once and, having then destroyed it, can create it again. We talk of "managed wilderness" as if we understood the delicate balances. In our self-appointed stewardship, we make what we call informed decisions, many of which are dead wrong.

With this self-importance, this illusion of control, we rob ourselves of a sense of being part of something larger. We rob ourselves of the mystery of life.

When I first started writing in and about the national parks, I was a law enforcement ranger on Isle Royale in Lake Superior in Michigan. Isle Royale has a small staff—at least at the south end in Windogo where I worked. So, in addition to my patrol duties, I gave a couple of campfire programs each week.

Something I noticed in the rangers as well as the visitors was an aura of complacency, the feeling that we are the master of our environment. We the puppeteers, the earth and its denizens the puppets. This was most evident when mother nature turned on a tourist and they were injured or frightened in the back country. They were outraged. Litigious. The government, the park service, somebody was at fault. Somebody should pay—somebody besides the idiot who had done every stupid thing he could think of, then invented a few more.

If we are all powerful then, by definition, we are all responsible.

No gods, no magic.

For this reason (and because I basically didn't know anything then either), instead of telling the people who came to my programs about the flora and fauna of the island, I decided to invent new myths for them. Tell them stories that would leave them wondering, scare the pants off of them. I gave them a sense of the mystery that surrounds us every day.

There are multitudinous questions science cannot answer. Seldom, however, is the phrase "I don't have a clue" used in scientific treatises. I tried to find the things that science had glossed over, failed to define, and put forth nonscientific answers. The point being that we don't know, that we are not in control, that the magic isn't gone, and we'd best watch our step, show a little respect.

On Isle Royale one among the questions that remain unanswered is how the wolves came to the island and why they have ceased to thrive. At Guadalupe National Park, the mystery was what happened to the twenty radio-collared lions. In Mesa Verde, what caused a bustling civilization to pack up and abandon their homes and cities virtually overnight. On the Natchez Trace, where I most recently worked, Meriwether Lewis of the Lewis and Clark Expedition is buried. There's a controversy over whether he committed suicide, as history would have us believe, or was shot by a jealous husband.

My research is as much to uncover what we don't know as to arm myself with the facts that we do know. My husband jokes that we split the marital duties right down the middle: he deals with reality and I don't. There's something to that. Questions without answers are the beginning of my dreams.

I've always marveled that we can answer such questions as what does Jupiter weigh? And how many hamburgers laid end to end would it take to reach Alpha Centauri? But answers to the tiny questions of life, the important questions, remain elusive. From the shallow: What does your husband do those final forty-five second he always spends in the car after you have leaped out and are standing in the rain? To the bone-deep: Would I kill somebody? Am I a coward? A hero? What would push my panic button?

For me the national parks, the wilderness, provide a catalyst for the study of these captivating human mysteries.

Pretty doggone profound, huh?

I must confess this is not an original idea. I've come to the conclusion—also not original, I believe Aristotle was the first to go on record with this conclusion—that there is nothing new under the sun.

The wilderness is the place where we traditionally go to meet our inner demons: Christ in the desert, Indians on spirit quests, Gurus on the mountain tops. Clubs and organizations have sprung up around the concept: Outward Bound, Wilderness Inquiry. The idea is that, shorn of our customary crutches and comforts, we will finally be forced to face our fears. For people, these are the things of epiphany. For the writer they are the ingredients for character development and the building of tension.

With the various settings I have chosen, I have been able to explore some of the primal fears haunting mankind. Haunting me. Fear of the dark, of enclosed spaces, of abandonment, fear of failure, of letting others down, fear of heights, fear of being the hunted and not the hunter, fear of hunger and thirst and isolation.

When we as a country—or as taxpayers—talk of saving the wilderness, we customarily discuss it from the aspect of saving wildlife, scenery, natural resources, historical sites, and recreation areas. One of the greatest gifts our vast outdoors gives us is a place to challenge ourselves. Even those of us who will never wander the tundra in Alaska, face the grizzlies in Yellowstone, or ride the white water through the Grand Canyon, need to know those places exist, to know that there is a world where a Visa Gold card and a cell phone won't solve life's dilemmas. This is a necessary exercise for the mind and for the soul.

Not to mention a fertile field for the mystery writer. On my list of "Things People Want to Get and Things People Want to Keep" the foremost is arguably beliefs. Throughout history the human being has been more likely to kill in defense of what he believed in, to attain a place to believe as he chose, and to murder others for refusing to embrace his beliefs, than he has to kill for any other reason. This is the stuff not only of murders but of wars.

The national parks are in the middle of a number of ideological wars that have erupted in violence more than once. Reintroduction of the wolves into Yellowstone challenged the ranchers on the outskirts of the park in two ways. It challenged their belief that wolves were varmints, inherent evils that came by night and preyed upon women, children, and other livestock. And it threatened their belief that, as human beings, they have the right to life, liberty, and the pursuit of happiness far and above any rights to those things that might be claimed by the animal kingdom.

In Texas, Guadalupe Mountains National Park was carved out of old grazing and hunting grounds. The American taxpayers paid the original owners for those lands. Well and good, but with park regulations, suddenly lands that had always been the personal stomping grounds of a number of old families were now closed to hunting, to camping in certain areas, to dogs, to motor vehicles. Despite the change of titles on paper, the descendants of those who sold the property still believe they have an inherent right to that property. A right of birth. A right that could not be sold away.

In the Southwestern parks—parks, that showcase and preserve our Native American heritage—there are those among the Native American population who believe these places are not museums for white people but living breathing history belonging solely to them. Theirs to walk and explore. Theirs to share with their children. Park rules and regulations forbid climbing on walls, going into fragile ruins, the taking of artifacts. Many places are closed totally to the public and are only visited by rangers. Usually white rangers.

Every decision made about our infinitely precious and irreplaceable heritage is fraught with controversy.

› › ›

My next book is set in Lechuguilla Cave. Lechuguilla was discovered on the lands of Carlsbad Caverns National Park in the mid-eighties. It is a world-class cave. There are formations in Lechuguilla that are found nowhere else. And formations in such profusion as have never seen before. Though it's not yet fully explored, there is the possibility that Lechuguilla will be the deepest and the longest cave in the United States—maybe in the world.

But it's desperately fragile. Caves have no way to regenerate. No winds or waters to cleanse the filth we leave behind. Formations are created on a time line where humanity is just a blip, a recent occurrence. By the act of walking into a cave we destroy it. Urine upsets the delicate balance of this closed environment. A footprint remains forever. Even the air we let in when we dig a new entrance brings in microbes, dust, pollens, new life forms.

So the battle begins.

Do we explore the cave and to hell with the damage? Do we do it with care to limit the damage? "Limit the damage?" How much damage is okay? A little, a lot? Who decides where the line is drawn? Do we close the cave to protect it? If it is closed, is it closed to everybody? Or just to those the national park service says it's closed to? Can researchers go in? Rangers?

Superintendents? You can bet your ass superintendents can go in, but can you? And is the cave of any value if it's not to be enjoyed by the public? After all, these are public lands, are they not? They belong to you and me. Who are you and me? I'm relatively young and strong. I can hike and climb in to see these wonders. How about the old and the infirm, the disabled? Should they be shut out? If not, then we must build ramps and elevators, trams to the tops of the mountains and paved paths through the meadows. Can we all go? If we all go to the resource, it will be trampled, loved to death. If not all, then who?

The questions that arise over each decision have the power to boil somebody's blood, to bring the murderous instincts to the surface.

For years I made my living as a park ranger. I adore the parks, think of myself a loyal employee. Yet there are decisions made I would consider chaining myself to a tree or pouring a cup of sugar into a gas tank to abort.

These are the questions you as a taxpayer, a lover of the wilderness, an explorer, a recreator, a parent, a responsible citizen must find an answer for, or risk losing it all.

And this is fertile ground for the writer of murder mysteries. For me. It is what tickles my fancy and urges me to put pen to paper page after page, year after year.

Photo Credit Tommy Bennett

Nevada Barr

Biography

Born in the small town of Yerington, Nevada, and raised on a mountain airport in the Sierras—her parents and sister Molly all became pilots—the author fell into the theater when pushed out of the nest. She earned an MFA in Acting before tackling Manhattan and Minneapolis, and for years worked on stage, in commercials, in industrial training films, and doing voice-overs for radio. Interest in the environmental movement led to working in National Parks during the summers: first Isle Royale in Michigan, then Guadalupe Mountains, Texas, Mesa Verde, Colorado, and eventually the Natchez Trace Parkway in Mississippi. A constant thread running through these disparate careers was a love of storytelling and writing, leading to the publication of her first novel, *Bittersweet*, in 1983. A decade later came her first mystery, a debut so dramatic it won both the 1994 Agatha and Anthony

Awards. At the time of writing this paper, the author lives with new husband, Broderick, in Clinton, Mississippi, and keeps her ranger's skills alive on the Trace while writing the sixth Anna Pigeon, *Blind Descent*, set in Lechuguilla Cave in New Mexico. A self-admitted claustrophobe, Nevada believes if she can communicate one tenth of the suspense she feels about researching the book on the finished page, she should sweep the 1999 awards fields.

She has continued to write a new Anna Pigeon mystery each year and remains an awards contender.

Bibliography

The Anna Pigeon Novels:
    Track of the Cat, 1993
    A Superior Death, 1994
    Ill Wind, 1995
    Firestorm, 1996
    Endangered Species, 1997
    Blind Descent, 1998
    Liberty Falling, 1999
    Deep South, 2000
    Blood Lure, 2001
    Hunting Season, 2002

Other:
    Bittersweet, 1983

Sharyn McCrumb

◇

Rank Strangers:
The Celts and the Appalachians

Rank Strangers:
The Celts and the Appalachians

My favorite story to illustrate character of the Appalachian Celtic people is an incident that happened in 1960 in the mountains of western North Carolina.

If you were on the East Coast in 1960, you may remember that it was a terrible winter. In North Carolina in particular, the March weather was fierce. That month it snowed every Monday. That's much more snow than North Carolina usually gets. With this steady fall, the snow did not melt. It just kept piling up and piling up. The North Carolina transportation department did not have the resources to deal with a snowfall of this magnitude. The accumulation was so great that back in the western mountains of the state, the roads, especially unpaved rural back roads, never got cleared and soon became impassable. People who lived in cabins way back in the coves couldn't get out. Because many of them were elderly, the Red Cross was called in to try to get help to these elderly citizens trapped back there, deep in the mountains.

Two Red Cross workers had heard about an old woman—in her eighties—who lived in a cabin way back in the hills, and they volunteered to take a jeep to bring help to her. The two volunteers drove up the ice-bound road as far as they could, abandoned the jeep when the road became impassable, got out snow shoes, wrestled them on, and helped each other tramp through the waist-deep snow until, finally, they saw the little curl of chimney smoke up on the ridge that told them they'd found her. They managed to hike to the cabin on the top of the hill, stomped up on the porch, and rapped on the door. Finally the old lady opened it.

The rescuers announced proudly. "We're from the Red Cross."

"Oh honey," she replied. "It has been such a hard winter, I don't think I can help you this year."

That's us: proud, independent, and willing to go through a good bit of hardship.

My family settled the western North Carolina mountains in 1790. The story of my family origin is something I learned only in the last year. I was tracking down the histories of the people of Mitchell County as part of the research for a novel I'm writing about Frankie Silver, the first woman hanged for murder in North Carolina (The *Ballad of Frankie Silver,* Dutton, May 1998). Frankie Silver came from Mitchell County. In the course of my research there, I discovered an enormous number of cousins. One of them is a professor of theology at Duke University who has done a lot of our family research. He was able to tell me about our first ancestor who came and settled in the mountains. It's a better story than most of mine.

Malcolm McCourry was born on the island of Islay off the west coast of Scotland. In 1750, when Malcolm was a child of eight, he was kidnapped from Islay and made to serve as a cabin boy on a sailing ship. He spent the rest of his childhood on the ship, but when he was in his late teens he was either let go or escaped, and he made his way to Morristown, New Jersey. There he read the law with an attorney and set up a law practice. During the American Revolution, he served as quartermaster with the Morris Militia. After the war, many soldiers were given land grants as a reward for military service, and Malcolm took his land in the mountains of western North Carolina. You understand that land grants aren't given for places like downtown Baltimore, but for some remote territory that no one else wants to homestead—in this case, Indian land. Malcolm took his grant, moved south, and settled in Mitchell County. I'm descended from Malcolm McCourry, and from another eighteenth century pioneer family: the Arrowoods (pronounced Arwood).

Malcolm would have come to America sometime in the early 1770s, a time when a great deal of the Celtic migration was happening. People came along in the 1600s and 1700s, and especially after 1746 when the Jacobite rising in Scotland failed. That was the last attempt to restore a Stuart and a Catholic—Charles Edward Stuart, known as Bonnie Prince Charlie—to the throne. The Highland Clearances followed, a forced exit of both Jacobite rebels and of crofters driven from the land to make room for sheep. The political effect of the Clearances is probably not as important as the cultural effect. What the English did, after they defeated the Scots, was to change the entire culture. They wanted to anglicize Scotland, anglicize Celtic Britain. The whole lifestyle of Scotland was foreign to the English way of doing things. In Scotland the Laird or chief and his extended family, which was called the clan, was the focal point of the social order, and the pastoral economy of tending herds necessitated a tribal lifestyle. The English and the Celts even differed on the use of surnames. The Scots custom of taking as your surname your father's first name wasn't going to work for the English bureaucracy. One's patronym would change with every generation, which would muddle the tax people, and the lawyers, and central government. The British wanted things a little more regimented.

The Highland Clearances were often effected by taking a sailing ship up to an island, telling the people in the cottages that they had until sundown to get on the ship, and at sundown, burning the cottages. The ship then sailed for America, and wherever it docked, the people were let out.

That was it. Go find a home. So, between 1763 and 1775, more than 20,000 people from the Scottish Highlands came to the colonies or to Canada—somewhere in North America—and settled. In 1775, the British banned emigration to the soon-to-be United States. We know why: The American Revolution. People might arrive, grab a musket, then face the other way. Especially the Celts.

The first US Census was in 1790. It is not terribly helpful for modem researchers because only the head of the household is listed by name. The wife and any children, dependents, or household members such as servants are listed merely by sex and age, which is not helpful in determining your great-grandmother's name. However, it did list the surname of the household. The people who analyze sociological data say that by 1790, seventy-five percent of New England was Anglo-Saxon, while more that seventy-five percent of Pennsylvania and the lands to the south and west of that state were Celtic. What this set up was a difference in culture in our country that was profound and continues to resound to this day.

There is some argument about the identity of the people we call "Appalachian." One school of thought states that because they came down from the north, they are not Southern, but are more like New Englanders. I don't think they came from far enough north for that to be true. Here's what happened. The Appalachian Mountains form a barrier which extends south/southwest all along the Eastern seaboard. The easiest way to get into the mountains is not to start at the coast of, say, Charleston (SC) or Richmond (VA) or Wilmington (NC), and go due west. The best way is to get into the mountain chain around Pennsylvania and work your way south at an angle, following mountain passes between the ridges. The migration patterns do reflect this. The people who settled the mountains moved down from the north going south/southwest. The people who settled the coastal plain landed there in the first place, or else they started in the mid-

Atlantic and went west until they got to Statesville (NC) or to some inconvenient place where the mountain barrier was difficult to pass, so they quit and either stayed there or turned back east. They didn't want to live in the mountains, anyway. The people who did were the people who were used to a Highlands sort of existence.

When I was writing *She Walks These Hills*, I studied the geology of the region, because I'm very interested in making the connections, culturally, and any other way, between Britain and Appalachia. One of the most delightful things I learned came from a textbook by Kevin Dann. It was published by Rutgers University in a print run probably large enough to fill his entire Christmas card list, but I managed to get hold of a copy. What Dann had done was to analyze the mountain structure, taking into account plate tectonics, orogeny, and all that, and to conclude that the mountains of Appalachia and the mountains of Great Britain were once joined together. The Appalachians start in Birmingham, more or less at Red Mountain right there in the city itself, and the mountain chain runs up through Georgia, up through South and North Carolina, Tennessee, Virginia, West Virginia, Pennsylvania, and New York. I realize that the stereotypes stop about Pittsburgh, but the mountain chain itself, not the culture, extends through New York and New England and finally ends in Nova Scotia. There the Appalachians stop. If you did soil samples in the Atlantic, you wouldn't find that vein of serpentine, which is the genetic DNA of the Appalachian mountains, this green mineral that rises in Georgia, follows the chain to Nova Scotia, and quits...until it reappears in the west of Ireland. You've skipped the Atlantic ocean, which is recent by geological standards. The mountains of Connemara contain the same vein of serpentine as our mountains. The serpentine chain extends through Cornwall, up through Wales into the north of England, and on to Scotland, the Orkney Islands, and finally ends in the Arctic Circle.

I thought that was a wonderful reinforcement of what I had felt about the migration patterns. Here are these people who left a land that they loved, that they were known to love—the whole idea of nature and place was so treasured by the Celtic people—and were forced to resettle. They come to this country, they look around, they get in covered wagons, and they keep going. Richmond is too flat, and too hot, people live too close together. It's not right in Raleigh. It's not right in Statesville. They keep going, and finally they get to a place where the ridges rise, where you can see the mountains and the trees in the distance, and it looks right, and it feels right. Like home. Like the place they left. With them they brought fiddle tunes, quilt patterns, folk tales, all kinds of wonderful things that, although they've changed over time, still show the family resemblance, the way there is between cousins. *And they were right back in the same mountains they had left behind.*

◇◇◇

This summer I took a six-week-version of today's lecture with a professor of folklore who is the model for the real Nora Bonesteel. We went to Ireland, rented a car, and proceeded to put 1800 miles on that car in a country about the size of Maryland. We went to all the pre-Christian sites we could find, to all the different ruins that we could find, and we looked for connections between the culture we knew in the mountains of the South and the Irish culture. If you are interested in going yourself, there are places I'd recommend.

One is the Craiganouwen Project in County Clare, an hour or so from the Shannon airport, near Quin. There a group of archaeologists have recreated the different types of dwellings that people lived in from prehistoric times through the middle ages in Ireland. They constructed the beehive huts that the Celts used, and the crannogs, man-made islands that the ancient Irish used to protect themselves from enemies. They would build an artificial island in the middle of a lake.

They'd put the beehive huts out on this island, which was built by piling rocks into the lake, and finally covering the projecting mound with dirt—not a quick process. When it was finished, the crannog-dwellers would put down a path of stepping stones leading from the shore to the island. The rocks were slightly submerged so that they couldn't be seen, so that anyone who wanted to cross over to the island had to memorize the route. The theory is that when you're being chased by the enemy of the month, you go running through the woods, get to the lake, skip across to the island, and mount a defensive with arrows or spears while the enemy is forced to pause and pick its way along, searching for the submerged path of rocks.

If you drive around Ireland, you won't see the ancient beehive huts. They've been gone for thousands of years, but you will see lots of little islands in Irish lakes. They are not natural formations. They were put there. If you excavate, as archaeologists are doing, you will find traces of that ancient civilization. The Craiganouwen Project, not wanting to destroy an actual archaeological site, built its own island on a lake in an estate and constructed a nice new beehive hut using wattle and daub, weaving willows together. You can visit it. Occasionally a fellow dressed in hides will greet you and answer the odd question or two. Also on display is a log canoe made by burning the wood until you get a dugout boat. In the forest, the project builders have erected a palisaded ring fort, huts surrounded by a tall wooden fence much like the basic army forts built along our own frontier. The most ingenious thing about the ring fort was its escape route. There was only one gate—apparently the only way in and out of the stockade. But if the enemy is at the gate, the villagers could go into one of the huts. Concealed in the earth floor there is a trap door. Pull it up, go down the ladder, and you find a little tunnel that comes out in the woods. It's a back door. So while the enemy is beating on the front gate, trying to break in...the villagers make their escape. Assuming you close the trap door behind you, they might never guess how you got away. My nine-year-old son loved this.

Finally there is Tim Severn's reconstruction of the boat that, according to legend, St. Brendan used to voyage to the new world in the sixth century. He made it! He also wrote the first bestseller after he made it back. His book was the story of his voyage in a coracle or leather-covered boat. Many scholars scoffed at this legend, saying St. Brendan couldn't possibly have reached America in a leather-covered boat a thousand years before Columbus. But Tim Severn sailed from that same little bay, Brendan Bay, on the Dingle peninsula, where St. Brendan is said to have departed, in the same kind of boat, and Tim Severn made it to Canada. And I say, if Tim Severn did it, St. Brendan did it. When my daughter's third grade class had Columbus week, and everyone had to do a project commemorating the voyage to the Americas, Laura, who'd been to the project with me, produced her photos and map, and gave a lecture on St. Brendan: "How the Irish Discovered America."

The other places I recommend for studying American-Irish connections are the Bunratty Folk Park and the Ulster Folk Park: they are similar reconstructions of the past. The Bunratty Folk Park, in County Clare, has constructed replicas of Eighteenth and Nineteenth century farm houses, manor houses, and little villages. They are artificial, but reasonably accurate. In Ulster, the folk park features actual dwellings, located throughout Ireland, and then moved to the Folk Park for preservation. Thus you can see the real buildings there, just south of Belfast.

My mother-in-law made this trip with us. Her ancestors had come over from Sligo three generations ago, during the potato famine. She had always wanted to go back to Ireland, but part of our itinerary on that trip was Ulster, and she was terrified of Northern Ireland. She updated her will, and told everybody goodbye before we left, vastly amusing the real Nora Bonesteel. As we headed north, through Donegal, Charlotte said to my mother-in-law, "Nancy, we're coming up on Northern Ireland, you'd better get ready." Nancy rummages for her passport, finds the rental car papers, prepares to convince the armed guards that we're just harmless tourists—she figures with me and Charlotte along they're going to need convincing—and presently we come up to this little toll booth off to one side of the road. There's a stout fellow in a sleeveless shirt standing out front, and, as I slow down to thirty-five miles per hour, he snaps a wave, I snap one back. And that's the Irish border crossing. In Ulster, Charlotte and I saw no on more dangerous than ourselves.

Northern Ireland was wonderful. In Armagh you can visit the site of Navan, the Camelot of Ireland, home to Cuchulain and the cattle raiders of Cooley, all the Irish heroes like Ossian (pronounced O'Sheen). The court of the king was at Navan, and their visitor center has one of the best audiovisual programs I've ever seen.

It occurred to me on this trip that one might discover over there a folk song or a quilt pattern, and think, "Aha, this familiar bit that I know from back home must have come from Ireland," but file this story away as a cautionary tale. We were going through the Ulster Folk Park looking at things like cabins because Charlotte contends (and she's right) that you can look at a cabin on our frontier—and certainly at the barns—and tell by the architecture where its builders came from. The structure of the rooms, and the building techniques, are clues to whether those who settled there were German, Irish, English: every ethnic group had its own style. People brought the old ways with them to the New World, and they continued to use them. We were looking at the patterns in the Ulster Folk Park to see what we could learn, when we reached the nineteenth century section. We saw a little urban house that dated from 1890's Belfast. All the dwellings were furnished with period pieces, with sofas, chairs, clocks, and so on. My mother-in-law spotted a clock on the mantelpiece. She recalled that her grandmother had a clock just like it, so she thought she was really onto something about the origin of a family heirloom. Her Irish ancestors had settled in Pennsylvania, north of Pittsburgh. She wanted to know all about this Irish clock. The curator came and, when she asked him where the clock came from, he replied that it had come from Pennsylvania, north of Pittsburgh. Many clocks had been made there, he said, and many of them had been exported *to* Ireland in the late nineteenth century. So I'm glad we asked instead of jumping to conclusions. Sometimes the transmission of cultures goes in the opposite direction from the one you were expecting.

Quite a number of scholars that I know are interested in all these cultural connections. Dr. Betty Fine, head of the Appalachian Studies Program at Virginia Tech, gives a wonderful one-hour lecture that she has yet to put into print. I keep urging her to write a book about it. Dr. Fine takes quilt patterns and traces them back several thousand years. For example, she will show you a photograph of a quilt and then display a photograph of a rock from the Orkney Islands bearing the same pattern. What she contends (and a moment's thought will show you the logic) is that the quilters have long forgotten why they do particular patterns like the log cabin or the bear claw, or the wedding ring, or some intricate design, but that originally all these patterns were luck symbols, symbols of magic from an older civilization. Think about it: if you're making a coverlet to put over your loved one in the dark, and if you come from a time when people believed in demons and spirits, of course you're going to put symbols of protection on this blanket, that's why we have quilt patterns. I'm delighted that scholars are looking into so many aspects of this ancient heritage.

〉〉〉

The songs, even songs that we don't think of as being Scottish or Irish, sneak up on you. We know ballads like the *Rising of the Moon* or *Barbara Allen* come from the British Isles. But consider the origins of other familiar folk songs, often assumed to be authentic American tunes. *The Bard of Armargh*—we call it *The Streets of Laredo*. The Irish version predates our cowboy song by one hundred years. Quite a lot of songs are like that. In *If Ever I Return, Pretty Peggy-O*, I mention a song called *The Knoxville Girl*, which was originally the Irish ballad *The Wexford Girl*. When a similar murder case took place in Tennessee, the ballad-maker changed the locality of the borrowed song.

Another ballad whose origin surprised me was one I knew in the 1960s when Peter, Paul, and Mary recorded it. The song, set in Kentucky, is called *The Lily of the West*. I knew that in the early 1800s, the west *was* Kentucky. (It keeps moving.) For instance, when it was written, *The Last of the Mohicans* was a perfectly good western set in New York state. But *The Lily of the West* begins, "When first I came to *Louisville*, some pleasure there to find…" The girl in the song was a dance hall girl called Flora, the Lily of the West. Last summer, I went into a pub in County Clare, and there was someone singing, "When first I came to Ireland…" and the girl in his song was Flora, the Lily of the West. I thought: "Wait a minute, that girl's from Kentucky," but no, she's from the west, originally meaning the west of Ireland, County Clare, Connemara, Galway, all still called The West. In the 1600s when Cromwell was destroying Ireland, the place to go for a dangerous time was to the wild west, *the west of Ireland*. Then in the 1700s, the concept of the wild west changed to mean the eastern seaboard of North America, where you could have adventures and fight Indians like the Shawnee. By the 1800s, danger receded to Kansas, then to Colorado, then Arizona. Today the West may be Australia.

Just wait, it'll be back. My ballad novels point out that the Appalachian stereotype comes from a time when Appalachia was "The West." In *The Rosewood Casket,* Daniel Boone's experiences are contrasted with events that are taking place today.

Speech patterns: the cadence of a Tennessee accent has that same lilt found in Irish speech. In *The Story of English,* a book and a video made in the 1980s, Cratis Williams of Appalachian State University talks about being able to place people according to where their ancestors came from by listening to their pronunciation of certain key words. He says some of these regional speech patterns transfer. So do some of the words, like poke for paper bag, common to Tennessee and common to Scotland generations ago. To redd, a verb, as in "to redd the room." Nobody in Minnesota's going to understand that, but it will be understood in Tennessee, and in Scotland. It's one of those key words…actually, it may be Scandinavian in origin, so maybe they would understand it in Minnesota.

American square dancing is very similar to Scottish or Irish country dancing.

Folk customs from Britain are still remembered on this side of the Atlantic, although they are now forty or fifty years out of date since Appalachia, like everywhere else, has CNN and other homogenizing forces at work to obscure the past. People who were old when I was a child would remember customs like telling the bees when someone dies, or putting a cloth over the mirror, or putting a little ball of salt on the window sill in the home of the deceased. All these are ancient traditions that go all the way back to Celtic Britain.

The Long Black Veil, the origin of my book title *She Walks These Hills,* is not an old ballad, although it sounds like one. It was written in 1959 by Nashville songwriter Danny Dill. It's a kind of *faux* cowboy ballad: it sounds like one but it isn't. I found a wonderful version of *The Long Black Veil* that

I play sometimes in my lectures, and I love to ask people in Appalachia who they think is singing. When I play this in Appalachian Study lectures, Willie Nelson gets the most votes, but people often suggest that the song is being performed by a local, nonprofessional singer. It's Mick Jagger of The Rolling Stones. This Mick Jagger recording of an American song has managed to fool professors of linguistics. I was very proud of him. I found a scholar who did her Ph.D. in Kentucky speech patterns, and when she heard it, she said "Well, that's not a professional singer, it's probably your uncle and you stuck a microphone in his face." She thought it was the real, genuine, Appalachian article. Finally, we were so puzzled by Mick Jagger's ability to sound authentic that we faxed Hodder, my publisher in London, to ask "Where's that boy from?" They replied, "We think he's from Kent, but his mother's Australian. That probably explains it." I don't think that does explain it. I expect what's happened is that Jagger has hung out for so many years as a professional musician with Willie Nelson, Johnny Cash, and so on—and he's an extraordinarily good mimic—that I think he picked up the accent. Trust me, his vowel sounds are perfect! That's my favorite recording of *The Long Black Veil*, the one by Mick Jagger.

One of the reasons that I write the books to explain the Appalachian lifestyle is to combat the hillbilly stereotype, this whole *"Deliverance* was a documentary" type of thinking. At first, I thought that people just bought into *L'il Abner*— Al Capp spent an entire seventy-two hours in the mountains before he made a living from his cartoon stereotype—or *The Dukes of Hazzard,* which is Hollywood getting everything wrong. But I found that stereotyped thinking went back farther than that. Let me tell you about where some of the customs came from and what they mean.

In some cases, I wrote my books before I found out where the custom in question came from. There is a tradition in the mountains—and here again, thirty or forty years ago it was probably more necessary than now—called "helloing the house," which means one doesn't just approach a house and knock on the door, the visitor calls out first to announce his presence. In rural areas, you let people know you are coming. In this passage from *The Rosewood Casket,* Frank Whilescarver, the evil realtor in East Tennessee, is trying to buy the farm from a family because the father is dying and the realtor realizes that none of the boys wants to come back and take over the land.

> He parked his Jeep Cherokee, noting the old truck and the other late-model car, and hoping the latter wasn't paid for. He helloed the house. He probably didn't need to with a younger generation of town boys in residence, but it was a habit worth keeping in the wilder parts of the mountains. People didn't like you to sneak up on them. A holdover from who knew what terrible times in the past. Revenue men, armed for a raid, perhaps, in the early part of the century. Or Civil War guerillas who turned the war in the southern mountains into a house-to-house feud, stealing livestock and ambushing the householders. You might even trace their wariness of strangers back to Scotland, the Rising of 1745, when the Duke of Cumberland sent his soldiers into the Highlands to kill the Jacobites—that is, anyone they could find. Many of the ones who hid—who distrusted strangers, and therefore survived—ended up here. The lessons of the past would not desert them easily. They distrusted trespassers instinctively. Frank didn't blame them. Even today, a trespasser might be a hunter who would shoot your cow by mistake, or a tourist who figured that the whole state was a theme park, open to the public. He had learned to smile broadly, and to use the front path.

That's helloing the house. One of the places that gave rise to it was Scotland after the Jacobite Rising when any stranger could kill you. Another source was in Ireland. The Irish penal laws were pretty instructive in not trusting your fellow men. These came after the Battle of the Boyne in 1690. The English decided that "they wanted the Irish to become insignificant slaves, fit for nothing but to hew wood and draw water." So, they barred the Catholics from the Army, the Navy, the law, commerce, and from every civic activity. "No Catholic could vote, hold any office under the Crown, or purchase land. Catholic estates were dismembered by an enactment saying that at the death of a Catholic owner, the land must be divided among all his sons, not given to the oldest son," which meant that in three or four generations, a great landholder's descendants have become a bunch of small farmers. Educations was made almost impossible since Catholics could not attend nor keep schools, nor send their children to be educated abroad. Priest hunting was considered to be a sport. So, the old families disappeared, the old estates were broken up, and no one could be trusted.

> His religion made him an outlaw. In the Irish House of Commons, the Irish peasant was described as 'the common enemy'. To whom could he look for redress. To his landlord? Almost invariably an alien conqueror. To the law? Not when every person connected with the law from jailer to judge was a Protestant who regarded him as the common enemy. And so he learned to take the law into his own hands, to keep his own business secret, to distrust strangers. These were dangerous lessons for any government to compel its subjects to learn, and a dangerous habit of mind for any nation to acquire. [*The Great Hunger.*]

We see the ramifications still, hundreds of years later, hundreds of miles from Ireland.

The other thing that the Irish and Scots share with their Appalachian descendants is love of land. Before the potato famine, very few Irish emigrated. In a contemporary account of the 1845 famine when conditions had become severe, the Earl of Derby underscores this love of country. He wrote: "Only during the famine did the Irish immigrants leave the country willingly, without the weeping and wailing, the shrieks of anguish, the keening as for the dead which could be witnessed in the west of Ireland at the departure of the immigrants." They hated to go.

I picked up on this, not by knowing that it was something we brought with us, but by seeing how people felt about the Appalachian mountains. In a scene in *The Hangman's Beautiful Daughter,* on a Saturday before Christmas, Sheriff Spencer Arrowood is out on a hillside near the railroad tracks. There's a custom called "The Santa Claus Train" in which the coal companies who owned so much of the land and the resources in the mountains, get together a bunch of presents, load them on a train, and run that train a hundred miles or more through coal country, throwing the gifts off to the children waiting along the tracks. Spencer is there to keep order and to make sure no one gets hurt. In this passage, the sheriff is looking at the people he sees waiting there on the tracks for the Santa Claus Train.

> Spencer adjusted his brown Stetson and strolled down to the track. The steel rails stretched away between the cuts in the mountain pasture land, curving out of sight at the bend where the forest began. His boots crunched on the gravel siding as he leaned out to look along the length of track facing east. All was still. He turned and waved to the crowd camped on the hill. Some of them had brought blankets to sit on; others stood and talked, cigarettes dangling from their fingers, as shrieking blond children chased each other through the clumps of people and into the weeds.

There was a sameness to them, he thought, scanning the faces. Many of the women were overweight from a lifetime on the diet of the poor. The deep-fried and starchy foods that are both filling and cheap make pasty complexions and lumpish bodies. The men were short and gaunt, a combination of ancestral genetics and poor nutrition. Beer and cigarettes in lieu of vegetables and jogging didn't help any, either. But they were honest people, and if there was work to be had, they'd put in long hours without a murmur.

People he knew from Knoxville and from the flatlands were always saying how great the house prices were in east Tennessee, and how cheap it was to live in the mountains, but Spencer reckoned that living in the mountains cost most of those people on the hillside ten years of their lives. And maybe a future for their children. But they wouldn't leave-not for jobs or love. Those that did leave sickened in exile in the ugly cities of the Midwest, pining for the hills of home. Even people who weren't poor, like himself or Dallas Stuart's young law partner, J.W. Lyon, could make more money and advance their careers by moving elsewhere, but they continued to stay in the shadows of the mountains. Why can't we just get out of these hills? He wondered for the thousandth time. Why are we so willing to sacrifice so much to live in this beautiful place? If this were the Garden of Eden, God couldn't drive us out of here with a flaming sword. We'd sneak back when the angel wasn't looking.

The sad thing was that the poverty wasn't natural to the region. The livestock business had thrived before the chestnut blight, and just to the north of Hamelin, lay land that bore the richest deposits of anthracite coal in the world. You could stand by this railroad track at any hour of any day you chose and watch a mile-long coal train hauling the natural resources away. The coal mines weren't locally owned, and they didn't put much back into local taxes, either. The mine owners could afford lawyers and lobbyist to see to that. Spencer had once read that 90 percent of the state of West Virginia was owned by absentee landlords.

The coal companies would be running the train today; the only of the year that didn't haul coal. At least they made this gesture; offered a little money to the people. But maybe if things had been different politically, there wouldn't have to be a train like this.

I thought that was ironic. If West Virginia, just by itself, seceded from the United States, it could be the fifth richest industrial nation in the world. But as it is, all the minerals are hauled away, and once a year they bring this train through and throw toys to the children. Not good. Not new, either.

The last thing I want to talk about is art—the art of war. The next book that I do, if and when I finish *Frankie Silver,* will talk about the Civil War in the mountains. That conflict was not the Civil War in the *Gone with the Wind* sense, but much more the Civil War in the sense of Afghanistan or Bosnia. It was a terrible, terrible time. When I started looking into the methods and traditions of warfare, I discovered that the American Civil War was essentially Super Bowl 1863, and that we had been fighting that same damned war for more than 2000 years. Not only fighting the same war, but fighting it in the same sort of way and not learning a whole lot. In case you or anyone you know plans on going to West Point, please listen carefully.

In 225 BC, the Celts had moved into Western Europe. They started out as people in Eastern Europe, and you can find the early Celtic artifacts and burial sites there. But by 225 BC they had moved west into France, and they had come to northern Italy in the Po Valley. The Romans did not like that. There had been border raids and the usual bad blood skirmishes between two cultures. Finally the Romans sent troops up there to confront the Celts. They lost a few of the battles, but finally the big one came at Telemon, in 225 BC in the Po Valley. The Celts did what they always do, they attacked. They had swords that were good for cutting, not for thrusting. They let out enormous war cries, and they charged. They wore very little, no armor, and their shields were small. The Romans, however, had been fighting them for some years and had been taking note. Roman soldiers wore metal armor, had sharp swords that thrust as well as cut, and they carried shields as tall as they were. When the Celts came charging up to the enemy, they met a solid metal wall: the Romans had put all the shields together and stood behind them. Another problem for the Celts: their metal working was less sophisticated than that of the Romans. When they cut or hacked with their swords, the weapons bent. To use the sword again, you'd have to unbend it. So, there you stood with your foot straightening out your sword. Guess what happened next....

The Celts lost 40,000 soldiers in that one battle, and 10,000 more were taken prisoner. That was pretty much the end of them as a threat to Rome.

They migrated west after that, into Britain. I could keep giving you accounts of cross-cultural skirmishes, but we can skip all the way to Culloden in 1745. From Marcy Moor outside the little town near Inverness, April 16, 1746, the Jacobites commanded by Bonnie Prince Charlie meet the English commanded by the Duke of Cumberland. The earl of Murray was the quartermaster for the Prince's army. He had left the food in Inverness. He brought the wrong size ammunition. The men marched for twenty-four hours, largely on empty stomachs, before the battle, so they were exhausted. Their swords this time were huge claymores, hardly able to be lifted, no armor.... It's the Duke of Cumberland's birthday, literally and figuratively. His men are well armed, they have bayonets on the end of their muskets, they have very effective cannons. And what do the clans do? The same thing they did in 225 BC. They all lined up in a straight line, and then they *charged* with heavy sword towards the *bayonets*. The English rifle drill taught the soldier not to bayonet the attacker coming straight on, but to aim at the one to the side. If everyone works together, that's a killer. The man rushing towards you has his arm raised with the sword, so if you go in from the side, he's unprotected and you've got him. Two thousand soldiers were killed that day on the Scots side. British losses: fifty men. And that was the beginning of the conquest of Scotland, that led to the Highland Clearances, and that whole chain of events that ended with so many people coming to America.

I contend that if you want to understand the American Civil War, forget *Gettysburg.* The film you really ought to watch is *Braveheart,* because there it is. Remember? seventy-five percent of New England: English, seventy-five percent of the South: Celtic. Super Bowl 1863. Gettysburg, Pennsylvania.

The other factor to remember is that Celts don't like trench warfare. They don't like entrenchment, barricades, and breastworks. They don't like hiding behind stuff. I wish they would learn! There's no lack of courage or determination, but they honestly think that if you charge and yell, you're strong and brave—that you can overcome guys who are hiding behind fortifications. Gettysburg. Here are all these men up on the hill with cannons and rifles, and the South tries to take the hill. What they also didn't realize is that much earlier in the war, the rifles used by the Union—*but not by the Confederacy*—had gained twice the range of the old weapons. So the boys in grey are still fighting the Mexican

War, the Battle of Culloden, Telemon, but the weaponry is advanced. You're trying to charge, and they can get you half a mile away. Out of 75,054 Confederate troops at Gettysburg, 22,634 were killed. Let me put that in perspective for you: they lost this number in just two days in Pennsylvania in 1863. We lost 55,000 in the whole Vietnam war, in more than ten years. The Celtic soldier...

Barry Sadler, who wrote the song *The Green Berets*, also wrote a book called *The Universal Soldier*, a kind of science fiction/fantasy thing. In it, the hero was a kind of Roman Soldier. He can't die. He just keeps being a soldier in various armies all the way through history, and finally he gets to Vietnam. It's kind of a Sgt. Rock sort of book, but Sadler is on to something. If you watched the movie about Audie Murphy, the highly decorated hero of World War II, you saw that in a way Audie Murphy *was* the Universal Soldier. I can see him, that same Steve McQueen body type, at Telemon, with his short sword and his inadequate shield. There he is at Culloden, trying to lift that big Claymore sword to charge against bayonets and cannons. There he is at Gettysburg in Pickett's charge up against excellent, state of the art rifles and fortifications. Audie Murphy, East Texas, yet one-hundred-and-ten percent Celt.

Culture doesn't go away. In art, in music, in rural customs, and even in war, if you go back far enough, everything starts to make sense, and you begin to see the patterns, the family resemblances. Or as Pinero said: "I believe the future is simply the past, entered through another gate."

Photo Credit: Jerry Bauer

Sharyn McCrumb

Biography

Sharyn McCrumb, currently living in the Virginia Blue Ridge, is the great-granddaughter of circuit preachers in North Carolina's Smoky Mountains. The author says it's from these ancestors that she gets her storytelling ability, her regard for books, and her love for the Appalachian region. Her Celtic ancestors seem to have blessed her slightly with the Sight, or at least with a special lens through which she brings the past richly to life while hinting at the future. Her novels, whether centered on Elizabeth MacPherson, Jay Omega, or the Ballad Series characters, strongly weave contemporary issues into their rich tapestries. Sharyn has won all of the major mystery awards: the Edgar Allan Poe Award for Best Paperback Original (*Bimbos of the Death Sun*, 1988), the Anthony, Agatha, Macavity, and Nero Wolfe Awards, and been nominated for the Independent Mystery Bookseller's Dilys Award for the "book most fun to sell." Her books have been named Notable Books of the Year by *The New York Times* and the *Los Angeles*

Times. She is the recipient of numerous scholarly awards iincludiing Outstanding Contribution to Appalachian Literature and Southern Writer of the Year. Married to David, with three children, she divides her time between writing and traveling either across the Atlantic to her Celtic heritage, or around the United States lecturing on the cultural significance of the Ballad novels at universities, libraries, and museums.

Bibliography

The Elizabeth MacPherson Novels:
    Sick of Shadows, 1984
    Lovely in Her Bones, 1985
    Highland Laddie Gone, 1986
    Paying the Piper, 1988
    The Windsor Knot, 1990
    Missing Susan, 1991
    MacPherson's Lament, 1992
    If I'd Killed Him When I Met Him . . .,1995
    The PMS Outlaws, 2000

The Ballad Novels:
    If Ever I Return, Pretty Peggy-O, 1990
    The Hangman's Beautiful Daughter, 1992
    She Walks These Hills, 1994
    The Rosewood Casket, 1996
    The Ballad of Frankie Silver, 1999
    The Songcatcher, 2001

The Jay Omega Novels:
    Bimbos of the Death Sun, 1987
    Zombies of the Gene Pool, 1992

Short Story Collection:
    Foggy Mountain Breakdown, 1997

Philip Craig

◇

Bogs, Beowulf, and Baubles…

Bogs, Beowulf, and Baubles...

Martha's Vineyard is an island that lies just off the southern coast of Massachusetts. It's roughly triangular in shape and consists of about 125 square miles of land. In the summer it houses 100,000 visitors. In the winter, its population is about 12,000. There are six townships on the island, and each is different in character and topography. Once famous for its farms and whaling ships, its principal economy now is tourism, its second is fishing.

I first went to Martha's Vineyard in the spring of 1955, when, quite on the spur of the moment, I decided to go there instead of returning to Colorado and putting in another summer as a lumberjack. My principal reason for doing this was a girl, Shirley, who lived on the island. A second reason was that I had never been to an island and had always wanted to see one. I expected the Vineyard to be a mound of sand with a palm tree growing in the middle of it, and thus was quite surprised to discover that it had electricity, cars, and all of the other conveniences of the mainland.

But it was better than the mainland. I had never seen a village as clean and neat as Edgartown. Coming from southwest Colorado where dust is the prevailing condition, and, more recently, having spent a college winter in Boston, I was enchanted by Edgartown's green lawns, swept streets and sidewalks, flower gardens, and perfectly maintained houses. It was like a make-believe place, like a creation of the imagination.

I found Shirley's house and I got a job working on a barge and repairing docks destroyed by the previous year's hurricane. I went back to the island the next summer and the year after that I married Shirley. We've been summering on the island ever since. Our children, fourth generation Vineyarders, were born there.

The Vineyard is a perfect place for a writer to set stories. Its population includes the rich and the poor, the famous and the unknown, the good and the bad. Its topography varies from coastal plains to rolling hills and includes fresh water streams, brackish ponds, and salt water bays.

It's surrounded by a sea full of fish, and its ponds are rich with shellfish: scallops, oysters, clams, and mussels. Its citizens include every sort of human being alive: Gay Head is home to Wampanoag Indians; Oak Bluffs is a renowned summer colony for Afro-Americans and has been for a hundred years; Edgartown and Vineyard Haven are famous yachting ports; West Tisbury and Chilmark are homes for artists and farmers.

In short, the Vineyard is a beautiful microcosm of the world; anything that can happen anywhere can happen on the Vineyard, so a writer can set a thousand stories on the island and never run out of tales yet to tell. In my own case, being a writer of mystery novels, I like to contrast the popular view of the island as a sort of paradise with a darker side of Vineyard life that few tourists see: the poverty and the evil doings that are normally known only to the cops, the medical community, and the social workers. This Serpent in Eden concept is central to most of my stories.

◇◇◇

I've not thought of myself as an author who makes consistent use of art in his novels, but manifestations of my lifelong interest in history and antiquities do pop up in my books fairly often. When this happens, I typically have to do research to create the impression that I know more than I really do, and to employ some tricks of the con man's trade to persuade my readers that I'm more honest than is actually the case.

When I was a kid, one of the most influential books that I read was Richard Halliburton's *Complete Book of Marvels.* My mother gave it to her children when I was six years old, and I loved it. If ever I win the lottery, my plan is to go around the world following Richard Halliburton's routes and visiting all the wonderful old places he wrote about.

Even in our pre-lottery-winner current state, when my wife and I travel, we often visit places that consist of piles of broken rock: ruined cities, standing stones, and the remains of cathedrals and castles. This interest in antiquities and ancient places is reflected in my mystery novels.

In *The Woman Who Walked into the Sea,* for example, the motive for a murder lies in a character's obsession with some ancient standing stones on Martha's Vineyard, the island as I've mentioned is my wife's ancestral home, and which is the location of my series of novels featuring Jeff Jackson. Apparently I was reasonably successful in creating the impression that those fictional standing stones are real, because I still have readers come up to me to ask where they can be found.

Actually, the whole notion of such stones existing on the Vineyard is not as far-fetched as it may initially seem. There's a group of out-of-the-mainstream archaeologists, anthropologists, and linguists whose members are rigorous advocates of the argument that there was extensive pre-Columbian European, African, and possibly Oriental contact with the Americas, and that those contacts are reflected in both the language of modern Amerindians and in the archaeological remains of past American civilizations. It's an idea that has interested me since I was very young, since it seemed to me then—and seems to me now—that there are remarkable similarities between the ruins of the high cultures of pre-Columbian America and those of ancient civilizations across the Atlantic and Pacific oceans.

Some strange looking rock constructions in New England, for instance, have been interpreted by advocates of these theories as being similar to the great stone structures found in such places as Avebury, Stonehenge, Malta, and Carnac. Traditional scholars are inclined to dismiss such notions, but whatever the proper interpretation of such structures, there is one such ancient stone construction on Martha's Vineyard that nobody's been able to explain: The Chilmark Quoit, which consists of vertical stones topped by a capstone. It's less impressive in size than similar quoits in Europe, but someone lost in the mists of history built it, and no one today knows the who or why of it.

There is also a "Viking gravestone" in the Martha's Vineyard Museum. There have been other rumored rocks on the island—from time to time someone staggers out of the woods to report a strange stone covered with what appears to be ancient writing, but no one is ever able to find it again. Such tales have been circulating around the Vineyard for centuries, rather like the Arizona stories of gold mines such as the Lost Dutchman Mine wherein an ancient prospector makes friends with a local grocer who stakes him to enough money and food to go into the Superstition Mountains where, by God, the old prospector finds the gold and comes out, then dies before he can reveal the mine's location but leaves an enigmatic map in the hands of the grocer, who never actually has time to go look but leaves it to his grandchild, who in turn hikes in but is never able to follow the map to the treasure.... The same thing happens in the case of Martha's Vineyard's fabled rocks.

We also have rumors of Viking encounters, a popular notion that Martha's Vineyard is the Vinland mentioned in the Viking explorations. I've done a good deal of reading on this topic, and I'm not convinced that the Vikings got as far south as Martha's Vineyard, but many people are. It's all great; if you're a romantic—or a novelist—you can't do any better than this.

The plot I constructed in *The Woman Who Walked into the Sea* stems from an old scholar who is persuaded that he has found some genuine pre-Columbian standing stones on the island. That belief becomes the motive for a murder. The scholar is strapped for cash and it looks ominously like he'll have to sell his land to the dreaded developers, the eternal villains on the Vineyard, but he manages to avoid doing that while keeping his beloved stones protected. To persuade my readers that those fictional stones actually exist, I had characters in the book refer to the real Chilmark Quoit and to a number of other well known but enigmatic stone structures such as Mystery Hill in New Hampshire. It's near my home and is an impressive site. Since my readers can, if they wish, verify the existence of such real sites, they are inclined to accept my fictional ones as well!

This technique is well known to con men and to writers of mystery novels. Most of these wizards, at least of the modern species, tend to try to create the illusion of reality in their books rather than presenting some kind of science fiction or fantasy where readers know right away that they aren't dealing with truth, except metaphorically. If you, the author, want to persuade the reader that an untruth is a truth, you tell the truth, tell the truth, tell the truth, lie; tell the truth, tell the truth, tell the truth, lie...."

It's an old but always viable scam technique, and one I recommend to all would-be mystery writers. That's the technique I used in this book with the stones, pointing out that you can drive right up to the Chilmark Quoit and see it. I tell you right where it is. Then, in the middle of the story, I have the murderer discover some rocks that only exist in my imagination. I am playing a sort of con game of my own, feeding in all the information I'd gleaned about new world structures and creating something that makes perfect sense, but is just sufficiently enigmatic so that the reader can't be absolutely sure the stones are there, or what they are for if they do exist, which is what happens when we look at the actual monuments. No one knows exactly what was going on in Stonehenge. We can go there and eyeball it, or eyeball Avebury or Carnac, but nobody can tell us why they were built, or what purpose they served. They remain…a mystery. The same thing happens here in Indian ruins like Chaco canyon. The structures are clearly oriented to the sun but precisely why, and who built them and then left, shrouds them in an aura of mystery that probably lends itself very nicely to my profession.

In the same novel, I also used this technique to introduce a Shakespearean theme involving the discovery of a fragment of a play about King Arthur, reputedly written by the Bard. I did this to bolster creation of a *faux* ruin—one fake supported by another.

King Arthur's story is the most famous and most often retold tale in British literature; the legend and its characters, its great romances and griefs, have never lost their power to fascinate. I have long wondered why Shakespeare, who wrote about many a lesser king, bypassed Arthur. Why not tap into this? I'm not a true scholar, I lack the love of drudgery that marks him, that sends him into a roomful of dusty books to emerge with a tiny nugget of undiscovered information, but I admire his ilk, and occasionally swipe ideas from accounts of their feats. Thus, to correct an obvious omission on Shakespeare's part, I had scholars in *The Woman Who Walked into the Sea* discover a fragment of what may have been just such a play! I created a circumstance within which my scholar would actually find this lost manuscript fragment in a believable and deceptively casual way. It's not a whole play—I thought this might be too much to swallow—but it's enough.

Of course, the question that immediately arises in the book, as it would arise in real life if such a fragment were actually discovered, is: is it a fake? In respect to this question, it's perhaps important to remember that controversies swirl about not only the authenticity of "Shakespearean" writings, but about the very identity of the man whom we know as Shakespeare, with respectable scholars waging intellectual war on both sides of the issues. Just as I did with the theme of the standing stones, I dealt with the Shakespearean issue by mixing facts and literary arguments with my own imaginings, and creating, I hoped, the illusion that the latter were as real as the former.

Shakespeare "borrowed" ideas and characters himself. I thus felt I could "borrow" from him to put a manuscript fragment into my mystery with the question of whether or not it's genuine encapsulated in larger questions of authenticity, and use this as the hook that brings the scholar/victim to Martha's Vineyard. And I had a lot of fun writing a mystery novel that included such arcane considerations.

Having said all this, I'm sorry to report that *The Woman Who Walked into the Sea* is out of print.

In another book, *Death on a Vineyard Beach*, I dealt with a different sort of antiquity, a Martha's Vineyard cranberry bog, an ancient topographical feature highly valued for this delicacy. There are bogs all over New England like those on the Vineyard where it's the great local berry. The tale is placed within real and ongoing land disputes on the island. The story follows the course of a dispute about the ownership of an ancient bog in Gay Head, the Vineyard's westernmost village, where a group of Wampanoag Indians live. In my book, some of the Wampanoags are intent upon recovering the bog, arguing that their ancestors were cheated out of it. Opposing them is the current owner of the bog which is part of a large Gay Head estate that he's purchased. He did it in all innocence, but the Indians claim the bog was stolen from them—probably true. This current owner is a wealthy but aging retired Mafioso who's set on keeping his property intact. Then someone takes a shot at him, and he hires Jeff Jackson to figure out who the shooter might be. Can it be someone from Boston where he has criminal interests? or from New York or the Cape, same reason? or is some local hood trying to knock him off? Jeff's first suspects are, of course, the Wampanoags who are angry with his employer for refusing to return what they believe to be "their" cranberry bog to the tribe.

There are some hot and heavy arguments on the Vineyard today about these lands. I find that people generally do not kill each other over important reasons, but over something more trivial like a nickel, a spilled drink, a casual remark...a bog. But that which is trivial to some is major to others, and so a matter for murder might arise over this topographical phenomenon that stems from antiquity and continues to be meaningful and controversial right up to the present day.

By the way, in this dispute is a character I've created, Joe Begay, who is half Hopi and...well, he doesn't claim any particular ancestry, perhaps part Navajo, and per his claim, part anyone else who wandered by during the past four hundred years. He's cast aside the notion of tribal identity and that's an issue that I find interesting: how do we define who we are racially? I have no answers, but I find that the older I get, the less it matters. I also choose not to use real historical personages in my books even though the one I've just written involves the kidnapping of the American President's daughter.

Just as historic arguments and disagreements about standing stones, Shakespeare, and a cranberry bog are of major importance in the books I've already mentioned, so history literature, and myth have also provided central themes in others. My first published book, *Gate of Ivory, Gate of Horn,* is about a group of adventurers looking for the tomb of Beowulf. If you reach into the far corners of your memory you may extract a recollection of the great Geatish hero who, in or around the Sixth Century, lived on the coast of what is now Sweden. He it is who slew Grendal and Grendal's mother, who died in old age while killing a dragon, and whose body was burned in a great funeral pyre atop a cliff overlooking the sea.

If Beowulf actually existed, and there is some reason to believe that he did, then, I reasoned, his tomb might also exist. If so, it would be worth finding, for it is described in the poem as a tower built by his followers. They built a tower and put his jewels in it and him atop, and then set it on fire so that the smoke would rise toward heaven. The tomb was filled with treasure worthy of a great king.

So I decided to find it in fiction.

I studied atlases, maps, and sea charts so my characters would know where to sail. I created two great cliffs on the Swedish coast thrusting into the sea, and I placed an ancient ruined tower on top of one of them. Since the dragon that killed Beowulf, and was at the same time slain by the hero, had previously showered fire on a nearby town, I created such a town, making it a Roman city. Even though the Romans, as far as I knew, had never reached Scandinavia, I couldn't see any reason why they could not have, so I had them establish an outpost there which, by the time of Beowulf's life and death, was already greatly in ruins.

Having created an imaginary geography and history, and combined those elements with a good deal of medieval myth and real history, I wrote my book and had a fine time doing it.

It is, of course, out of print.

Moving on from bogs and Beowulf to baubles, we come to the sequel to *The Woman Who Walked into the Sea*, a novel titled *The Double-Minded Men*, which is third in the Jeff Jackson series.

I wrote it because I wanted to write an "impossible crime" story. I wanted to steal a precious necklace in full view of two hundred people and not have them realize that a crime had even occurred.

But first, I had to make a necklace that was worth stealing.

What about one made of emeralds and gold? I like emeralds but am bored by diamonds. Actually, I like opals best, but it seemed unlikely anyone would go to such lengths for an opal necklace, so I settled for the emerald.

In order to make my story, and the necklace, believable, and to create an impression that I knew what I was talking about, I had to ask and answer some necessary background questions, then do the required research on jewelry. Where do emeralds come from? I think mine ended up coming from Columbia after I did some research on their source. What do the rough stones look like? How are they cut from the raw crystalline form? How are they set into a necklace? Who designs and makes this bauble? Can I use some killer pearls to make the completed necklace more valuable, something worth stealing?

Once I knew these things, I needed a history for the necklace. Where was it kept, and how and why did it come to Martha's Vineyard so I could arrange to steal it? It had to happen there, on the island, for purposes of my series. This led me to create its country of origin. In the book, this nation is called Sarofim. It's located between Iran and India, a spot which, after I consulted my atlas, seemed to me like a good one for the country I needed.

When I had it, I realized it needed to be a believable place and I needed to know a lot about it. After doing research into Iran and India, and assuming that Sarofim probably would be defined by similar influences, I created its national economy, its history, its political system, its religion, and its topography, and made the necklace a part of its national treasury. Then I asked, "Why was the necklace one of its treasures? Why would this bauble move across the Atlantic to my little island?"

The answer to this was somewhat elaborate. It required that I create a series of dynastic leaders who in its history had ruled Sarofim at one time or another, and thus a ruling class. In a dictionary I stumbled across the word "padishah", a variation on the word "shah" (like the Shah of Iran; remember him?). A padishah is basically a ruler. I thought, "that sounds good, it's got a ring to it, so let there be the Padishah of Seraphim." And, lo! it was done.

Now, I needed a Padishah to ascend the throne in such a manner that he would lose the emerald necklace. He did it in the standard way: in the 18th Century, my guy overthrew a previous regime. How did he do it? He got the help of a renegade British officer who organized the aspirant's ragtag army, trained the troops, and engineered a *coup d'état*. Good, we were now in power. But then the Englishman, a soldier of fortune and wised up about the habits of dictators when it comes to payoffs, stole his reward—my emerald necklace—and a great deal of gold from the royal treasury of Sarofim and took it back to England.

In order to do all that, I got out the atlas and found the places, I got out my geographic atlas and found out what kind of land they had between Iraq and India—was it mountains? was it deserts? What kind of economy would there have been, and how did the people stay alive there? Well, there's a trade or shipping route that runs east to west, so I created a bunch of corsairs or robbers who worked out of the port of what later became Sarofim. They raided trading convoys, and made themselves rich through piracy until finally the British got sick and tired of their ships being plundered and moved in to establish themselves and bring order, the kind of stuff they typically did to build an Empire in the Eighteenth and Nineteenth Centuries. On this bloody past, and on what I thought was a plausibly legitimate history for Sarofim and my necklace, and also for my soldier of fortune, who becomes rich and famous and marries advantageously, as did his descendants, I built my story. I actually had to work out all this stuff—even Sarofim's religion, which is an offshoot of Islam but they eat meat—so that I would know how my necklace got to Martha's Vineyard and started my plot rolling. I finally get the necklace to the Vineyard because a series of marriages between American and English branches of the soldier's family establish a dynasty here, and one of its heirlooms is...the necklace.

Now we fast jump ahead to this century to how I steal the necklace. To do that I had to create an international event. The Padishah is negotiating with the United States for the right to put a deep water military establishment in Sarofim, which by now has significant military and strategic importance. The United States wants to get its military into Sarofim, and the Padishah's position is that maybe something can be worked out, but in exchange for the base, what about the return of the royal treasure that was stolen two hundred years ago? The American who now owns the necklace is desperate for a position in the diplomatic corps, and agrees—for a price—to return the necklace at a posh event at a great house on Martha's Vineyard where Presidents, movie stars, and other such famous folk cavort. This is a lot of background work for a pretty small incident, but it allowed me to do some real digging around, something I enjoy, a sort of fake research.

Jeff Jackson gets involved because there's a need to beef up security for the transfer ceremony, and he's a former cop. The security risk is seen as stemming from some anti-Padishah activity going on, a revolutionary group of Sarofim students in America who'd love to embarrass the regime. As one of the extra security people, Jeff is on hand when the big event takes place. The big event is staged on the Vineyard because the Padishah loves Superman movies and he wants to make a splash. To that end, he's hired a Hollywood director to create a major event. And the event is that's there's a real necklace, and there's a paste necklace, and the United States gets to keep the paste replica which is destined for the Smithsonian as a relic of one of the great works of the jeweller's art. On the night of the ceremony, the fake necklace is brought to the assembly to be admired and passed over to the museum. Then the donor goes back upstairs to bring down the real thing, and, surprise, it's gone...out of a locked room.

The question is not only who did it and why, but how? I wanted to steal that necklace in front of a throng looking right at it—and I did. Everything in the book led up to that scene, and then everything that happened after the robbery led away from that scene. That scene, in fact, is the only reason I did all of the research required to paint its background canvas, the only reason I wrote the book. My hero spends the rest of it figuring out the who, the why, and the how.

Need I say that *The Double Minded Men* is out of print?

You've probably noticed the obvious, that in my books I'm always dealing with artifice, with lies, fakes, questions of ownership, identity, and history. Did a pre-Columbian European culture assemble Martha's Vineyard's stone monuments, or did some farmer just want to get rocks out of his field? Is this a real emerald necklace or is it paste? Who owns that cranberry bog? Who's lying about what to whom, and why? What's the truth? It's all a lot of fun. I think one of the most enjoyable parts of writing mysteries is the research you have to do, not only on technical questions like types of poison and proper police procedure, so as to get it right, but to pick up little idiosyncratic bits of information that normally you wouldn't need to know in a million years in order to grab your readers.

By the way, the way you steal things from a locked room is a scam, sort of the way you work a magic trick: "look at this hand! but this is the hand you should be watching." Magicians work that way. Sleight of hand magic is based on "my hands can do things faster than yours can while you're looking somewhere else." Big deal magic like sawing the woman in half or hiding the elephant takes a lot of preparation, especially in equipment. You set it all up, just like you do a scam, and direct people to look at what they think they should be seeing, what they want to see, while you're really showing them something else. This works in part because in our common experience, most of the time, people don't lie to us. People tell the truth. That's how we live: we live a life of trust, even the most cynical of us. The light is green, it says you walk, and you think the cars will stop, so you step off the curb. And the cars almost always do. You trust people who are in professions or businesses to do what they are supposed to do. You shop for food at the grocery, and you assume it isn't poisoned. We all live lives of incredible confidence in each other. And that's why con artists are so successful. That's why my locked-room mystery worked.

We mystery writers are con artists. We go to great lengths to weave elaborate webs of deception, to create the impression that one thing is happening when something else is actually going on. We labor long to create convincing realism, and we not only earn some money but take delight in literary sleight of hand, in adorning our tales with frauds, fakes, and felonies…in making murder artful.

Philip Craig

Biography

Phil Craig grew up on a small cattle ranch in southwest Colorado. The family did without running water or electricity when he was little, but it did have shelves of books because mother had been a school teacher. Phil learned to read when he was five and by grade school started writing poetry and prose—neither very well. Mad about Tarzan, he collected the books and quickly became the Tarzan expert of La Plata County. Years later, barely surviving Boston University where he earned a degree in Philosophy and Religion but actually majored in fencing and minored in bridge, he tackled the University of Iowa Writers Workshop for an MFA in prose fiction. Landing a job at a small college, he worked during summers in Edgartown on the Vineyard, writing novels on his lunch hour. He never intended to write mysteries, but when his novel *Gate of Ivory, Gate of Horn* published in 1969, it surprised the author as a Crime Club selection. The die was cast.... Long married to Shirley Prada Craig, Phil has retired from his post as professor of literature at Wheelock College and now lives year round on Martha's Vineyard. One Craig child lives in Colorado so they sometimes come West as well.

Bibliography

The Jeff Jackson Novels:
> *A Beautiful Way to Die*, 1989
> *The Woman Who Walked into the Sea*, 1991
> *The Double Minded Men*, 1992
> *Cliff Hanger*, 1993
> *A Case of Vineyard Poison*, 1994
> *Off Season*, 1995
> *Death on a Vineyard Beach*, 1996
> *A Deadly Vineyard Holiday*, 1997
> *A Shoot on Martha's Vineyard*, 1998
> *A Fatal Vineyard Season*, 1999
> *Vineyard Blues*, 2000
> *Vineyard Shadows*, 2001

With William G. Tapply, *First Light*, 2001

Other:
> *Gate of Ivory, Gate of Horn*, 1969

Elizabeth Peters

◇

The Famous Egyptologist
Takes to Crime

The Famous Egyptologist
Takes to Crime...

We have a joke in the writing business about the questions we find most exasperating. Probably the most exasperating is the good old, "Where do you get your ideas?" Think about it for a few minutes, and try to understand why this innocent question should annoy us so much. In part it's because of the ambiguity of the word "ideas." Do you mean it would be nice to write a book about the ancient Etruscans? That's an idea, but it's a long way from being a book. Books require more than ideas; they require things called plots. As for where you find ideas, you don't. They are omnipresent. If you aren't on the lookout for them, you don't see them, and if you've trained yourself to spot them, they are all over the place.

Another question I find personally frustrating is "How did you become interested in Egyptology?" I've reached the point where I want to say, "Why isn't everybody interested in Egyptology?" I think all young people—I was about to say bright imaginative young people, but that sounds a little conceited—become fascinated by Egypt at a certain age. The implication of this is that some of us stayed in our first childhood all our lives. Possibly that is true, but it's what happened to me. I can't account for it, I can only say that of all the things that interest me—and a great many things do—Egypt is the one subject that interests me most. I've come back to it through all sorts of vicissitudes—such as children and marriage and other distractions.

I feel very fortunate to have been able to use my Egyptological training as I have. I was very young when I got my doctorate (twelve years old in case anybody is counting) and I had of course hoped to go into the field. At that time it was a great deal more difficult for women than it is today. It wasn't only because I was female; it was because I made the mistake—whoops, I was about to say "the horrible mistake"—of getting married. Getting married is not a mistake, but it was a mistake for a woman who wanted to be an Egyptologist if her husband was not one. Back in the Fifties it was not acceptable to abandon your husband and infant child and go haring off to Egypt.

When I began writing mystery stories, the beleaguered heroine, especially of the Victorian era, was very popular, so that was the first kind of mystery I wrote—a rather unoriginal version of the "governess romance," as I call them. However, as soon as I started the Elizabeth Peters books, I set the first one in Egypt. I had a wonderful time writing that book because I was able to discover the lost tomb of Akhenaton and Nefertiti. (I threw them both in just for fun.) However, my nefarious career didn't actually take off until someone suggested I do a Victorian novel set in Egypt. I had done several novels with Victorian settings, so I said, right, fine, and started to write a conventional book about a conventional heroine who went to Egypt, got lured into tombs and other dangerous places, and found a handsome romantic hero. I don't know how I ended up with a heroine like Amelia Peabody. She's totally unlike any heroine I had written about up to that time; in fact, I think she's unlike any heroine anybody had written about. She was speaking in her own voice, because I had decided to use a first person narrator, and I found her developing in a way I had not expected.

The opinionated, independent Victorian gentlewoman was unusual but not totally fictitious. Amelia B. Edwards is of course the person from whom I got Amelia's name. I have been quoted as saying Miss Edwards wrote "third rate thrillers", which is not fair. I don't think many of them are easily readable today; but for her time she wrote pretty good books and she earned a good living. It was not until after she made her first trip to Egypt that she wrote her best book. *A Thousand Miles Up the Nile* is not a thriller, it is a classic travel book, and still enormously enjoyable. I referred to it quite often while I was writing *The Crocodile on the Sandbank*, but, except for her name and a few other minor details, Amelia Peabody bears very little resemblance to Amelia B. Edwards who was a well behaved, proper Victorian lady.

I had to find a match for my opinionated, unconventional heroine. Searching for a model, I came upon William Flinders Petrie. When he was a young man, Petrie was quite good looking, with a lovely black beard and flashing dark eyes. He also had a terrible temper and a big mouth. He was very critical of other archaeologists—with some reason—so I thought it would be fun to have a hero who was like Petrie, only more so—even louder, even more opinionated and much, much sexier. I designed Emerson to be a foil for Amelia and I don't think she could have functioned without him. Even though people refer to these books as the Amelia books—I do myself—it's the two who work so well together.

However, when I wrote *Crocodile on the Sandbank*, I did not intend it to be the first of a series. I don't know that I should tell you this—you may find it disillusioning—but you should know that we in the writing game are not inspired solely by noble motives. When an editor said to me, "Why don't you write a mystery series, they are very popular?" I said—since I have no scruples—"Certainly, I will do that if it will make me lots of money."

On the surface, Amelia was a totally unsuitable candidate for a series, because I had not only married her off at the end of the first book, I had gotten her pregnant. (Or, to be more precise, Emerson had gotten her pregnant.) There is nothing more devastating to a female hero than having a baby. Even marriage is something of a handicap. Most husband-wife teams in detective fiction end up with one partner or the other serving essentially as comic relief. I wanted my protagonists to be equals, not only maritally, but insofar as the investigation of the crime was concerned.

The second book of the series was called *Curse of the Pharaohs*—and I would like to state here in public that I had nothing to do with that title which I think is one of the most unimaginative ever invented. My original title was *The Heart in the Cedar Tree*. The reference is to a classic Egyptian story called "The Tale of the Two Brothers." My editor thought this was too obscure, and that it sounded like a romantic novel. He changed the title to you know what. I've been trying to live it down ever since.

As I was saying, in that book there was this baby, and I wanted to get the Emersons back to Egypt, *sans enfant*. Again the Victorian setting gave me some help, because in those days parents of a certain socio-economic class didn't see that much of their children. The servants would trot the kiddies down at tea time all dressed in their best clothes and trot them back up to the nursery afterward. I figured Amelia could probably dispose of the baby for the winter easily enough, which she proceeded to do.

But from that point on I really did have to cope with Ramses. Ramses is, of course, the son of Amelia and Emerson. Opinions about the boy seem to be rather violently divided. You either loathe Ramses or you adore him. I must warn you that I do not take kindly to suggestions that I dispose of Ramses. This has been suggested, more than once, and I take umbrage at the idea.

Ramses is a perfectly nice child, if unusual.

As Amelia once remarked, "What can I say about Ramses? I have raised a son, and I assure you that in a lot of ways Ramses is no worse than any normal boy." I believe I need say no more on that subject.

The other thing about this series that I thought was going to be an enormous handicap was the fact that I had nailed it down in time. I had a good reason for doing this: historical fiction gains authenticity if it is related to specific historical events. I don't know why I picked the year 1884. I suppose I wanted to bring in the Mahdi, and the dervishes in the Sudan and so on. That was harmless enough, but once Ramses was born I was stuck with a definite chronological sequence. I didn't specify the year he was born, but I had given enough clues so that a reader with *that* kind of mind could easily ascertain what year it was—and I have readers with that kind of mind. They will spend hours looking through old almanacs to find out if there really was a full moon on the night of October 12, 1889. I knew that when I said in a particular book that Ramses was eight years old, those readers would be counting on their fingers and figuring out what year it was. Consequently I had to ascertain, in each book, precisely was going on in Egypt and the rest of the world in that year, in that very month.

For example, in *The Hippopotamus Pool*, Amelia says casually, "Oh, yes, we hear that dear Howard has just been appointed Inspector of Antiquities for Upper Egypt." I made it clear at the beginning that the book opens in Cairo, on December 31, 1899—New Year's Eve. The Emersons arrive in Luxor about two weeks later—mid-January, 1900. I had to make certain that Howard Carter had taken up his appointment by then. (He had.) I also wanted the Emersons to visit the tomb of Amenhotep II, which had been discovered the year before. (In case you don't know, though I'm sure you do, this was another cache of royal mummies.) There was considerable argument as to whether the extraneous royals should be moved to the Cairo Museum. In the end they were moved—but when? I needed to know how many mummies there were in the tomb when the Emersons went there. The sources did not all agree, so I amused myself for two weeks trying to find out the precise date. (January 1900.)

This is the kind of nit-picking research I love to do, and I believe it is this kind of nit-picking detail that readers appreciate. Even if you are not nasty-minded souls who relish picking holes in other peoples' work—even if you don't always catch a particular error—it seems to me there is a kind of climate created by repeated errors. Something makes you uneasy—something doesn't sound exactly right—and then your willing suspension of disbelief ceases and you aren't going to continue reading.

I also have fun with my Egyptological jokes. I have been known to cackle hysterically over things like having the Emersons miss the tomb of Tutankhamon by twenty feet or so—and Howard Carter's remark, to the effect that he doesn't want to work for rich American or English dilettantes.

Carter has been a friend of the Emersons for some time; he pops in now and then, and has little chats with them. I use other historical personages as minor characters, but I don't like to use them as major characters. A slight digression here, if I may; it is not so much of a digression as it may seem at first. Some of us who are interested in the field collect awful books about ancient Egypt. One of the worst I've ever read— I have forgotten the name, which is just as well, because now I can't be sued for slander—featured Howard Carter as the hero. At the end of the book he married the heroine, whom he had rescued from assorted villains. This was a totally fictitious account of the life of a real individual whose life is known in detail. I disapprove of this sort of thing, and I think my readers would agree.

The next book in the Amelia series takes place during the 1903-04 season, and one of my major problems is going to be with Ramses—the consequence of pinning myself down in time. Ramses was born in 1887—July—he's a Leo—somehow I wasn't surprised when I figured that out. He's now an adolescent, which is fun, but sooner or later he is going to be an adult. What sort of person will he be when he's grown up? He is an individual, with distinctive personality traits, but he is also a product of his time. His mother and father are getting older, too. I fully intend to have them continue their energetic activities—of all kinds—until they're a hundred years old. Even so, they are changing, as real people change. At least one hopes people do, acquiring more wisdom and more tolerance.

Seeing a Large Cat is number nine in the series, and I expect to carry it on through number twelve. I have it all worked out....

Well, I have a lot of ideas. All I need now are the plots.

*Paper first given at the University of Penn. Museum, March 22, 1996.

Photo Credit: Kristen Whitbread

Elizabeth Peters

Biography

Barbara Mertz, who writes fiction as Elizabeth Peters and Barbara Michaels, was born in Canton, Illinois, 1927. She earned a Ph.D. at the University of Chicago's Oriental Institute in 1952. An authority in Egyptology, she has written two nonfiction books and many scholarly articles, and draws upon her expertise in her popular fiction. As Elizabeth Peters, she writes several series characters—Amelia Peabody Emerson, Vicky Bliss, and Jacqueline Kirby—as well as standalone novels. (As Barbara Michaels she has written 29 suspense novels.) In 1989, she won the Agatha for Best Mystery with *Naked Once More* at Malice Domestic, a fan convention originally convened in her honor. In 1998, the Mystery Writers of America named her a Grand Master.

The author was married to Richard Mertz in 1950 (now divorced) and has one son and one daughter. She is an enthusiastic grandmother.

A Partial Bibliography

The Amelia Peabody Series:
The Crocodile on the Sandbank, 1975
The Curse of the Pharaohs, 1981
The Mummy Case, 1985
The Lion in the Valley, 1986
The Deeds of the Disturber, 1988
The Last Camel Died at Noon, 1991
The Snake, the Crocodile, and the Dog, 1992
The Hippopotamus Pool, 1996
Seeing a Large Cat, 1997
The Ape Who Guards the Balance, 1998
The Falcon at the Portal, 1999
He Shall Thunder in the Sky, 2000
Lord of the Silent, 2001
The Golden One, 2002
The Jacqueline Kirby Series:
The Seventh Sinner, 1972
The Murders of Richard III, 1974
Die for Love, 1984
Naked Once More, 1989
The Vicky Bliss Series:
Borrower of the Night, 1973
Street of the Five Moons, 1978
Silhouette in Scarlet, 1983
Trojan Gold, 1987
Night Train to Memphis, 1994
Egyptology, as Barbara Mertz:
Temples, Tombs and Hieroglyphs, 1964
Red Land, Black Land, 1966

Barbara Peters

◇

Riding with the
Wildcat in China…

Riding with the Wildcat in China...

I've said for the past few years that a more accessible China is bound to become the new theater for the thriller—especially now that the Evil Empire has crumbled and The Third Riech is so often revisited. But China is also ripe for use in the modern mystery, lagging just behind Japan. When the chance to join a Northwestern University alumni trip presented itself to me, my husband and I seized it. We were prompted by curiosity about China, not to mention my husband, Rob's, perpetual quest for the perfect meal, and were anxious to see Hong Kong before its transfer from Britain to China. So, we prepared to depart on 9 September, 1996, through San Francisco to Tokyo and thence to Beijing, our gateway to the Mysterious East.

International datelines being what they are, the flight across the Pacific seems to cover two days, while the return flight is compressed into an afternoon. Thus we enplaned at a Monday lunchtime on a beautiful late summer day by the bay, and arrived at Narita on Tuesday afternoon. There was very little to see, and no sense of Japan to be had along its concourses. We rather quickly boarded our four-hour flight to Beijing which, oddly, is one hour less far in time from the US than is Japan (because, they tried to explain, the time zone revolves west to east). We finally reached our destination about 9 p.m. on Tuesday, and were greeted by a True

Character, whom we came to know over the next sixteen days as Philip, our immensely suave escort. Accompanying Philip was a professional Chinese guide, a member of China's department governing tourists. She was very Western in jeans and tee and carrying a flower-patterned umbrella that became our standard and rallying-point. Her name was Jenny and she proved to be exceptional.

Our five-star hotel, the Palace, was a longish bus drive, but welcomed us with efficiency and elegance, and many warnings about drinking nothing but the bottled water or special tap water provided and using only this liquid for brushing teeth. I recalled an old story about an Indian maharajah who, after vowing water would never touch his lips, brushed only in Scotch. And I remembered a Virginia Bar trip to Peru where all those who wanted ice in their drinks paid a severe price. Following these injunctions, we awoke full of vigor to launch ourselves on Beijing.

What can I say about the capital city? For one thing, it's an unlikely location for the center of government, being stuck up in the northeast corner of the vast territory of China, quite near the fabled Great Wall. During much of China's history its capital was in the southern or middle territories where it was not only more central but easier to protect, but the Manchus fixed it firmly in the north during their final reign and there it remains. The climate is harsh, very cold in winter, very hot in summer, very dry and dusty, but our trip was timed to cash in on the temperate autumn and we were lucky here.

The old city, formerly surrounded by ancient walls that the Mao regime demolished in favor of easing traffic, has some elegance and order compared to the rampant, ugly growth of the new, a series of ugly concrete towers and boxes housing people and small businesses that spill over to the sidewalks and streets. The older compounds, called *hutongs*, are more picturesque, but are being rapidly replaced. Their low roof lines and walled compounds make them not unlike the adobes of Rob's longtime home, Santa Fe.

The traffic is unbelievable and anarchic despite some occasional police direction from towers erected at intersections. Lights are a mere suggestion, lanes are a laugh, left turns are for the bravest. Vehicles have the right of way, but only good luck lets the driver avoid pulverizing the teeming bicycles and bicycle-powered loads or trailers of goods and people, not to mention the pedestrians. A small blue truck was ubiquitous, much like the old Ford Model T must have been on American roads. We were astonished at the loads that were managed on bicycles or pulled by bicycles with trailers. While our hotel was theoretically just around the corner from the fabled palace of The Forbidden City, in practice it was a forty-five minute struggle to gain our first destination.

While China's modern urban architecture is a staggering disappointment, lacking the picturesque qualities of ancient or Third World buildings or the polished efficiencies of contemporary structures, the preserved buildings of Imperial China—and there aren't as many as such an ancient culture might have bequeathed since the main material was wood and conquest or domestic turbulence levelled a lot of that, as did fires and the passage of time—are truly staggering, more magnificent than imagined. The scale is vast, the detail and decoration overwhelming, the rhythmic outlines and soaring roofs breathtaking, the colors stunning, and the sense of history weighty. The urban palace, the Summer Palace, the pagodas, temples, monuments, the mosque later seen in Xi'an, completely satisfied our expectations and sharply underlined the architectural contrast between the past and the uninspired present.

Those who had seen the film, *The Last Emperor*, had the benefit of an image full of life and people to superimpose on the quiet grandeurs standing behind the monumental walls and gates. The main access to The Forbidden City is through Tiananmen Square and under a gateway hung with a huge portrait of Chairman Mao, another of those striking contrasts between today and yesterday. The Chairman's mausoleum is also at hand. Philip—or was it Jenny?—informed us that as the years pass, the lighting in the mausoleum's viewing room is going down as the corpse deteriorates. We appreciated this tidbit more when we later saw a several thousand year old mummy in Wushan that's holding up just fine. Apparently modern embalming techniques are not a patch on the ancient.

Just a cursory inspection of the palace occupied the whole morning. We ended in the magnificent gardens. Despite the enormous number of tourists, native and foreign, there was no sense of crowding in these huge courtyards and buildings, even in the imperial museum with its dusty treasures where visitors donned paper overshoes to protect the floors. The rich ox-blood of the royal walls, the remarkable Imperial-gold tiled roofs, the rich blues and greens, made both colors and shapes a feast for the eyes. The carved marble bridges and slabs provided bright accents to the dark hues. The fantastic guardian beasts—the female lion with a paw on her cub, the male with a paw on a globe—the giant urns and braziers, and the dragons that filled the same gutter-spout roles as European gargoyles, enhanced the magic. Even more fun was to discover that Chinese doorways have raised sills—just as the famous moon gates make their circles well above ground level—in order to cut down on ghost traffic. These spectres are thought to be kneeless and are thus unable to step up and over the raised door sills.

Next, a long drive northwest brought us to the lake and vast grounds of the Summer Palace. Its serpentine covered walkway along the shore boasting incredible painted ceilings, the hillside ramparts, the marble boat forever moored to its dock, the dragon boats on which we sailed back to the entry gate, gave just a hint of the grandeur—and artificiality—of imperial life, especially that enjoyed by the formidable Victorian Tsui-Hzi, the ruthless Last Empress.

Thoroughly exhausted, Rob and I abandoned thoughts of the Peking Opera for a foray into Peking Duck. This proved a disappointment at the restaurant we selected, but was remedied by a sensational meal the next evening in...our hotel. For Westerners and the privileged, it's often better to eat in the luxury hotels where ingredients are much higher in quality than the average restaurant can provide.

The next day took us on another bus ride to The Great Wall. The roadway was under construction. Observing one or two workers driving modern machinery while crews of others used shovels and brooms, we realized the effect of the Cultural Revolution had been to wipe out a generation not only of scholars, artists and artisans, but of skilled workers able to use modern technology. Only now is a new generation coming up to fill those places.

As with The Forbidden City, the scale of The Great Wall, the only man made structure visible from space, defies appreciation anywhere except atop the structure itself. It marches up and down the crests of the mountains in gradients that are—well, gruelling. Lacking engineering expertise, the second century BC work crews ignored valleys, chasms— whatever needed bridging—and just overbuilt the natural contours. Thus the Wall snakes down, seems to turn on itself more than once, and snakes on. Since it only goes in two directions, forward and back, thirty nine of our group were bemused to discover when reconvening on the bus near the aerial tramway that one of us was missing. This lone gentleman, a retired banker and aspiring poet, had sat down to meditate and compose—and upon arising, taken a wrong turn. He and the never-flustered Philip reappeared later that afternoon among the tombs of the Ming Emperors many miles away, having missed an excellent lunch at the Beijing Golf Club.

The Ming tombs and temples, reached via a long pathway guarded by human and animal statues, situate in the rather remote countryside, are another reminder of times past and a site well worth visiting. En route back to Beijing we made a stop at a cloisonné factory that took us a step back in time to a more primitive industrial age and a step forward in souvenir shopping.

Friday saw us at the Temple of Heaven for a morning of unalloyed pleasure strolling its vast premises and parks. Round in shape to simulate the heaven of Chinese cosmology, sporting a blue tiled roof like the sky instead of the imperial yellow of the palace roofs, the temple remains…awesome. The park attracts hordes of citizens and is worth a whole day in itself.

The afternoon was occupied by a flight to Xi'an, what proved to be my favorite city. We met a new national guide, Wei-wei, a friend of Jenny and a real boon. It was she who arranged the fabled dumpling banquet we enjoyed our on our second night in Xi'an, a twenty-two-course gustatory delight at a crowded but pleasant restaurant near the old city walls that also got us out for a look at Xi'an at night during Autumn Festival, an event filled with dragons, kites, and mooncakes, a sticky sweet shaped like sickle moons. Our first night had been marked by a banquet and costumed floor-show, pure tourist attraction but fun and a chance to hear Chinese music and voice. It compares to the obligatory Hawaiian luau on the tourist bill. Were we to return, I'd hunt up more dumpling or noodle houses in the city's endless and fascinating narrow streets. In fact, we'd hire our own Chinese guide and abandon group travel, it's easy to arrange and no more costly.

The third grand sight many of our party anticipated after the Forbidden City and the Great Wall was the famous tomb of the Emperor Chin and his army of terra cotta warriors. No one was disappointed by the vast enclosed structure housing the currently excavated statues and those awaiting resurrection. Remarkably, the clay warriors were not stamped to a single pattern but display individual features and personalities. A staggering circular cinematic portrayal of the birth and destruction of this imperial monument to a man who founded a one-person dynasty, but imprinted the country with his name for all time and carried out other vast projects like the Great Wall, made a memorable finale. I carried away in my mind a picture of his imperial chariot, round like a yurt and constructed with a false floor into which pieces of ice were inserted to provide the royal party with primitive air-conditioning. When the emperor unexpectedly died on one of his journeys, his son kept the body on ice, covering it with layers of fish to conceal the smell—and postponing dynastic controversy for many months. He was right to take this drastic step; ultimately a revolt ended the Chin reign and wreaked havoc on the terra cotta army as well. One has to wonder if the long absence of the current Chinese leader from public view hints at a replay. [Note: said leader has since officially expired.]

The actual tomb of the Emperor Chin [circa 222 BC] has yet to be opened under its hill behind the buried warrior guardians. The river of mercury upon which the coffin floats is so highly toxic it has so far defeated tomb robbers and archaeologists; the warriors, in fact, were intended as the dead emperor's advance guard and, in the event, faithfully performed their assigned role.

A visit to the deservedly praised provincial Shaanxi Museum and its ancient artifacts collections rounded out the day. Xi'an, among the most ancient of Chinese cities and capitals, is definitely on the move as a modern urban center. Interestingly, it still boasts its ancient city walls which we can hope escape the traffic engineers for all time.

Sunday began auspiciously with an early departure for the airport and our flight to Chong Qing via an ancient mosque in the old city. What a treasure this was. Gateway to the Silk road, Xi'an had a large Moslem population. The mosque, erected in Chinese style, blends two cultures and faiths to create a timeless oasis in the sea of commerce that surrounds it. Trading was brisk on the crowded streets, food service, largely prepared on oil drums or portable grills, infinitely varied. Rob, of course, was in heaven, if one populated by dumplings. I ventured quite a few bites myself and loved the tastes and textures. The trick is not to eat anything uncooked that can't be peeled, and not to drink anything unbottled or unboiled. Neither of us became ill from eating as we pleased bearing these strictures in mind.

The rest of the day was a nightmare of delayed flights. China does not have enough planes to accommodate demand, nor nearly enough routes (only two or three flights a day from Xi'an to Chong Qing as compared to hourly Phoenix-LA service, and just a few to Beijing). Planes [at the time of this writing] are often buckets of bolts, maintenance being weak and use high; flight schedules function as mere suggestions (like Chinese traffic lights); airports are minimal and rest rooms unspeakable. In short, this is the least attractive part of touring and the most nail-biting. You can't get to Chong Qing from Xi'an over the mountains other than by air, unless you have several days to spend traveling, so our trip to the Buddhist caves the next day was in some jeopardy. However, a late night departure finally got us to Chong Qing and all was well. Our subsequent flights from Wushan to Shanghai and from Shanghai to Hong Kong went more smoothly.

Buddhism is the predominant religion of China, with Taoism, Mohammedanism, Christianity, and Confucianism taking smaller roles. The temples are everywhere and well worth visiting. One of the most impressive of the various shrines is located at Dazu, in the hills north of Chong Qing, the city that commands the major western access to the mighty Yangtze River. Many of our group were exhausted or apprehensive about a long bus trip, so we halved, which made a much more comfortable and relaxed day. The drive to and from the shrine was fascinating, taking us out into rural China. On the return we stopped at a typical communal farm, where animals and people occupy one rambling structure, and cooking fire smoke, dust, and animal odors make breathing a labor.

Dazu itself was an astonishing array of religious art and carvings right into the living stones. The overall impression was akin to Bruegel with much medieval imagery, but the subjects were staunchly Eastern and therefore oddly unsettling to the Western visitor. Viewing progress is made downhill through a natural canyon. It was a glorious day, perfect for admiring the Sleeping Buddha and the full panoply of bodhisattva and ordinary mortals. The large temple at the entrance was especially interesting. Noteworthy were the signs next to the coin boxes with this injunction: "Pay money, become Buddha."

Back in Chong Qing, we had time to visit a renowned painters' village where many of us bought original paintings directly from the artists. Our one regret was the dearth of time to appreciate their wonderful work. During the two weeks in China we were able to visit a cloisonné factory—as mentioned, a frightening glimpse into the early Industrial Revolution as it existed pre-OSHA and unions—a silk factory, a lacquer works, coops with wonderful carpets displayed among other wares, museum gift shops, temple gift shops, a jewelry design firm in Hong Kong, and innumerable markets of various sorts including an excellent Farmer's Market in Xi'an where Rob was stunned by the range of chiles heaped on display. Some of our group experienced credit card meltdown. I couldn't resist a replica of a Tang Dynasty flying horse in bronze, nor a water color painted for us on the river cruise, nor a jade bracelet and lots of cloisonnés and silk scarves as gifts. Rob loved two paintings from the Shanghai Children's Museum; he paid $5 a piece for the paintings and over $300 for the subsequent framing! China is no longer the shopper's bargain paradise it once was, nor is Hong Kong, but there is still a rich variety of reasonably priced merchandise and art to enrich the experience.

The next day after a short ride through the city, the Second World War stronghold of General Chiang. It was also home base to the famous Flying Tigers who landed their planes on a large island in the river that is now partly covered by a bridge. The Yangtze is so impassable through its famous gorges that the Japanese could never transport sufficient troops upriver to pacify the western provinces. One criticism among the many levelled at the massive projected single dam for the river revolves around security; others target changes in weather, seismological conditions, build up of silt at the dam's base, possible self-rerouting of the river, the destruction of ecology and natural beauty, safety…an endless list. The "Great Wall Mentality" is perhaps a serious blindspot for China; changes in government, the fate of the current Chairman who many believe is actually dead but reigning through deputies, and an upcoming congress may redirect a project that the famous Belgian hydraulic experts hired to consult labelled as undoable. Having flown China's airlines, I think its government's trust that Chinese engineers can overcome all obstacles is misplaced.

Boarding our ship, the newest of the Victoria line cruising from Chong Qing to Wushan, we got useful advice:

From the ever well-spoken Philip: "If you are having an animated discussion with your cabin mate, bear in mind you will be entertaining those in cabins near and far." In other words, it's tight quarters so be tight lipped.

From the cruise director: "The ship is slightly higher than the river is deep. If we run into trouble, we can gather on the top deck and drain the bar while awaiting rescue."

The cruise takes three days and is marvelous if the weather cooperates, pretty much a bust if it rains which it often does—

and did. We needed a rest so all was not lost and we were able to observe our passage through the new locks. Some of our group discovered a fondness for bridge. The ships cuisine was uneven but several dinner dishes were splendid. The ice cream treat, made with evaporated milk, was not to our taste. Happily, fruits and vegetables, especially melons, were luscious, seafood was fresh, lots of beer and bottled water and tea were offered to wash it all down. Despite stuffing ourselves, Rob and I lost weight during our stay.

The Three Gorges are among China's most renowned scenic highlights, resembling in their contours the landscape of Scotland as well as its color: predominantly green with brown accents. So much of China's land is put to agricultural use that gardens of flowers are minimal, but lots of blooms are displayed in pots. The famous hanging coffins along the river are startling when first espied. There are tow paths on both sides. Navigation is treacherous. The weather precluded our sampan tour of the Little Gorges, eleven tourists having drowned on the last attempt under rainy conditions. The amount of water pouring forth from the surrounding mountains is vast; the incredible force of the waterfalls and the occasional bridal veils reminded me of Yosemite. Kilns stand everywhere and discharge their wastes into the river. Terraced hillsides march along, populated by goats and monkeys, the only visible animal life. Isolated villages and farmhouses were glimpsed; all these, and substantial portions of several cities, will be forcibly relocated before the water rises several hundred feet behind the new dam.

Musings while on the river:
Chinese women have a natural elegance and are bred in the bone clothes-horses; the diet helps. Hair is generally gleaming and black. Features can be delicate or when not, still handsome. The men are often tall and muscular. They all seem to age well. Teeth are the problem. Everyone wears

Western clothes, often the cheap polyester varieties, in lots of colors. Little denim, no Mao jackets. The women have a weird fashion of wearing anklets or knee-high stockings, under sandals, with skirts of all lengths, shorts, whatever. The upper class Chinese, especially the business class, are totally Western in appearance with New York or British suiting and razor haircuts. Few Chinese wear glasses; eye exercises are taught from childhood and faithfully practiced.

The Cultural Revolution destroyed not only the scholarly and privileged class in place but the next generation as well. Only now, some thirty years later, has a middle or management class begun to reemerge. As a result, much of sloppy, aimless work, whether street cleaning, construction, whatever, can be attributed to a lack of direction and supervision, there being just those at the top and those who labor. "Aimless" and "random" describe so much of the casual labor force. Roads despite sweeping remain full of debris and litter is everywhere, compounded by the advent of US fast food service and its takeaway packaging. The opening of Colonel Sanders is the current excitement, as we saw in Shanghai. The new slogan for the Chinese is "Personal Responsibility," which is replacing the Red Guard watch. We were surprised at how little the military were present where we went, although we were sure the state security apparatus was still powerful.

A clear return to capitalism, or rather a modified capitalism with socialist aspects, is in progress. It's not too different from our system. Joint venture companies appear to be doing well. Workers for joint ventures have to pay one hundred percent of their way, while workers for the government are about eighty percent subsidized for housing, education, medical care. Working conditions in manufacturing, at least in small enterprises, are primitive, with poor light, poor ventilation. Many of those who work on the cloisonné retire very young with bad lungs or ruined eyes. Early retirements must be cheaper for management than providing proper conditions.

Many people live over the shop, protecting their street level premises with a pull down metal shutter. Hazardous conditions thus often characterize living arrangements. We saw one family along the highway to Dazu with three petrol pumps in their front room. The farm house we visited was filled with dust and smoke; the cleanest things were the pigs and their sty.

The one-child per family rule is very evident in the lack of children to be seen. Exceptions to the standard are made for parents with a handicapped firstborn. Fines are steep for second children and much state aid is withheld from city dwellers. Rural families get more leeway. The rule can lead to abortion, infanticide, and offering up girl babies to the black market for adoption since boys are still preferred. Marriage is delayed.

The most difficult thing for tourtists to deal with is the sanitation. The public restrooms are appalling, much worse for women where flushing is required than for men where water can just run. The use of plumbing has to be taught, and it isn't. Even places like airports are disgusting. We learned to hold Kleenex over our noses, and never to be without it as toilet paper is not provided. Julie, our alumni representative, discovered her sunglasses had slipped from her nose into the pit while she was squatting in some stop or other—she never considered trying to retrieve them. We quickly learned it was far easier to tour in a skirt than to struggle with pants in the privies.

The hot book in China was *China Can Say No*—to the US position on Taiwan. A large clock in Tiananmen Square is counting down the seconds to the Hong Kong takeover. In Hong Kong we subsequently learned that while the Territories were under the lease, the city itself had been fully ceded to Britain and Mrs. Thatcher had for some reason, probably the unlikelihood of defense, offered the whole kit and caboodle back to China without negotiating, a fact that's left the Hong Kong residents pretty bitter. Macao is scheduled to revert from Portugal to China in 1999. No one in Hong Kong wants to predict how things will go since China has indicated little interest in agreements made before June, 1997.

Gambling is a Chinese vice. Little games were going on all over sidewalks, in tea houses, wherever. Mah jong is still very popular, and played intensely.

Back to Touring

We disembarked on Friday for a tour of Wushan and its excellent museum and pagoda, then flew to Shanghai where our Sheraton was sadly not on the exciting waterfront but out in the new area across from a huge stadium. Shanghai is the most westernized city, the most attractive to Western eyes, the most dynamic and exciting. To our surprise, we liked it better than Hong Kong. It's a place we've marked for a further visit. We had a great meal in the hotel that night, and a splendid full day tour on Saturday that included a visit to historic Yu Garden, a tea house, a walk through the old quarters with its picturesque shops, lunch at a Mongolian barbecue joint, a visit to the Children's Museum where we observed classes in calligraphy, ballet, violin, chorus, and other cultural pastimes…and lost our hearts to the attractive, charming children. The museum's gift shop did a brisk trade. The silk company was also poplar, as were the carpet vendors.

◇◇◇

Commerce is the backbone of Shanghai; the architecture here reflects Western influence, capital, and joint ventures more than most other sites we saw. Our day was rounded off by a Chinese acrobat show after dinner at an elegant hotel. Everyone was sorry to have such an abbreviated time in this pulsating place.

The flight to Hong Kong went without a hitch. When we arrived, we were offered a bus tour across the city stopping at the famous western beach market, for a sampan ride among the vanishing boat people in the harbor, a visit to the jewelry designers, and ended up atop Victoria Peak where we queued for the famous tram ride. The views were superb and, as it happened, were the last to be enjoyed before monsoon weather struck. As a result our touring in Hong Kong was dampened, as it was also by the realization that we should have come a generation ago if we wanted to see it as a British colony. That has now departed along with the administrators, the army, the colonials, and many Chinese-born citizens. It was fascinating to trace the growth of the area into a corner of empire—the settlers imported sufficient turf from Britain, for example, to create a nine-hole golf course and a cricket ground—and to imagine what a privileged life it was for some.

Our day visit to Macao via the swift and smooth hydros was another glimpse into a colonial past. We had a superb lunch and *vinho verde* at a Seventeenth century Portuguese inn, now a thriving small hotel. The marine museum was excellent and offered a real glimpse into the local fishing economy as well as into centuries of exploration, trading, and the merchant marine. It was right on the harbor's edge; behind up the hill rose a small temple for fisherfolk. Casinos are the lifeblood of this city today, sucking in visitors and money. Who knows what will happen at the takeover?

A superb collection of Chinese porcelain in a museum owned and housed by a bank, breakfast in a tea house, a wander through the aviary, many trips on the ferry to Kowloon, and our favorite meal, a luscious Cantonese cuisine at the famous Regent Hotel, much tastier than tea at the Peninsula Hotel that proved a less appealing spread than that found at New York's Plaza or Phoenix' Phoenician hotels, were highlights of our stay, along with a glorious dim sum lunch with Art Professor Larry Silver, Rob's evil twin. This knowledgeable man's lectures on China and particularly its Buddhist art were informative and exciting, enlivening our entire journey.

Some final observations from tour guide Jenny, whose English led her towards an occasional Malapropism:

"I will be standing on my toes to answer all your questions."

"The crane is the national bird of China. Why? China is a very modern nation—there is much construction."

We found that the traveller's maxims applied, except for "Eat it today, wear it tomorrow." "Travel light, travel right" is excellent advice. Rob had the best souvenir, the good luck he achieved by spinning about, then pointing to the money symbol at Fengdu, the famous ghost temple high above the Yangtze. We thought it no accident he then won the ship's betting pool on how many seconds it took to close the lock gates. But we're hoping the other shoe will still fall, as the final souvenir of this or any other trip is the trailing credit card charges that eventually catch up with you....

By the way, I draw the title of this travel memoir from the University's athletic teams' mascot, the Northwestern Wildcat.

Barbara Peters

Biography

Barbara Peters, a native of Winnetka, Illinois, graduated from Stanford University (BA, Northwestern University (MA), the University of Tennessee (MSLS), a postgraduate Intern program at the Library of Congress, and read for the Virginia Bar. In 1989, she founded The Poisoned Pen, A Mystery Bookstore, in Scottsdale, Arizona, as a retirement present to herself. In 1992, she helped founded the Independent Mystery Booksellers Association, and remains active in promoting the specialty book trade. In 1997, she joined the faculty at Arizona State University, teaching a spring semester undergraduate class, Murder They Wrote: A History of Crime Fiction, while continuing to oversee an active events program and bookselling schedule at The Poisoned Pen. Foreseeing the need to keep crime backlist books in print, she cofounded Poisoned Pen Press in January, 1997. Devoted to Excellence in Mystery, the press publishes a *Missing Mysteries* line, original crime fiction, and reference works. Barbara has been nominated for an Edgar (Best Critical/Biographical Work) and in 2001 the MWA awarded her its Raven, Mr. Poe's bird.

Bibliography

AZ Murder Goes... Classic, 1997
AZ Murder Goes... Professional, 2002

Louis Silverstein

with Barbara Peters

◇

Bibliography of Art,
Architecture, and
Antiquity Mysteries

Bibliography of Art, Architecture, and Antiquity Mysteries

(This bibliography has been compiled by two retired librarians, Louis H. Silverstein (Yale University Library) and Barbara G. Peters (Library of Congress). While comprehensive, it is by no means complete, but reflects books read and enjoyed by one or other of the compilers. Many, but not all, of the titles listed, both old and new, are currently in print or should be available in library collections. Titles are arranged by author and then chronologically. For additional titles, pre-1990, the reader is referred to Albert J. Menendez, *The Subject Is Murder, Vol. 1*. New York: Garland, 1986; *Vol. 2*. New York: Garland, 1990.

Ackroyd, Peter. *Hawksmoor*. London: Hamish Hamilton, 1985. (Odd happenings surround the famous 17th Century British designer who completed Castle Howard.) [Architecture.]

Adler, T. C. *see* Van Adler, T. C.

Allingham, Margery. *Look to the Lady*. London: Jarrolds, 1931. (US title: *The Gyrth Chalice*). (A treasure hidden in a country manor has a surprising—and awesome—guardian; an Albert Campion mystery.) [Antiquities.]

Allingham, Margery. *Death of a Ghost*. London: Heinemann, 1934. (An artist dead for decades reappears at a showing of his work; an Albert Campion mystery.) [Art.]

Allingham, Margery. *Black Plumes*. London: Heinemann, 1940. (The slashing of a valuable painting starts a fatal imbroglio at London's posh Ivory Gallery.) [Art.]

Andrews, Sarah. *Bone Hunter*. New York: St. Martin's Press, 1999. (Geologist Em Hansen finds herself among paleontologists and bones ancient and modern in Utah.) [Antiquities.]

Angus, Sylvia. *Death of a Hittite*. New York: Macmillan, 1969. (Anatolia is the scene for dark deeds then…and now.) [Antiquities.]

Angus, Sylvia. *Arson and Old Lace*. Cleveland: World, 1972. (Someone takes a burning interest in the gimcrackery invading a beautiful historical New England fishing village.) [Architecture.]

Angus, Sylvia. *Dead to Rites*. New York: Crown, 1978. (Mrs. Wagstaffe is with a tour group exploring Mayan ruins when she spots a girl floating in the sacred pool of the virgins….) [Antiquities.]

Ardin, William. *Some Dark Antiquities*. London: Headline, 1994. (The sale of a medieval reliquary leads to intrigue and deceit; a Charles Ramsay mystery.) [Antiquities.]

Ardin, William. *Light at Midnight*. London: Headline, 1995. (Chasing to Stockholm after a swindler, Charles Ramsay discovers antiques and murders.) [Antiquities.]

Ardin, William. *The Mary Medallion*. London: Headline, 1996. (A modern Scots painter sinks in treacherous sands and leaves a killer legacy behind; a Charles Ramsay mystery.) [Art.]

Arnold, Margot (Petronelle Margaret Mary Cook). (The Penny Spring and Sir Toby Glendower mysteries. A series featuring elderly American anthropologist Penny Spring and aged archaeologist Sir Tobias Glendower. Locations given with each title.) [Antiquities.]

> *Exit Actors, Dying*. New York: Playboy, 1979. (Turkey).
>
> *The Cape Cod Caper*. New York: Playboy, 1980. (Cape Cod).
>
> *Zadok's Treasure*. New York: Playboy, 1980. (Israel).
>
> *Death of a Voodoo Doll*. New York: Playboy, 1982. (New Orleans).
>
> *Death on the Dragon's Tongue*. New York: Playboy, 1982. (Brittany).
>
> *The Menehune Murders*. Woodstock, Vt.: Foul Play, 1989. (Hawaii).

Lament for a Lady Laird. Woodstock, Vt.: Foul Play, 1990. (Scotland).

Toby's Folly. Woodstock, Vt.: Foul Play, 1990. (Wales).

The Catacomb Conspiracy. Woodstock, Vt.: Foul Play, 1992. (Rome).

The Cape Cod Conundrum. Woodstock, Vt.: Foul Play, 1993. (Cape Cod).

Dirge for a Dorset Druid. Woodstock, Vt.: Foul Play, 1994. (Dorset).

The Midas Murders. Woodstock, Vt.: Foul Play, 1995. (Greece).

Asher, Michael. *Eye of Ra.* London: HarperCollins, 1999. (Maverick archaeologist Omar Ross wonders why his famous Egyptologist colleague is dead at the foot of the Giza pyramid.) [Antiquities.]

Asher, Michael. *Firebird.* London: HarperCollins, 2000. (Dr. Adam Ibram is murdered, bringing local Egyptian police and an FBI agent to the Great Pyramid.) [Antiquities.]

Atkins, Charles. *The Portrait.* New York: St. Martin's Press, 1998. (A psychological thriller involving a successful artist who finds his life in shreds. [Art.]

Bagley, Desmond. *The Vivero Letter.* London: Collins, 1968. (A swashbuckling adventure through the Yucatan where Mayan ruins and bronze mirrors are the prize). [Antiquities.]

Banks, Oliver T. *The Rembrandt Panel.* Boston: Little, Brown, 1980. (Featuring "art cop" Amos Hatcher.) [Art.]

Banks, Oliver T. *The Caravaggio Obsession.* Boston: Little, Brown, 1984. (Featuring "art cop" Amos Hatcher.) [Art.]

Barnard, Robert. *The Corpse at the Haworth Tandoori.* London: HarperCollins, 1998. (Murder and mayhem in an artist's colony outside Haworth with keen insights into the sources of artistic inspiration.) [Art.]

Barr, Nevada. *Ill Wind.* New York: Putnam, 1995. (UK title: *Mountain of Bones.*) (Park Ranger Anna Pigeon, unmasks evil at Mesa Verde's Anasazi ruins.) [Antiquities.]

Barr, Nevada. *Blind Descent.* New York: Putnam, 1998. (Park Ranger Anna Pigeon descends to Lechuguilla Caverns, an ancient cave in New Mexico that proves the site of modern murder.) [Antiquities.]

Barr, Nevada. *Liberty Falling.* New York: Putnam, 1999. (Park Ranger Anna Pigeon finds murder at the Statue of Liberty National Monument and in the deserted buildings of Ellis Island.) [Antiquities; Architecture.]

Barron, Stephanie. *Jane and the Wandering Eye: Being the Third Jane Austen Mystery.* New York: Bantam, 1998. (The practice of painting portraits of eyes in the early 19th century provides a clue in this mystery.) [Art.]

Bayer, William *see* Hunt, David.

Berkley, Roy. *A Spy's London.* Casemate, 1997. (136 sites in Central London relating to spies, saboteurs, and subversives including Ian Fleming.) [Architecture.]

Berne, Karen. *False Impressions.* New York: Popular Library, 1986. (Santa Fe adobes house a variety of art world figures, some bent on making a killing....) [Art.]

Birmingham, Ruth. *Atlanta Graves.* New York: Berkley Prime Crime, 1998. (Sunny Childs, the lead detective at Peachtree Investigations, attempts to find a stolen painting.) [Art].

Black, Veronica. *A Vow of Sanctity.* New York: St. Martin's Press, 1993 (Sister Joan journeys to Scotland to make a retreat. Her painting leads her to a troubled family and...murder.) [Art.]

Bleeck, Oliver (Ross Thomas). *The Brass Go-Between.* New York: Morrow, 1969. (Professional go-between Philip St. Ives is assigned to recover a rare tenth-century African brass shield stolen from a Washington museum.) [Antiquities; Art.]

Block, Lawrence. *The Burglar Who Painted Like Mondrian.* New York: Arbor House, 1983. (The theft of a valuable painting propels a caper where among those framed is bibliophile burglar Bernie Rhodenbarr who began it by stealing the Mondrian to get his girl's cat back from a museum.) [Art.]

Boast, Philip. *Resurrection.* London: Headline, 1997. (Beneath London's St. Paul's Cathedral rests an ancient secret...the lost gospel of Judas Iscariot. Generations play out their lives around this holy place, the story's main character.) [Architecture.]

Bonfiglioli, Kyril. *Don't Point That Thing at Me.* London: Weidenfeld, 1972. (Art dealer Charlie Mortdecai, unlike his art dealer creator, sells stolen paintings). [Art.]

Bowen, Michael. *Badger Game.* New York: St. Martin's, 1989. (Former bar member Thomas Curry is a kind of freelance legal investigator in 1962 New York. With his family firm's girl Friday, Sandrine Cadette, he agrees to help an artist in a tricky lawsuit with a jealous rival. Then, the client artist dies, his nearby painting slashed to ribbons....) [Art.]

Bowen, Rhys. *Evan Can Wait*. New York: St. Martin's Press, 2001. (British art treasures are stashed in Welsh slate mines during the war and result in murder at century's end.) [Art.]

Boyle, Josephine. *Holy Terror*. London: Piatkus, 1993. (A newly-wed professional embroiderer and her husband move into an old cottage adjacent to a huge stately home of many architectural periods that has hidden priest holes, at least one ghost, and a strong link to the village's 17th Century religious martyr.) [Antiquities; Art; Architecture.]

Bradberry, James. *The Seventh Sacrament*. New York: St. Martin's Press, 1994. (An architectural competition on a secluded Italian estate leads to deadly results for a young American contender; a Jamie Ramsgill mystery.) [Architecture.]

Bradberry, James. *The Ruins of Civility*. New York: St. Martin's Press, 1996. (Architecture professor Ramsgill's Cambridge mentor is murdered after upsetting his own farewell party by rescinding his resignation from college, leaving Jamie to follow the crime's blueprint to a killer.) [Architecture.]

Bradberry, James. *Eakins' Mistress*. New York: St. Martin's Press, 1997. (An unknown version of an Eakins' masterpiece leads to the ruin of an architect; a Jamie Ramsgill mystery.) [Architecture; Art; Forgeries.]

Braun, Lilian Jackson. *The Cat Who Could Read Backwards*. New York: Dutton, 1966. (Introducing Jim Qwilleran and his two Siamese cat sleuths who come together when a gallery owner, then the newspaper's art critic, are murdered.) [Art.]

Braun, Lilian Jackson. *The Cat Who Saw Red*. New York: Jove, 1986. (Qwill and the cats solve a puzzle featuring pottery.)[Art.]

Brett, Simon. *Mrs. Pargeter's Point of Honour*. London: Macmillan, 1938. (An unusual twist on a stolen art theme where a terminally ill widow, with the assistance of Edith J. Pargeter, tries to restore anonymously to their rightful owners all the Old Masters her husband lovingly collected.) [Art.]

Brown, Dan. *Angels and Demons*. New York: Pocket, 2000. (A modern intrigue propels a glorious tour of Rome's Renaissance

architecture which holds the key to a mystery involving the
Illuminati society v. the Vatican.) [Antiquities; Architecture.]

Bryers, Paul. *The Prayer of the Bone.* London: Bloomsbury, 1998.
(An archaeological dig one the site of two 'lost' 17th century
settlements in northern Maine reveals answers to murders past
and present.) [Antiquities.]

Burley, W.J. *Wycliffe and the Winsor Blue.* London: Gollancz, 1987.
(The Cornish detective was bound to encounter a case centered
on art during his long career.) [Art.]

Buss, Louis. *The Luxury of Exile.* London: Cape, 1997. (When a
mildly shady antique dealer gone into the antiquarian book
business discovers a cache of old letters, it starts him on a trail
that ends devastatingly in an old Neapolitan palazzo, his career
and marriage in ruins, suicide a possibility. The letters have prom-
ised to reveal the possible whereabouts of Lord Byron's memoirs, a
great lost treasure of English literature.) [Antiquities.]

Carvic, Heron; Crane, Hamilton (Sarah Jane Mason); Hampton,
Charles (Peter Martin aka James Melville).

The Miss Seeton series. (Retired British art teacher Miss Seeton
often puts her sketches to good use in tracking crooks.) [Art.]

> *Picture Miss Seeton* (Carvic). London: Geoffrey Bles, 1968.
>
> *Miss Seeton Draws the Line* (Carvic). London: Geoffrey Bles,
> 1969.
>
> *Miss Seeton Bewitched* (Carvic). London: Geoffrey Bles,
> 1971. (US title: *Witch Miss Seeton.*)
>
> *Miss Seeton Sings* (Carvic). London: Davies, 1974.
>
> *Odds on Miss Seeton* (Carvic). London: Davies, 1976.
>
> *Advantage, Miss Seeton* (Hampton). New York: Berkley
> Books, 1990.
>
> *Miss Seeton at the Helm* (Hampton). New York: Berkley
> Books, 1990.
>
> *Miss Seeton, by Appointment* (Hampton). New York: Berkley
> Books, 1990.
>
> *Miss Seeton Cracks the Case* (Crane). New York: Berkley
> Books. 1991.
>
> *Miss Seeton Paints the Town* (Crane). New York: Berkley
> Books, 1991.
>
> *Hands Up, Miss Seeton* (Crane). New York: Berkley Books,
> 1992.

Miss Seeton by Moonlight (Crane). New York: Berkley Books, 1992.

Miss Seeton Rocks the Cradle (Crane). New York: Berkley Books, 1992.

Miss Seeton Goes to Bat (Crane). New York: Berkley Books, 1993.

Miss Seeton Plants Suspicion (Crane). New York: Berkley Books, 1993.

Miss Seeton Rules (Crane). New York: Berkley Prime Crime, 1994.

Miss Seeton Undercover (Crane). New York: Berkley Prime Crime, 1994.

Starring Miss Seeton (Crane). New York: Berkley Books, 1994.

Sold to Miss Seeton (Crane). New York: Berkley Prime Crime, 1995.

Sweet Miss Seeton (Crane). New York: Berkley Prime Crime, 1996.

Bonjour Miss Seeton (Crane). New York: Berkley Prime Crime, 1997.

Miss Seeton's Finest Hour (Crane). New York: Berkley Prime Crime, 1999.

Caudwell, Sarah. *Thus Was Adonis Murdered*. London: Collins, 1981. (London barrister Julia Larwood goes on holiday to Venice where a handsome young sculptor ends up dead in her bed; a Hilary Tamar mystery.) [Art.]

Caunitz, William. *Black Sand*. New York: Crown, 1989. (A case for the cops involves a deadly hunt for a priceless ancient artifact). [Art.]

Caverly, Carol. *Frogskin and Muttonfat*. Aurora, Colorado: Write Way Publishing, 1997. (Antique and modern jade cast a glow over the Old West still found in Wyoming's jade fields; a Thea Barlow mystery.) [Antiquities.]

Chadwick, Whitney. *Framed*. London: Macmillan, 1998. (Art historian Charlotte Whyte begins her first case with the murder of the curator of the San Francisco Art Museum and proceeds to a tangle of art looting by the Nazis.) [Art.]

Charles, Kate. *Dead Men Out of Mind*. New York: Mysterious Press, 1994. (A valuable historical silver collection of St. Margaret's Parish disappears, leaving local laypersons and clergy open to question.) [Antiquities.]

Christie, Agatha. *Murder in Mesopotamia*. London: Collins, 1936. (Mrs. Leidner's murder on the Tell Yarimjah excavation puzzles everyone but Hercule Poirot.) [Antiquities.]

Christie, Agatha. *Five Little Pigs* (US title: *Murder in Retrospect*). London: Collins, 1943. (Amyas Crayle was famous as a painter and infamous as a lover. It was not thus surprising when his widow was convicted of his murder. Years later, his daughter comes to Hercule Poirot in hopes he'll reopen the investigation.) [Art.]

Christie, Agatha. *Death Comes at the End*. London: Collins, 1944. (Newly widowed Renisenb comes back under her father's roof whereupon sudden death strikes the ancient Egyptian household). [Antiquities.]

Christie, Agatha. *They Came to Baghdad*. London: Collins, 1951. (Dr. Pauncefoot Jones' Babylonian dig is the scene of a scheme threatening the too trusting Victoria Jones.) [Antiquities.]

Christie, Agatha. *Come, Tell Me How You Live*. London: Collins, 1946. (A fascinating factual account—perhaps slightly fictionalized by storyteller Christie—of her life with her second husband, archaeologist Sir Max Mallowan, on his Middle Eastern excavations.) [Antiquities.]

Cleveland, David Adams. *With a Gemlike Flame*. New York: Carroll & Graf, 2001. (A 15th Century masterpiece by Raphael was seized from a Venetian Jewish family during the war and supposedly destroyed until Renaissance Art scholar Jordan Brooks is caught in a modern imbroglio....) [Art.]

Clinton-Baddeley, V.C. *Death's Bright Dart*. London: Gollancz, 1967. (A Cambridge College Conference registers a murderer who apparently draws inspiration from a collection of primitive Borneo artifacts.) [Antiquities.]

Coel, Margaret. *The Story Teller*. New York: Berkley Prime Crime, 1998. (19th Century Arapahoe legend books and their art hold the key to a modern murder mystery; a Father John O'Malley and Vicky Holden mystery.) [Art.]

Coker, Carolyn. The Andrea Perkins series. (Art restorer Andrea Perkins performs her magic—and solves mysteries in several locations which are given with each title.) [Art.]

> *The Other David*. New York: Dodd, Mead, 1984. (Florence.)

The Vines of Ferrara. New York: Dodd, Mead, 1986. (Ferrara.)

The Hand of the Lion. New York: Dodd, Mead, 1987. (Venice.)

The Balmoral Nude. New York: St. Martin's Press, 1990. (Scotland).

Appearance of Evil. New York: St. Martin's Press, 1993. (Pasadena, CA.)

Collins, Wilkie. *The Moonstone*. London: Tinsley, 1868. (The theft of an enormous diamond is accompanied by somnambulism, clever scheming, and some Oriental magic.) [Antiquities.]

Connor, Beverly. *A Rumor of Bones*. Nashville: Cumberland House, 1996. (Who is the woman buried in the Jasper Creek dig, an ancient Indian village in the Southeast? A Dr. Lindsay Chamberlain novel.) [Antiquities.]

Connor, Beverly. *Questionable Remains*. Nashville: Cumberland House, 1997. (The 429-year-old tale of renegade conquistadores sets up a modern archaeological murder trail across the Southeastern United States; a Dr. Lindsay Chamberlain novel.) [Antiquities.]

Connor, Beverly. *Dressed to Die*. Nashville: Cumberland House, 1998. (Old bones, Native American artifacts and archaeologist grandfather figure in a most engrossing mystery; a Dr. Lindsay Chamberlain novel.) [Antiquities.]

Connor, Beverly. *Skeleton Crew*. Nashville: Cumberland House, 1999. (Salvage work on an old shipwreck requires a coffer dam that proves to be a killer; a Dr. Lindsay Chamberlain novel.) [Antiquities.]

Connor, Beverly. *Airtight Case*. Nashville, Cumberland House, 2000. (A dig in a Smoky Mountains pioneer settlement apparently unearths a haunted house; a Dr. Lindsay Chamberlain novel.) [Antiquities.]

Cook, Petronelle Margaret Mary *see* Arnold, Margot.

Craig, Philip R. *Gate of Ivory, Gate of Horn*. New York: Doubleday, 1969. (The tower of Beowulf remains a magnet drawing the curious to Scandinavia.) [Antiquities.]

Craig, Philip R. *The Woman Who Walked into the Sea*. New York: Scribner, 1991. (Ancient stone cairns reputed to stand on Martha's Vineyard are just one of the elements baffling sleuth former Boston cop Jeff Jackson.) [Antiquities.]

Craig, Philip R. *The Double Sided Men*. New York: Scribner, 1992, (An antique bauble unbalances J. R. Jackson and the Martha's Vineyard security for a Sultan.) [Antiquities.]

Craig, Philip R. *Death on a Vineyard Beach*. New York: Scribner, 1996. (An ancient cranberry bog belongs to the island's Wampanoag tribe and to a wealthy but mysterious couple; a J. R. Jackson mystery.) [Antiquities.]

Crane, Hamilton *see* Carvic, Heron.

Crider, Bill. *Murder is an Art*. New York: St. Martin's Press, 1999. (The chairman of an art department is found murdered after admitting to painting a nude portrait of an attractive female student.) [Art.]

Crosby, Ellen. *Moscow Nights*. London: Piatkus, 2000. (Journalist Claire Brennan arrives in Moscow just in time to ID her lover at the morgue. Refusing to believe Ian was a thief, she winkles out the facts which include a cache of art either held in Russia since the war or native to the old culture.) [Art.]

Cullen, Robert. *Dispatch from a Cold Country*. New York: Fawcett Columbine, 1996. (Art masterpieces in the Hermitage are the currency of high-flying Soviet or Nazi officials brought low by the forces of history.) [Art.]

Cussler, Clive. *Inca Gold*. New York: Simon & Schuster, 1994. (An ancient Andean civilization hid its golden hoard from the Conquistadores in an inland sea. Dirk Pitt's 1998 dive into an ancient sacrificial pool draws him into the vortex of a syndicate that's traced the treasure from the Andes along a hidden underground stream flowing beneath a Mexican desert.) [Antiquities.]

Cussler, Clive. *Atlantis Found*. New York: Putnam, 1999. (Dirk Pitt battles Neo-Nazis in Antarctica over artifacts of Atlantis, the lost civilization.) [Antiquities.]

Cussler, Clive. *Valhalla Rising*. New York: Putnam, 2001. (The Vikings crossed to North America and left a legacy faced by Dirk Pitt and company.) [Antiquities.]

Davis, Lindsey. *Silver Pigs*. London: Sidgwick, 1989. (Ancient silver coins in Roman Britain prove expensive for sandaled gumshoe Falco and for a Senator's daughter.) [Antiquities.]

Davis, Lindsey. *Poseidon's Gold*. London: Century, 1992. (An ancient sculpture holds the secret as Falco tries to clear his family name of murder and intrigue.) [Antiquities.]

Davis, Lindsey. *One Virgin Too Many.* London: Century, 199. (A murder forces Falco to take on the Vestal Virgins and ancient cults.) [Antiquities.]

Davis, Lindsey. *Ode to a Banker.* London: Century, 2000. (Falco faces a body found in a rich Roman's library.) [Antiquities; Architecture.]

Davis, Lindsey. *The Body in the Bath House.* London: Century, 2001. (Falco and family are sent to Britain where chicanery piles up bodies at the building site of the governor's manse, known today as Fishbourne Palace.) [Antiquities; Architecture.]

Davis, Sedona. *Concha.* Phoenix: C. F. Abanico Press, 1998. (The theft of antique silver belts embroils Drew Whittaker in a complicated investigation.) [Antiquities.]

Dawkins, Cecil. *The Santa Fe Rembrandt.* New York: Ivy Books, 1993. (The part-Sioux assistant director of Santa Fe's art museum copes with a stolen Rembrandt and a temperamental artists colony.) [Art.]

Dawkins, Cecil. *Turtle Truths,* New York: Ivy Books, 1997. (When a very rich Jamaican woman dies in a young artist's home—and her necklace is found in his luggage—he takes off for the island's Turtle Bay to snag the real killer.) [Antiquities.]

Dean, Elizabeth. *Murder is a Collector's Item.* New York: Doubleday, Doran, 1939. (A look behind the scenes at a Boston antique shop where a body has been stumbled across.) [Antiquities.]

Delaney, Frank. *Pearl.* London: HarperCollins, 1999. (Architect Nicholas Newman accepts a design commission from a Dutch footballer and discovers violence stemming back to the Second World War comes with the plans.) [Architecture.]

Delaney, Frank. *At Ruby's.* London: HarperCollins 2001). (Wealthy architect Nicholas Newman is again embroiled against his will in a thriller that opens in a corporate boardroom where the chairman faces down a challenge from another director.) [Architecture.]

Delving, Michael (Jay Williams). *Smiling, the Boy Fell Dead.* New York: Scribner, 1967. (A charming Connecticut antiques and rare book dealer specializing in old manuscripts encounters a remote English village and a formidable, elderly lady of the manor; a Dave Cannon mystery.) [Antiquities.]

In the later books, Dave,—and sometimes his partner, Bob Eddison—pursues antiquarian treasures in Gloucestershire and Wales:

> *The Devil Finds Work.* New York: Scribner, 1969 (an ancient barrow).
>
> *Die Like a Man.* New York: Scribner, 1970 (a gold-rimmed wooden bowl reputed to be the Holy Grail).
>
> *A Shadow of Himself.* New York: Scribner, 1972 (Cannon's partner, Bob Eddison, a Cherokee Indian, who also marries an Englishwoman, detects.)
>
> *Bored to Death.* New York: Scribner, 1975 (a 15th Century gilt casket).
>
> *No Sign of Life.* London: Collins, 1978 (an ancient torque).
>
> And: *The China Expert.* New York: London: Collins, 1976. (Not a Cannon/Eddison, but focused on an American specialist in Chinese porcelain who becomes embroiled in espionage.)

Dexter, Colin. *The Jewel that was Ours.* London: Macmillan, 1991. (Inspector Morse investigates an American tour group, trying to figure out who pilfered the Wolvercote jewel, an Anglo-Saxon buckle destined for the Ashmolean Museum.) [Antiquities.]

Dickinson, Peter. *Some Deaths Before Dying.* New York: Mysterious Press, 1999. (A missing pair of antique dueling pistols resurfaces in mysterious circumstances.) [Antiquities.]

Dickson, Carter (John Dickson Carr). *The Curse of the Bronze Lamp.* New York: Morrow, 1945. (UK title: *Lord of the Sorcerers.*) (A bronze lamp from Egypt carries a curse that presumably causes the disappearance of its owner; a Sir Henry Merrivale mystery.) [Antiquities.]

Doherty, P.C. *Satan's Fire.* London: Headline, 1995. (The great treasure of the dissolved order of the Knight's Templar fuels fatal fires in 1309 York; a Hugh Corbett mystery.) [Antiquities.]

Doherty, P.C. *Ghostly Murders.* London: Headline, 1997. (The ghosts of Knights Templar murdered in 1308 Kent continue to protect their treasure in 1389; The Priest's Tale on Pilgrimage to Canterbury.) [Antiquities.]

Dolson, Hildegard. *A Dying Fall.* Boston: Lippincott, 1973. (A girl and her beau decide to start an art museum filled with *avant garde* sculptures. In the controversy about leveling a prize rose garden for the site, the beau is tossed onto a statue and punctured; a Lucy Ramsdale/James McDougal mystery.) [Art.]

Dunbar, Catherine. *False Images*, London: Robert Hale, 1999. (A picture conservator is hired to restore a picture that turns out to be a forgery; in the process images from her past begin to awaken fearful memories.) [Art.]

Durant, Isadore. *Death Among the Fossils*. Albuquerque: Univ. New Mexico, 2000. (Academic infighting besets anthropologists combing Africa's hot and harsh terrain for early hominids. It ends in a young scholar trapped by his supervisor's lack of scruple and a murder.) [Antiquities.]

Dymmoch, Michael Allen. *The Death of the Blue Mountain Cat*. New York: St. Martin's Press, 1996. (Murder on Chicago's Magnificent Mile when a Native American artist is slain during a showing at an ultraconservative art museum.) [Art.]

Easterman, Daniel. *The Jaguar Mask*. London: HarperCollins, 2000. (The discoveries of an archaeologist on a dig deep in the Mexican jungle link the Maya to modern ritual murders in France.) [Antiquities.]

Echenoz, Jean. *I'm Gone*. France, 1999. US: New York: New Press, 2001. (Art dealer Felix Ferrer hunts for a trove of Inuit art preserved in an Arctic shipwreck and disrupts Parisian art circles.) [Antiquities; Art.]

Eco, Umberto. *The Name of the Rose (Il nome della rosa)*. Italy: Gruppo Editoriale Fabbri-Bompiani,1980. US: New York: Harcourt Brace Jovanovich, 1983. (In 1327, finding his sensitive mission at an Italian abbey further complicated by seven bizarre deaths, Brother William of Baskerville turns detective, penetrating the cunning labyrinth of the abbey and deciphering coded manuscripts for clues.) [Antiquities; Architecture.]

Elkins, Aaron. *Murder in the Queen's Armes*. New York: Walker, 1985. (Gideon Oliver checks into the Queen's Armes and at a nearby dig a battered body is discovered instead of the anticipated Bronze Age relic,) [Antiquities.]

Elkins, Aaron. *A Deceptive Clarity*. New York: Walker, 1987. (The Seattle art museum's Chris Norgren navigates the treacherous waters bubbling around museum politics and valuable art.) [Art.]

Elkins, Aaron. *Curses*. New York: Mysterious Press, 1989. (Forensic anthropologist Gideon Oliver digs into crime in the Yucatan; a Gideon Oliver mystery.) [Antiquities.]

Elkins, Aaron. *A Glancing Light*. New York: Scribner, 1991. (The Seattle art museum's Chris Norgren goes to Bologna to snoop into the theft of Italian art works.) [Art.]

Elkins, Aaron. *Old Scores*. New York: Scribner, 1993. (The Seattle art museum's Chris Norgren struggles with the pros and cons of accepting a dubious Rembrandt.) [Art.]

Elkins, Aaron. *Dead Men's Hearts*. New York: Mysterious Press, 1994. (The Valley of the Kings nearly entombs Gideon Oliver.) [Antiquities.]

Elkins, Aaron. *Loot: a Novel*. New York: Morrow, 1999. (A recently surfaced Velázquez provides clues to tracking down artworks looted during World War II.) [Art.]

Elkins, Aaron. *Skeleton Dance*. New York: Morrow, 2000. (Gideon Oliver visits the Dordogne caves where academic rivalries over the Neanderthal v. Cro Magnon Man erupt into murder.) [Antiquities.]

Elkins, Charlotte and Aaron. *Nasty Breaks*. New York: Mysterious Press, 1997. (Golf pro Lee Ofsted is invited to teach golf to employees of a Block Island marine Salvage company, which includes rescuing colonial glass and other artifacts, and finds herself embroiled in murder.) [Antiquities.]

Ellis, Kate. *The Merchant's House*. London: Piatkus, 1998. (The excavation of a Tudor merchant's house yields a body or two; one of which turns out to have been murdered in a manner paralleling a present day crime; a Wesley Peterson crime novel.) [Archaeology.]

Ellis, Kate. *The Armada Boy*. London: Piatkus, 1999. (The raising of a ship sunk during the invasion of England in 1588 and the discovery of the graves of the invaders parallels events that occurred during the 1944 D Day landings on the coast of Devon; events which resolved help to piece together the solution to a contemporary murder; a Wesley Peterson crime novel.) [Archaeology.]

Ellis, Kate. *The Unhallowed Grave*. London: Piatkus, 1999. (Why have two women been hanged from the same tree centuries apart? a Wesley Peterson crime novel.) [Archaeology.]

Ellis, Kate. *The Funeral Boat*. London: Piatkus, 2000. (The disappearance in Devon of a Danish tourist seems oddly linked to what may be a Viking burial; a Wesley Peterson crime novel.) [Archaeology.]

Ellis, Kate. *The Bone Garden*. London: Piatkus, 2001. (Digging up the 30-year-old garden at Earlsacre Hall reveals two bodies under a plinth, somehow linked a modern corpse found at a caravan site; a Wesley Peterson crime novel.) [Archaeology.]

Fairstein, Linda. *Cold Hit*. New York: Scribner, 2000. (DA Alexandra Cooper works two cases: a serial rapist who's come out of hiding and two murders linked to the nasty world of fine art.) [Art.]

Fairstein, Linda. *The Deadhouse*. New York: Scribner, 2001. (DA Alexandra Cooper is fascinated by the history of Blackwells Island in Manhattan's East River and learns the legacy of its plague victims.) [Antiquities; Architecture.]

Fiedler, Jacqueline. *Tiger's Palette*. New York: Pocket, 1998. (Introducing wildlife artist Caroline Canfield.) [Art.]

Fiedler, Jacqueline. *Sketches with Wolves*. New York: Pocket, 2001. (Wildlife artist Caroline Canfield travels to Wolf Prairie to observe the habitat and finds a savaged corpse...). [Art.]

Fiffer, Sharon. *Killer Stuff*. New York: St. Martin's Press, 2001. (Antique picker Jane Wheeler turns a hobby into a business while plagued by the murder of her neighbor.) [Art.]

Fitzgerald, Penelope. *The Golden Child*. London: Duckworth, 1977. (An offbeat story set in a London museum where the ancient, gold covered corpse of the Ruler of Garamantia arrives from Africa. It instantly becomes the center of a web of intrigue spun by museum personnel, especially the triumphant archaeologist, a guard, and hapless junior Waring Smith who is nearly strangled by a golden wire from the Child one night. Who? and moreover, how could the wire still be so strong?) {Antiquities].

Follett, Ken. *The Modigliani Scandal*. London: Collins, 1976. (First published under pseudonym: Zachary Stone.) (A lost masterpiece inspires forgery, theft...and murder.) [Art.]

Follett, Ken. *Pillars of the Earth*. New York: Morrow. 1989. (Building a 12th century British cathedral.) [Architecture.]

Ford, Peter Shann. *Keeper of Dreams*. New York: Simon & Schuster, 2000. (A debut thriller interweaves Aboriginal myths with modern science in an Australian Hillerman.) [Antiquities.]

Foss, Jason. *Shadesmoor*. Sutton: Severn House, 1995. (When an archaeologist is felled by a Stone Age axe at Shadesmoor Castle, who better to step into his boots than Dr. Jeffrey Flint?) [Antiquities.]

Fowler, Earlene. *Fool's Puzzle*. New York: Berkley Prime Crime, 1994. (The director discovers a body amidst an exhibition of handmade quilts in San Celina, California's Folk Art Museum; a Benni Harper mystery.) [Antiquities.]

Francis, Dick. *In the Frame*. London: Joseph, 1976. (Painter Charles Todd specializes in renderings of sleek horses. He faces a different sort of art at his cousin's home when a murderer polishes off Donald's wife.) [Art.]

Francis, Dick. *To the Hilt*. London: M. Joseph, 1996. (A Scottish artist is forced to abandon his hermit-like cell for the hurly-burly of business in London when his stepfather is savagely attacked.) [Art.]

Francis, Dick. *Shattered*. London: M. Joseph, 2000. (Glassblower Gerald Logan finds the death of a locket and a missing videotape might shatter his work and his life.) [Art.]

Frayn, Michael. *Headlong*. London: Faber & Faber, 1999. (Art historian Martin Clay espies a possible Bruegel in a chance-met Oxford couple's home and dives into double-dealing and a possible setup.) [Art.]

Furutani, Dale. *The Toyotomi Blades*. New York: St. Martin's Press, 1997. (Japanese American Ken Tanaka visits Japan where ancient samurai swords thrust him into murder.) [Antiquities.]

Fusilli, Jim. *Closing Time*. New York: Putnam, 2001. (A bomb injures the gallery owner who represented PI Terry Orr's dead wife, causing him to wonder if this art world crime is connected to the murder of a black gypsy cab driver.) [Art.]

Garcia-Aguilera, Carolina. *Havana Heat*. New York: Morrow, 2000. (Miami PI Lupe Solano, intrigued with modern Cuban art, ends up in Havana looking for a hidden art treasure: the "8th" unicorn tapestry.) [Art.]

Gash, Jonathan (Dr. John Grant). *The Judas Pair*. London: Collins, 1977. (Lovejoy, the rogue antiques divvy, has a long string of crimes related to antiques in this case involving dueling pistols.) [Antiquities.]

Gash, Jonathan. *Gold from Gemini*. London: Collins, 1978. (US title: *Gold by Gemini*.) (Lovejoy hunts for a hoard of rare Roman coins.) [Antiquities.]

Gash, Jonathan. *The Grail Tree*. London: Collins, 1979. (While chasing after priceless antiques, the smashing of a porcelain bowl brings tears to Lovejoy's eyes during a search for the Holy Grail.) [Antiquities.]

Gash, Jonathan. *Spend Game*. London: Collins, 1980. (Victorian villainy and the silver model of a railway engine power a Lovejoy caper.) [Antiquities.]

Gash, Jonathan. *The Vatican Rip*. (Lovejoy tackles the Vatican, attempting to retrieve a Chippendale table.) London: Collins, 1981. [Antiquities.]

Gash, Jonathan. *Firefly Gadroon*. London: Collins, 1982. (Decorating silver with dies—especially in the difficult Reverse Gadroon firefly pattern—might douse Lovejoy's light.) [Antiquities.]

Gash, Jonathan. *The Gondola Scam*. London: Collins, 1983. (Lovejoy becomes involved in a scheme to "rescue" every art treasure in Venice.) [Antiquities.]

Gash, Jonathan. *The Sleepers of Erin*. London: Collins, 1983. (Rather than witness the smashing of a 300 year old lock, Lovejoy blows his cover.) [Antiquities.]

Gash, Jonathan. *Pearlhanger*. London: Collins, 1984. (A precious pearl pendant sends Lovejoy on a quest around several amorous ladies.) [Antiquities.]

Gash, Jonathan. *Moonspender*. London: Collins, 1986. (Lovejoy tangles with "moonspenders," illicit treasure seekers with electronic metal detectors hunting for buried Celtic treasures). [Antiquities.]

Gash, Jonathan. *The Tartan Ringers*. London: Collins, 1986. (US title: *The Tartan Sell*.) (Why should Lovejoy leave the Highlands in peace when he's divvied everywhere else in the British Isles?) [Antiquities.]

Gash, Jonathan. *The Very Last Gambado*. London: Collins, 1986. (Consulting for a movie about a robbery at the British Museum launches Lovejoy into the ultimate antiques scam...) [Antiquities.]

Gash. Jonathan. *Jade Woman*. London: Collins, 1988. (Lovejoy in Hong Kong checking out antiques tangles with the Jade Woman.) [Antiquities.]

Gash, Jonathan. *The Great California Game*. London: Century, 1990. (Persona non grata in England, Lovejoy hits California where an illicit enterprise involves gambling antiques.) [Antiquities.]

Gash, Jonathan. *The Lies of Fair Ladies.* London: Century, 1992. (As part of an attempt to smoke out corrupt dealers, Lovejoy finds himself buying, selling and faking antiques.) [Antiquities.]

Gash, Jonathan. *Paid and Loving Eyes.* London: Century, 1993. (Lovejoy becomes embroiled in an international ring of smuggling, forgery, and exploitation.) [Antiquities.]

Gash, Jonathan. *The Sin Within Her Smile.* London: Century, 1993. (Sold as a slave-for-a-day at a charity auction, Lovejoy bids fair to be drawn into fraud involving a Sussex cache of early Celtic gold.) [Antiquities.]

Gash, Jonathan. *The Grace in Older Women.* London: Century, 1995. (Making love to a lady in the forest gets Lovejoy close to her precious collection of Bilston enamels.) [Antiquities.]

Gash, Jonathan. *Possessions of a Lady.* London: Century, 1996. (A thriving trade in fake Stone Age tools propels Lovejoy to London.) [Antiquities.]

Gash, Jonathan. *The Rich and the Profane.* London: Macmillan, 1998. (Abetting with the theft of an antique Buckingham jug inspires Lovejoy to greater heights amidst scams and murder.) [Antiquities.]

Gash, Jonathan. *A Rag, a Bone, and a Hank of Hair.* London, Macmillan, 1999. (As part of a quest to determine who has been passing off fake gemstones, Lovejoy finds himself involved with antique dealers in Chelsea). [Antiquities.]

Gash, Jonathan. *Every Last Cent.* London: Macmillan, 2001. (The sculptress Bernicka is Lovejoy's latest flirtation with disaster.) [Art.]

Gear, Kathleen and Michael. *The Visitant.* New York; Forge, 1999. (Modern archaeologist Dusty Stewart and arch-nemesis Dr. Maureen Cole find modern evidence of murders among the Anasazis.) [Antiquities.]

Gear, Kathleen and Michael. *The Summoning God.* New York; Forge 2000. (This time a serial murderer stalked the ancient peoples as revealed in a kiva filled with burned bodies.) [Antiquities.]

Gear, Kathleen and Michael. *The Bone Walker.* New York; Forge, 2001. [Antiquities.]

Gilbert, Michael. *The Etruscan Net.* London: Hodder, 1969. (US title: *The Family Tomb.*) (Deals with Etruscan antiques illicitly collected near Perugia; the amateur detective is the director of an art gallery.) [Forgeries.]

Gill, Anton. *City of the Horizon*. London: Bloomsbury, 1991. (The scribe Huy, a subscriber to the visionary philosophy of Pharaoh Akhenaten, faces hard times in Tut's reformist regime. A commission to delve into a tomb-robbing operation launches him into a new career as a private eye.) [Antiquities.]

Gill, Anton. *City of Dreams*. London: Bloomsbury, 1992. (A cache of papyri reveals a vicious killer plaguing Thebes to the scribe Huy, a man of natural forensic talent.) [Antiquities.]

Gill, Anton. *City of the Dead*. London: Bloomsbury, 1993. (Tut embarks on a hunting trip to celebrate his wife's first pregnancy and meets a horrible accident in the desert. Only Huy can discover what really happened and help the queen escape the rivals for the Golden Chair.) [Antiquities.]

Gilligan, Roy. *Chinese Restaurants Never Serve Breakfast*. Menlo Park, CA: Perseverance Press, 1986. (Carmel, a lovely artists colony on Monterey Bay, is the scene for a pleasant series, of which this is the first, with PI Pat Riordan.) [Art.]

Goddard, Robert. *Take No Farewell*. London: Bantam, 1991. (Cloud Frome was the first, and best, thing architect Geoffrey Staddon had done, although he personally betrayed its mistress. Twelve years later, in 1923, she's charged with murder...and he knows she's innocent.) [Architecture.]

Goddard, Robert. *Caught in the Light*. London: Bantam, 1998. (A photographer working in Vienna meets and falls in love with a woman who, if she really existed, may have invented photography some 170 years earlier in England.) [Antiquities.]

Gold, Alan. *The Gift of Evil*. Sydney, Australia: HarperCollins, 1998. (The key is an amulet with a history of violence and death.) [Antiquities.]

Goldman, James. *The Man from Greek and Roman*. New York: Random House, 1974. (New York's Metropolitan Museum exhibits...murder.) [Art.]

Gordon, Neil. *The Sacrifice of Isaac*. New York: Random House, 1995. (The death of an Israeli scholar involves his younger son in his elder's illegal antiques trade.) [Antiquities.]

Grant, John *see* Gash, Jonathan.

Grimes, Martha. *The Case Has Altered.* New York: Holt, 1997. (Antiques have a role to play in the 14th Supt. Richard Jury novel causing Melrose Plant to assume the role of an antiques expert.) [Antiquities.]

Hackler, Micah S. *Dark Canyon.* New York: Dell, 1997. (A rare amulet recently dug up by archaeologists may be a clue to the killings plaguing Sheriff Lansing's New Mexico community.) [Antiquities.]

Hamer, Malcolm. *Dead on Line.* London: Headline, 1996. (A golfing sleuth has to deal with murderous events surrounding valuable golfing antiques and paintings from wealthy clubhouses and collectors.) [Art; Antiquities.]

Hamilton, Lyn. *The Xibalba Murders: An Archeological Mystery.* New York: Berkley Prime Club, 1997. (A young woman archaeologist flies many miles to Mexico to participate in the search for a Mayan codex, challenging rebels who want to preserve their Mayan heritage, facing the Lords of Death themselves, and dodging murders...; a Lara McClintoch mystery.) [Antiquities.]

Hamilton, Lyn. *The Maltese Goddess: An Archaeological Mystery.* New York: Berkley Prime Crime, 1998. (Commissioned to collect antiquities to furnish a Toronto home, a antique dealer flies to Malta on her quest only to discover the body of her employer in a chest; a Lara McClintoch mystery.) [Antiquities.]

Hamilton, Lyn. *The Moche Warrior: An Archaeological Mystery.* New York: Berkley Prime Crime, 1999. (The discovery of a box of authentic Moche artifacts in a Toronto auction house triggers a chain of events resulting in a hazardous trip to Peru; a Lara McClintoch mystery.) [Antiquities.]

Hamilton, Lyn. *The Celtic Riddle.* New York: Berkley Prime Crime, 2000. (Lara McClintock travels to Ireland where a treasure hunt sends a circle of suspects after a rare Celtic manuscript.) [Antiquities.]

Hamilton, Lyn. *The African Quest.* New York: Berkley Prime Crime, 2001. (Lara McClintock travels to what was ancient Carthage with a tour group where the tale of an ancient sailor highlights a sunken treasure ship.) [Antiquities.]

Hampton, Charles *see* Carvic, Heron.

Haney, Lauren. *The Right Hand of Amon*. New York: Avon, 1997. (As a golden idol of the god Amon is moved up the Nile near Nubia in 1464 B.C. the corpse of a murdered soldier is discovered and dark, possibly treasonous, doings are investigated by Hatshepsut's Medjay Lt. Bak.) [Antiquities.]

Haney, Lauren. *A Face Turned Backward*. New York: Avon, 1999. (Medjay Lt. Bak searches the Nile for contraband, especially elephant tusks.) [Antiquities.]

Haney, Lauren. *A Vile Justice*. New York: Avon, 1999. (Medjay Lt. Bak is sent to Abu after a murderer.) [Antiquities.]

Haney, Lauren. *A Curse of Silence*. New York: Avon, 2000. (The arrival of the queen's Storekeeper of Amon at Buhren lead to a stabbing and the uncovering of a terrible secret.) [Antiquities.]

Haney, Lauren. *A Place of Darkness*. New York: Avon, 2001. (Exiled from Buhren, the Lt. Bak stops at the capital in hopes of investigating a troubling case of relics plundered from ancient tombs and smuggled through the southern frontier. Instead, he is sent to the partially built memorial temple of the divine Queen Maatkare Hatshepsut plagued by fatal accidents.) [Antiquities; Art.]

Hanson, Rick. *Still Life*. New York: Kensington Books, 1998. (Set in the Taos art world, sculptor Adam McCleet carves his way through crime with verve and zany humor.) [Art.]

Hardwick, Mollie. *Malice Domestic*. London: Century, 1986. (Antiques dealer Dorian Fairweather investigates a number of cases involving her profession. In the series debut, she comes to a tiny Kent village and a low-key romance with the young vicar. Soon they are hard-pressed to defy an evil that invades their lives.) [Antiquarian.]

Harrison, Ray. *Murder by Design*. London: Constable, 1996. (Art forgery rocks Victorian London but not Sgt. Cribb nor Constable Morton.) [Art; Forgeries.]

Hart, Carolyn. *Death on the River Walk*. New York: Avon, 1999. (A young girl disappears from a family owned Art Gallery in San Antonio and Henrie O learns about the trade in priceless art treasures as part of solving the mystery.) [Art.]

Hart, Roy. *A Deadly Schedule*. London: Macmillan, 1993. (A British policeman begins a case when he lends a hand to an archaeological dig on Crete; an Ins. Roper mystery.) [Antiquities.]

Hathaway, Robin. *The Doctor Digs a Grave.* New York: St. Martin's Press, 1998. (The body of a recently deceased young Native American Indian woman is discovered in an old Indian burial ground and gradually the murder is traced right into the elite of Philadelphia Society.) [Antiquities.]

Harvey, John. *In a True Light.* London: Heinemann, 2001. (An art forger just out of gaol is called to the deathbed of a dying lover. The stricken painter confesses she bore his child and sends him back into Manhattan's art circles to find her.) [Art; Forgery.]

Henry, April. *Circles of Confusion.* New York: HarperCollins, 1999. (The inheritance of a mysterious painting takes a young woman from Portland to an auction house in New York and embroils her in murder; a Claire Montrose mystery.) [Art.]

Hiaasen, Carl and Richard Montalbano. *Death in China.* New York: Atheneum, 1984. (The tombs of Western China have rich treasures that lead to trouble.) [Antiquities.]

Hill, John Spencer. *Ghirlandaio's Daughter.* New York: St. Martin's Press, 1997. (The corpse lay on its back sporting a bronze spear of a Mycenaean warrior from its chest, despoiling the beautiful Tuscan villa owned by international art dealer and patron Sir Richard Danvers, host to the poetry awards ceremony. Uglier are the events that follow and the secrets that emerge from the past as policeman/poet Carlo Abati investigates.) [Antiquities.]

Hillerman, Tony. *Thief of Time.* New York: Harper & Row, 1988. (Ancient artifacts on the Navajo reservation fuel scholarly rivalry and modern murder.) [Antiquities.]

Hillerman, Tony. *Sacred Clowns.* New York: HarperCollins, 1993. (A Taro kachina ceremony is the scene of a *koshare*'s murder, after which a mysterious artifact links a runaway, two bodies, tribal secrets, and crooked Indian traders.) [Antiquities.]

Holt, Tate. *Yamashita's Gold.* Berkeley, CA: Berkeley Hills Books, 1998. (Actually a business thriller, this book centers about a trove of plundered wealth from South East Asia's temples and treasures hidden for fifty years.] [Antiquities.]

Hook, Philip. *The Stonebreakers.* London: Hodder & Stoughton, 1994. (An art historian leads a convoy towards Dresden. Fifty years later, Oswald Ginn is sent a photograph of a masterpiece presumed destroyed in the bombing of Dresden. As the art world speculates, three people are propelled on an international search.) [Art.]

Hook, Philip. *The Island of the Dead.* London: Hodder & Stoughton, 1995. (While investigating the mutilation of a painting in a London gallery, journalist Minto Maitland finds himself drawn into a horrific story of brutality and betrayal during the Hungarian revolution.) [Art.]

Hook, Philip. *The Soldier in the Wheatfield.* London: Hodder & Stoughton, 1998. (A London art dealer spots an unheralded German landscape in a auction catalogue, hops a plane for New York and the auction, and traces its origins back to the Nazi art confiscations.) [Art.]

Hook, Philip. *An Innocent Eye.* London: Hodder & Stoughton, 2000. (A young man inherits his mother's diaries and learns her life in wartime France was more eventful than he'd imagined.) [Art.]

Hoving, Thomas. *Masterpiece.* New York: Simon and Schuster, 1986. (An international art intrigue featuring a painting by Diego Velázquez.) [Art.]

Hunt, David *see* Bayer, William.

Hunt, David (William Bayer). *The Magician's Tale.* New York; Putnam, 1997. (San Francisco photographer Kay Farrow suffers from a rare form of blindness. As an achromat she photographs nocturnal visions and steps into murder.) [Art.]

Hunt, David. (William Bayer). *Trick of Light.* New York: Putnam, 1998. (San Francisco photographer Kay Farrow deals with her dead Japanese mentor's legacy and engravings on rare guns.) [Antiquities; Art.]

Hunt, Richard. *Murder Benign.* London: Constable, 1995. (The murder of an archaeologist and the theft of his possessions including a clay tablet covered with cuneiform characters could have been a botched burglary....) [Antiquities.]

Iles, Greg. *Dead Sleep.* New York: Putnam, 2001. (Photojournalist Jordan Glass accidentally views an exhibition of paintings in Hong Kong that take as their subject women who are supposedly sleeping but certainly appear to be dead.) [Art.]

Innes, Hammond. *The Levkas Man.* London: Collins, 1971. (A cynical freebooter and his fanatical anthropologist adoptive father pursue the trail of earliest man from the docks of Amsterdam to the smugglers' harbors of the Aegean to a vast underwater cave below the Greek isle of Levkas where violence explodes and a startling discovery is made.) [Antiquities.]

Innes, Michael (J.I.M. Stewart). *The Mysterious Commission.*
London: Gollancz, 1974. (Charles Honeybath agrees to paint
the portrait of a elusive recluse and then finds himself held
prisoner in an isolated country mansion.) [Art.]

Innes, Michael (J.I.M. Stewart). *Honeybath's Haven.* London:
Gollancz, 1977. (An artist drowns and Charles Honeybath
becomes more than a little suspicious,) [Art.]

Innes, Michael (J.I.M. Stewart). *Appleby and Honeybath.* London:
Gollancz, 1981. (A locked room and a disappearing corpse
present a puzzle at a house party whose guests include an art
historian.) [Art.]

Innes, Michael (J.I.M. Stewart). *Lord Mullion's Secret.* London:
Gollancz, 1981. (While Charles Honeybath paints a portrait of
the mistress of Mullion Castle, he becomes embroiled in several
puzzles involving disappearing and reappearing art works.) [Art.]

Additional art related titles by Michael Innes (J.I.M. Stewart)
include:

> *From London Far.* London: Gollancz, 1946. {US title: *The
> Unexpected Chasm.*)
>
> *A Private View.* London: Gollancz, 1952. (Also published in
> UK with title: *One Man Show*; US title: *Murder is an Art.*)
>
> *Silence Observed.* London: Gollancz, 1961.
>
> *Money From Holmes.* London: Gollancz, 1964.
>
> *A Family Affair.* London: Gollancz, 1969. (US title: *Picture
> of Guilt.*)

Jahn, Michael. *Murder at the Museum of Natural History.* New
York: St. Martin's, 1994. (The opening night of an archaeological exhibit depicting the excavation of an old Silk road
showcases the brutal murder of the event's playboy host; a Lt.
Bill Donovan mystery.) [Antiquities.]

James, P.D. *Original Sin.* Toronto: Alfred A. Knopf Canada/Lon-
don: Faber, 1994. (For two centuries, Thames-side Innocent
House, replica of a Venetian palace, has housed Peverell Press
and shaped the lives of those who live and work there. The
firm's new chairman decides to sell it off, with fatal conse-
quences; an Adam Dalgliesh mystery) [Architecture.]

James, P.D. *Death in Holy Orders.* London: Faber & Faber, 2001. (A
theological college houses a stunning painting and other art treasures
that someone might kill for; an Adam Dalgliesh mystery.) [Art.]

Jardine, Quentin. *A Coffin for Two*. London: Headline, 1997. (Private Enquiry agent Oz Blackstone and his partner Primavera Phillips have abandoned all their cares for a new life in Spain…until a corpse nobody wants found and a painting that may be a lost masterpiece upset their idyll.) [Art.]

Jay, Charlotte. *Beat Not the Bones*. London: Collins, 1952. (A young Australian woman journeys to Marapai, New Guinea, to discover why her distinguished archaeologist husband has committed suicide. Soon she discovers the lure of antique gold and the magic with which the Papuans protect it—and themselves.) [Antiquities.]

Jeffries, Roderic. *An Artistic Way to Go*. London: HarperCollins, 1996. (An art dealer disappears on Mallorca; an Inspector Alvarez novel.) [Art.]

Johnson, Janice Kay. *Winter of the Raven*. New York: Forge, 1995. (A Victorian photographer from Victoria wants to inquire into her missionary father's fate and finds her passport to the Queen Charlotte Islands is to photograph the dying Haida culture and outwit rivalrous collectors.) [Antiquities.]

Johnston, Brian. *The Good Luck Murders*. New York: Pinnacle, 1991. (The picture-postcard-perfect village of Wistfield, New York, is shattered by architectural historian Winston Wyc's discovery of a corpse in the cornfield.) [Architecture.]

Johnston, Brian. *The Gift Horse Murders*. New York: Pinnacle, 1992. (Winston Wyc is lured up to the Hudson Valley village of Wistfield once again to help the local historical society decide the fate of an antiquated mansion.) [Architecture.]

Johnston, Brian. *With Mallets Aforethought*. New York: Penzler: 1995. (The architectural historian tries to pierce a modern American version of the classic country house murder complete with croquet on the lawn; a Winston Wyc mystery.) [Architecture.]

Jones, Liane. *Painting the Dark*. London: Headline, 1995. (A haunting tale of a painting that has the power to take a woman back to a former life, one she lived in Biblical times.) [Art.]

Kaiser, R.J. *Hoodwinked*. (Toronto: Mira, 2001. (A caper questioning the forgery of Van Gogh's "8th" sunflower painting, in question since WWII and now tantalizing the greedy gathering on St. Margaret, West Indies.) [Art.]

Karp, Larry. *The Music Box Murders: A Mystery*. Aurora, Colorado: Write Way, 1999. (Murder and mayhem amongst the underworld of music box collectors; a Thomas Perdue mystery.) [Antiquities.]

Karp, Larry. *Scamming the Birdman*. Aurora, Colorado: Write Way, 2000. (Collector Thomas Perdue learns a friend has had his world class collection of musical snuffboxes stolen.) [Antiquities.]

Karp, Larry. *The Midnight Special*. Aurora, Colorado: Write Way, 2001. (Neurologist Perdue is alerted to a very odd crime by a crooked antiques picker who leads the collector to a cache of important music boxes.) [Antiquities.]

Kaufelt, David. *The Fat Boy Murders*. New York: Pocket Books, 1993. (New England's Picturesque Waggs Neck Harbor has unexpected hazards for a real estate lawyer, an elitist men's club, and a famous artist.) [Art.]

Kearsley, Susanna. *The Shadowy Horses*. London: Gollancz, 1997. (An archaeologist travels to Eyemouth, Scotland where a dig gives evidence of the long-missing Roman Ninth Legion. A ghost centurion communicates through a small boy who is able to grasp classical Latin.) [Antiquities.]

Keating, H.R.F. *The Soft Detective*. London: Macmillan, 1997. (Det. Chief Ins. Phil Benholme investigates the death of 1945 Nobel Prize winner Professor Unwala and decides that he was murdered but for what reason: robbery? a racist assault? or a lead to a hoard of valuable Celtic coins buried nearby?) [Antiquities.]

Kelly, Mary. *The Spoilt Kill*. London: Michael Joseph, 1961. (A freelance detective is hired to determine which of a pottery's employees is spilling design secrets and murder complicates matters.) [Antiquities.]

Kennedy, Hugh. *Original Color*. New York: Doubleday, 1996. (Fresh and funny look at the contemporary Manhattan gallery scene with a particularly repulsive art broker center stage.) [Art.]

Kenyon, Michael. *Peckover and the Bog Man*. London: Macmillan, 1994. (Ins. Henry Peckover and wife attend the 170th Robbie Burns celebration where Britain's most eminent archaeologist, digging at Dundruming Castle, is slain amidst controversy over an unearthed ancient bog man....) [Antiquities.]

Kerr, Philip. *Esau*. London: Chatto, 1996. (A stirring inquiry into the possibility of Yeti alive in the Himalayas and all that portends to anthropologists and adventurers.) [Antiquities.]

Kerr, Philip. *A Five Year Plan*. London: Hutchinson, 1997. (A con man emerges from a Florida penitentiary having dreamed up a plan for a major final heist involving robbing a giant carrier ship which transports luxury yachts from Florida to the French Riviera, carrying their owners cash, jewels, and valuable works of art...and conveniently, a stash of freshly laundered drug money.) [Art.]

Kilmer, Nicholas. *Harmony in Flesh and Black*. New York: Henry Holt, 1995. (A malignant artist is murdered, leaving photographs to puzzle an expert; a Fred Taylor mystery.) [Art.]

Kilmer, Nicholas. *Man with a Squirrel*. New York: Henry Holt, 1996. (A Copley painting gets drawn and quartered and featured in satanic rituals; a Fred Taylor mystery.) [Art.]

Kilmer, Nicholas. *O Sacred Head*. New York: Henry Holt, 1997. (Italian religious paintings of the Baroque era are parodied in a gruesome decapitation; a Fred Taylor mystery) [Art.]

Kilmer, Nicholas. *Dirty Linen*. New York: Henry Holt, 1999. (A cache of erotic art works, possibly by an idolized Victorian artist, formerly cloaked in prudery, is uncovered at an estate sale resulting in murder and chicanery; a Fred Taylor mystery.) [Art.]

Kilmer, Nicholas. *Lazarus Arise*. Scottsdale: Poisoned Pen Press, 2001. (The fragment of a medieval manuscript missing since the Second World War ignites collector interest as well as Fred Taylor's interest in landscape artist Jacob Geist. Introduction by Art Professor Larry A. Silver.) [Art.]

King, Laurie R. *A Grave Talent*. New York: St. Martin's Press, 1993. (San Francisco's lesbian policewoman Kate Martinelli investigates an artist's colony in her first case.) [Art.]

Kingsnorth, Joss. *Landscapes*. London: Headline Review, 1996. (A family drama set in atmospheric Devon where renowned artist A.J. Monk has died, leaving a legacy with far reaching effects on the lives of his contemporaries as buried passions are now rekindled.) [Art.]

Knief, Charles. *Silversword*. New York: St. Martin's Press, 2001. (A hoard of ancient Hawaiian relics is a plot element in a thriller about Chinese triads and Hawaiian history and politics.) [Antiquities.]

Kruger, Mary. *Masterpiece of Murder*. New York: Kensington Books, 1996. (A turn-of-the-century theft of valuable paintings from the Manhattan Museum and the murder of the curator occupy newlywed sleuths.) [Art.]

Kurzweil, Allen. *A Case of Curiosities*. New York: Harcourt Brace Jovanovich, 1992 . (The imagined life of a French inventor and maker of automatons and other gadgets includes a glass-fronted box holding a collage of ten items has one empty compartment—a talking head. Was it guillotined?). [Antiquities.]

Kurzweil, Allen. *The Grand Complication*. New York: Hyperion, 2001. (A reference librarian and his pop-up book artist wife are confronted with a cabinet of curiosities that tell the life of an 18th Century inventor. The cabinet purportedly includes a clock belonging to Marie Antoinette.) [Antiquities.]

Lake, M. D. *Grave Choices*. New York: Avon, 1995. (A sculptor is bashed at the campus art museum, leading a campus cop into academic and artistic rivalries long suppressed.) [Art.]

Landrum, Graham. *The Historical Society Mystery*. New York: St. Martin's, 1996. (The ladies of Borderville mobilize under nonagenarian sleuth Harriet Bushrow when a valuable painting left to the Historical Society is stolen.) [Art.]

Langton, Jane. *Murder at the Gardner*. New York: St. Martin's Press, 1988. (Boston's Isabella Stewart Gardner Museum is a jewel box that proves too tempting, but our man Homer Kelly and wife Mary are at hand.) [Art.]

Langton, Jane. *The Face on the Wall*. New York: Viking, 1998. (A children's book illustrator finds her imagination becoming startlingly real; a Homer Kelly mystery..) [Art.]

Langton, Jane. *The Thief of Venice*. New York: Viking, 1999. (Homer Kelly is studying Renaissance manuscripts while Mary is seeing the city but the key here is the cache of art hidden by Venetian Jews during the Second World War.) [Antiquities; Art.]

Langton, Jane. *Murder at Monticello*. New York: Viking, 2001. (Any crime set at Jefferson's Virginia estate must have elements of architecture; a Homer Kelly mystery.) [Architecture.]

La Plante, Lynda. *Cold Heart*. New York: Random House, 1999. (A murder investigation reveals details of art scams and the shenanigans of gallery owners.) [Art.]

Laurence, Janet. *Canaletto and the Case of Westminster Bridge.* London: Macmillan, 1997. (The famous Venetian painter is in London, preparing to make a fortune with his brush, befriended by a young woman engraver, and beset with greedy villains and surprisingly modern developers.) [Art; Architecture.]

Laurence, Janet. *Canaletto and the Case of the Privy Garden.* London: Macmillan, 1999. (The painter is unprepared for a nightmare that descends while he's sheltering from a storm.) [Art.]

Law, Janice. *A Safe Place to Die.* New York: St. Martin's Press, 1988. (Pottery and murder mesh together; an Anna Peters mystery.) [Art.]

Lemarchand, Elizabeth. *Change for the Worse.* Loughton, Essex: Piatkus, 1980. (The author's interest in English history and archaeology runs through her numerous Det. Supt. Tom Pollard books. Here, a real art theft and a simulated one are juxtaposed to Pollard's personal life.) [Art.]

Lemarchand, Elizabeth. *Buried in the Past.* London: Hart Davis MacGibbon, 1974. (A medievalist seeking to debunk the charters of his home town and make a mockery of its millenary celebration turns up a modern corpse in an excavated Roman villa.) [Antiquities.]

Lemarchand, Elizabeth. *Unhappy Returns.* London: Hart Davis MacGibbon, 1977. (A pair of married writers receive their due while a medieval chalice is lost for the second time in its elusive history—and found again.) [Antiquities.]

Lemarchand, Elizabeth. *Suddenly, While Gardening.* London: Hart Davis MacGibbon, 1978. (A medieval pilgrimage route and a Bronze Age tomb housing a contemporary corpse merge into Pollard's vacation.) [Antiquities.]

Leon, Donna. *Acqua Alta.* London: Macmillan, 1996. (Commissario Guido Brunetti is roused one night with news that the director of Venice's most prestigious museum has been brained with one of his own artifacts. The killer narrowly missed murdering a prominent American archaeologist gaining fame on a dig in China.) [Antiquities.]

Lewis, (John) Roy(ston). *A Trout in the Milk.* London: Collins, 1986. (An old missal swiped from Willington Hall might yet save the estate...and lead to murder; an Arnold Landon mystery.) [Antiquities.]

Lewis, Roy. *Men of Subtle Craft*. London: Collins, 1987. (Arnold Landon is asked to assist an historian with research into a medieval mason which then provides him a foundation for finding the killer when a local magistrate is slain by a mechanism such as a medieval mason might have used.) [Antiquities.]

Lewis, Roy. *Bloodeagle*. London: HarperCollins, 1993. (While overseeing a medieval excavation Arnold Landon becomes embroiled in a series of murders.) [Archaeology.]

Lewis, Roy. *The Cross Bearer*. London: HarperCollins, 1994. (Arnold Landon is drawn into a web of intrigue and forgery involving the Knights Templar.) [Antiquities; Forgeries.]

Lewis, Roy. *Suddenly as a Shadow*. London: HarperCollins, 1997. (A Northumbrian burial ground becomes the focus of a bitter conflict. Arnold Landon is a British planning officer whose passion for architecture and antiquities gives him a penchant for solving crimes.) [Architecture.]

Additional art related (antiquities) titles by Roy Lewis featuring Arnold Landon include:

> *The Devil is Dead*. London: HarperCollins, 1989.
> *A Wisp of Smoke*. London: HarperCollins, 1991.
> *A Secret Dying*. London: HarperCollins, 1992.
> *Angel of Death*. London: HarperCollins, 1996.
> *Shape Shifter*. London: HarperCollins, 1998.
> *Ghost Dancers*. London: HarperCollins, 1999.
> *Assumption of Death*. London: Constable, 2000.
> *Dead Secret*. London: Constable, 2001.

Lieberman, Herbert. *The Girl With the Botticelli Eyes*. New York: St. Martin's Press, 1996. (A planned museum exhibition sends its curator hunting for Botticellis; he finds one of the painter's descendants...and death.) [Art.]

Lindsey, David L. *The Colour of Night*. New York: Warner, 1999. (A spy in from the cold turns his cover into a real art dealership and meets a Chinese-American with a cache of drawings she wants him to sell.) [Art.]

Lindsey, David L. *Animosity*. New York: Warner, 2001. (Sculptor Ross Marteau breaks up with his lover and returns from Paris to tiny San Rafael, Texas, where he is propositioned to sculpt a beautiful woman's lovely sister.) [Art.]

Llewellyn, Caroline. *The Masks of Rome*. New York: Scribner, 1988. (A young girl is enmeshed in suspense created by valuable Roman relics.) [Antiquities.]

Llewellyn, Caroline. *The Lady of the Labyrinth*. New York: Scribner, 1990. (Sicily's caverns shelter an ancient statue and modern murder as explored by the daughter of a famous archaeologist.) [Antiquities.]

Llewellyn, Caroline. *Life Blood*. New York: Scribner, 1993. (The Cotswold's Longbarrow Cottage is a poor refuge to a young widowed mother as ghosts rise from ancient—and modern—burial mounds to haunt her.) [Antiquities.]

Llewellyn, Caroline. *False Light*. New York: Scribner, 1996. (Antique photographs bring Victorian and modern Cornwall together in all their glamour and cruelty.) [Antiquities.]

Llewellyn, Sam. *The Sea Garden*. London: Headline, 1999. (An historic Cornwall garden serves as a grave.) [Architecture.]

Llewellyn, Sam. *The Malpas Legacy*. London: Headline, 2001. (Suspense on an Irish Georgian estate populated by follies human and architectural....) [Architecture.]

Long, James. *Silence and Shadows*. (London: HarperCollins, 2001. (A rural dig in Fawler reveals fragments of mosaics in the ruins left by the Romans and in solving modern crimes we learn the story of the German Queen.) [Antiquities.]

Loraine, Philip. *The Angel of Death*. New York: Mill, 1961. (Handsome John Lang sees in wealthy Pierro Fontana and his extraordinary art collection a way to boost his ambitions, so he sets in motion a deadly plot to steal Leonardo Da Vinci's famous painting, 'The Angel of Death.') [Art.]

Lott, Bret. *The Hunt Club*. New York: Villard, 1998. (Ancient slave relics and old burial grounds figure in this novel of murder, violence and sinister secrets set in South Carolina.) [Antiquities.]

Lovesey, Peter. *A Case of Spirits*. London: Macmillan, 1975. (Art collectors were just as greedy in Victorian times as present; a Sgt. Cribb and Constable Thackery mystery.) [Art].

Lovesey, Peter. *Waxwork*. London: Macmillan 1978. (A young woman poses nude for a photograph theoretically to be used by Frederick Leighton for a painting and as a result becomes involved in blackmail and murder; a Sgt. Cribb mystery.) [Art.]

Lovesey, Peter. *Bloodhounds*. London: Little Brown, 1996. (The forgery of a rare stamp causes someone to take a fatal licking.) [Forgeries.]

Lynds, Gayle. *Mosaic*. New York: Pocket, 1998. (Espionage in high places began with the mystery of the Tsars' famous Amber Room and currently strikes a blind concert pianist.) [Antiquities.]

Lyons, Arthur. *Other People's Money*. New York: Mysterious Press, 1989. (The investigation involves an art-collecting billionaire and, no surprise, smuggling; a Jacob Asch mystery.) [Art.]

MacDonald, John D. *A Deadly Shade of Gold*. New York: Fawcett, 1965. (Freewheeling Floridian Travis McGee runs into a case involving an Aztec idol made of gold.) [Art; Antiquities.]

Macdonald, Ross (Kenneth Millar). *The Blue Hammer*. New York: Knopf, 1976. (California's Lew Archer is hired to find a missing painting.) [Art.]

MacLeod, Charlotte. *The Convivial Codfish*. New York: Doubleday, 1984. (Art detective Max Bittersohn traces a valuable artifact stolen from a social club. Art expert Max Bittersohn and his Brahmin wife Sarah Kelling together are the scourges of Boston art thieves and cons.) [Art.]

MacLeod, Charlotte. *The Plain Old Man*. New York: Doubleday, 1985. (The disappearance of a valuable old portrait embroils Sarah Kelling and Max Bittersohn in murder.) [Art.]

MacLeod, Charlotte. *The Silver Ghost*. London: Collins, 1987. (The disappearance of a vintage 1927 New Phantom Rolls Royce leads Sarah Kelling and Max Bittersohn into another murderous adventure.) [Antiquities.]

MacLeod, Charlotte. *The Gladstone Bag*. London: HarperCollins, 1989. (Sarah Kelling's Aunt Emma, overseeing a summer artists' colony, gets caught up in murders.) [Art.]

MacLeod, Charlotte. *The Resurrection Man*. New York: Mysterious Press, 1992. (Expert forger of Byzantine icons Countess Lydia Ouspenska reports to Sarah Kelling and Max Bittersohn that restorer Bartolo Arbalest has set up a "guild" in Boston.) [Art.]

MacLeod, Charlotte. *The Odd Job*. New York: Mysterious Press, 1995. (Sarah and Max are challenged by the murder of the Wilkins' Museum administrator. An antique hat pin proves telling.) [Art.]

MacLeod, Charlotte. *The Balloon Man*. New York: Mysterious Press, 1998. (An attempt to steal a gold and ruby worn by the bride at a wedding hosted by Sarah Kelling requires Max Bittersohn's art theft expertise to resolve.) [Antiquities.]

Malcolm, John. *A Back Room in Somers Town*. London: Collins, 1984. (Camden Town artists and cosmetic and perfume interests embroil Simpson in murder; a Tim Simpson and White's Bank Art Fund mystery.) [Art.]

Malcolm, John. *The Godwin Sideboard*. London: Collins, 1984. (White's Bank Art Fund decides it needs embellishments of fine furniture and the resulting quest for an antique sideboard includes the usual accompaniment of murder; a Tim Simpson and White's Bank Art Fund mystery.) [Antiquities.]

Malcolm, John. *The Gwen John Sculpture*. London: Collins, 1986. (Venturing on the track of a Rodin sculpture leads to Gwen John; a Tim Simpson and White's Bank Art Fund mystery.) [Art.]

Malcolm, John. *Whistler in the Dark*. London: Collins, 1986. (A hunt for a Whistler results in murder; a Tim Simpson and White's Bank Art Fund mystery.) [Art.]

Malcolm, John. *Gothic Pursuit*. Collins, 1987. (On a hunt for a desk created by Richard Norman Shaw, Tim Simpson faces lethal weapons once again; a Tim Simpson and White's Bank Art Fund mystery.) [Art.]

Malcolm, John. *Mortal Ruin*. London: Collins, 1988. (Moreton Frewin and the Jeromes touch upon the fringes of the art world; a Tim Simpson and White's Bank Art Fund mystery.) [Art.]

Malcolm, John. *The Wrong Impression*. London: Collins, 1990. (Forgeries of Monet and Pissarro paintings done in 1870s London protesting the Franco-Prussian War inspire an attack on Ins. Roberts of the Yard and the best detecting efforts of his friend, Tim Simpson; a Tim Simpson and White's Bank Art Fund mystery.) [Art, Forgeries.]

Malcolm, John. *Sheep, Goats and Soap*. London: Crime Club, 1991. (Pre-Raphaelite paintings and Pears soap prove to be a lethal combination; a Tim Simpson and White's Bank Art Fund mystery.) [Art.]

Malcolm, John. *A Deceptive Appearance*. London: Crime Club, 1992. (A Paris cosmetics house and the lure of a James Tissot are conflicting interests that take a lethal turn; a Tim Simpson and White's Bank Art Fund mystery.) [Art.]

Malcolm, John. *The Burning Ground*. London: Crime Club, 1993. (On the track of a Nevinson in the Cubist/Futurist style Tim Simpson of the White's Bank Art Fund finds himself suspected of murder.) [Art.]

Malcolm, John. *Hung Over*. London: HarperCollins, 1994. (A collection of equestrian paintings featuring the work of Sir Alfred Mannings leads to murder; a Tim Simpson and White's Bank Art Fund mystery.) [Art.]

Malcolm, John. *Into the Vortex*. London: HarperCollins, 1996. (Banker Tim Simpson, chief agent for an art investment fund, grapples with the ghostly presence of Wyndham Lewis and a far too lively and aggressive tycoon; a Tim Simpson and White's Bank Art Fund mystery.) [Art.]

Malcolm, John. *Simpson's Homer*. London: Allison & Busby, 2001. (White's Bank faces various losses as Tim Simpson not only investigates murder but puzzles over the mysteries generated by Winslow Homer.) [Art.]

Malet, Léo. *Sunrise Behind the Louvre* (original French title: *Le Soleil Nâit derrière le Louvre*). London: Pan, 1991. (Paris PI Nestor Burma investigates an artful crime.) [Art.]

Marks, Peter. *Skullduggery*. New York: Carroll & Graf, 1987. (Fictionalized version of the Piltdown Man scandal of Sussex, with ties to London, where Wilde and Doyle are players. In 1953, the Man was proved to be a fake.) [Antiquities.]

Maron, Margaret. *One Coffee With*. Ontario: Raven House, 1982. (NYPD's Sigrid Harald finds love and death in a university art department.) [Art.]

Maron, Margaret. *Corpus Christmas*. New York: Doubleday, 1989. (Murder in an elegant Manhattan town house paints another crime scene for policewoman Sigrid and her artist lover.) [Art.]

Maron, Margaret. *Fugitive Colors*. New York: Mysterious Press, 1995. (The death of her artist lover leaves Sigrid bitter legacies, including his valuable collection of paintings; a Sigrid Harald mystery.) [Art.]

Maron, Margaret. *Uncommon Clay*. New York: Mysterious Press, 2001. (North Carolina Judge Deborah Knott untangles pottery family histories and the crimes they fired.) [Art.]

Marsh, Ngaio. *Artists in Crime.* London: Bles, 1938. (Supt. Roderick Alleyn meets painter Agatha Troy and pursues her and a killer.) [Art.]

Marsh, Ngaio. *Final Curtain.* London: Collins, 1947. (Agatha Troy is commissioned to paint the portrait of an elderly tycoon engaged to marry a chorus girl, a scene likely to end badly...; a Roderick Alleyn mystery.) [Art.]

Marsh, Ngaio. *Death of a Fool* (UK title: *Off with His Head*). Boston: Little Brown, 1956. (A peculiar case requires Alleyn to explore a folk tale and the ancient morris dance; a Roderick Alleyn mystery.) [Antiquities.]

Marsh, Ngaio. *Clutch of Constables.* London: Collins, 1968. (Painter Agatha Troy goes on a canal cruise through Constable country; a Roderick Alleyn mystery.) [Art.]

Marston, Edward *see also* Miles, Keith.

Marston, Edward (Keith Miles). *The Wolves of Savernake.* New York: St. Martin's, 1993. (William the Conqueror's census takers don't count on a wolflike killer or a ring counterfeiting coins of the realm to be housed in the Wiltshire village of Bedwyn. The presence of a licensed Royal Mint is always a potential occasion for...license.) [Antiquities.]

Marston, Edward (Keith Miles). *The Fair Maid of Bohemia.* New York: St. Martin's, 1997. (An Elizabethan players troop plagued by murder travels to Prague where the painter Arcimboldo has memorialized Rupert II). [Art.]

Marston, Edward (Keith Miles). *The King's Evil.* London: Headline, 1999. (After London's Great Fire of 1666 a young architect is hired to design a home for wealthy merchant whom he finds murdered in the cellar.) [Architecture.]

Mason, Sarah Jane (writing as Hamilton Crane) *see* Carvic, Heron.

Martin, David L. *Petikan.* New York: Simon & Schuster. 1999. (A Scam artist teams up with a group of nuns to recover a stolen religious icon.) [Antiquities]

Martin, James (writing as Charles Hampton) *see* Carvic, Heron.

Martin, Julia Wallis. *A Likeness in Stone.* London: Hodder, 1997. (A killer terrorizing Yorkshire has an odd connection with a sculptor.) [Art.]

Massey, Sujata. *Zen Attitude.* New York: HarperCollins, 1998. (In her second case, Rei Shimura sets up as a Tokyo antiques dealer and purchases a *tansu* or ancient chest of drawers that comes packed with trouble and leads to murder.) [Antiquities.]

Massey, Sujata. *The Flower Master*. New York: HarperCollins, 1999 (Japanese American antiques dealer Rei Shimura studies the ancient art of flower arranging which blossoms into murder.) [Art.]

Massey, Sujata. *The Floating Girl*. New York: HarperCollins, 2000. (Rei Shimura's 4th case explores the world of modern comics and the Japanese fascination with *manga*, animation.) [Art.]

Massey, Sujata. *The Bride's Kimono*. New York: HarperCollins, 2001. (Rei Shimura is asked to courier rare textiles to a small Washington, DC, museum where the exhibition opens up fraud and murder.) [Antiquities.]

Mathes, Charles. *The Girl with the Phony Name*. New York: St. Martin's Press, 1992. (A Celtic brooch and hits of buried treasure help Lucy MacAlpin Trelaine regain her identity.) [Antiquities.]

Mathes, Charles. *The Girl Who Remembered Snow*. New York: St. Martin's Press, 1996. (Memories of snow, a model ship, and a golden dragon whistle hold keys to Emma Passant's past.) [Antiquities.]

Mathes, Charles. *The Girl at the End of the Line*. New York: St. Martin's Press, 1999. (The accidental discovery of an old *Playbill* sends an antique dealer and her sister seeking clues to a family past and the solution to am unsolved murder). [Antiquities.]

Matteson, Stephanie. *Murder on the Silk Road*. New York: Berkley, 1992. (Elderly actress sleuth Charlotte Graham tracks a stolen Buddhist sculpture along an ancient Chinese trade route). [Art.]

Maxwell, A.E. (Ann and Evan). *The Art of Survival*. New York: Doubleday, 1989. (Fiddler and Fiora encounter Santa Fe artists, murder, fast cars—and each other—in an explosive mix.) [Art.]

Mayle, Peter. *Chasing Cézanne*. New York: Knopf, 1997. (An art scam involving a Cézanne is part of a scheme of hanky-panky on the international art scene.) [Art; Forgeries.]

McClendon, Lise. *The Bluejay Shaman*. New York: Walker, 1994. (How is a Salish bluejay pictograph tied to the weird behavior of rogue professor "Mad Dog" Tilden? An Alex Thorssen art historian mystery.) [Antiquities; Art.]

McClendon, Lise. *Painted Truth*. New York: Walker, 1995. (A Wyoming art expert wonders if the body cremated in a gallery fire is really an artist suicide?; an Alix Thorssen mystery.) [Art.]

McClendon, Lise. *Nordic Nights*. New York: Walker, 1999. (A gallery owner finds her stepfather standing over the body of a Norwegian artist—did he send the painter of myths on his voyage to Valhalla?; an Alex Thorssen mystery. [Art.]

McClendon, Lise. *Blue Wolf*. New York: Walker, 2001. (Jackson Hole gallery owner Alex Thorssen is mixed up in wolves back in the wild—and in the local arts community.) [Art.]

McCrumb, Sharyn. *Lovely in Her Bones*. New York: Ballantine, 1985. (Elizabeth MacPherson comes to an isolated Tennessee valley with an archaeological expedition hoping an old burial ground will help the Cullowhee Tribe save their land from strip miners, but finds new as well as old bones in the ancient earth.) [Antiquities.]

McCrumb, Sharyn. *Paying the Piper*. New York: Ballantine, 1988. (An archaeological dig into prehistoric burial sites on a small Scottish island leads to a murder that nearly unnerves forensic anthropologist Elizabeth MacPherson.) [Antiquities.]

McCrumb, Sharyn. *If Ever I Return, Pretty Peggy-O*. New York: Scribner, 1990. (Hamelin, Tennessee, gains a famous folksinger and a killer, linked by a voice from the Vietnam War.) [Antiquities.]

McCrumb, Sharyn. *The Hangman's Beautiful Daughter*. New York: Scribner, 1992. (Nora Bonesteel, who has the "sight," can't prevent dark deeds among her beloved mountains.) [Antiquities.]

McCrumb, Sharyn. *She Walks These Hills*. New York: Scribner, 1994. (An escaped convict making his way home across the mountains parallels a walk taken by a frontier girl kidnapped by Indians. The lines are tangled with a novice hiker, a talkative radio announcer, and other modern mountain folk.) [Antiquities.]

McCrumb, Sharyn. *The Rosewood Casket*. New York: Scribner, 1996. (A dying farmer's last request is that his sons fashion his coffin, but more distant corpses complicate the process.) [Antiquities.]

McCrumb, Sharyn. *Foggy Mountain Breakdown*. New York: Ballantine, 1997. (Appalachia is the scene for a short story collection.) [Antiquities.]

McCrumb, Sharyn. *The Ballad of Frankie Silver*. New York: Dutton, 1998. (Why was young 19th Century mountain wife Frankie Silver unable to secure a pardon for the murder of her

husband, an execution paralleling modern Tennessee justice.)
[Antiquities.]

McCrumb, Sharyn. *The Songcatcher: A Ballad Novel.* New York:
Dutton, 2001. (Not a mystery but a generational history of the
Malcolm McCourry family from his kidnapping from Islay to
his homestead in North Carolina and on down the line to the
present.) [Antiquities.]

McDermid, Val. *Clean Break.* London: HarperCollins, 1995. (The
theft of a Monet embroils Kate Brannigan in murder.) [Art.]

McGarrity, Michael. *Serpent* Gate. New York: Scribner, 1998.
(Involves an art heist from the office of the Governor of New
Mexico.) [Art.]

Melville, James (writing as Charles Hampton) *see* Carvic, Heron.

Mertz, Barbara *see also* Michaels, Barbara; Peters, Elizabeth.

Michaels, Barbara (Barbara Mertz). *Shattered Silk.* New York:
Atheneum, 1986. (Dwelling on antique clothing.) [Antiquities.]

Michaels, Barbara (Barbara Mertz). *Stitches in Time.* New York,
NY: HarperCollins, 1995. (Antique quilts pieced with vintage
clothing make for surprising suspense.) [Antiquities.]

Miles, Keith *see also* Marston, Edward.

Miles, Keith. *Murder in Perspective.* New York: Walker, 1997. (A
1920s murder at the Arizona Biltmore employs a concrete block
from Frank Lloyd Wright's unpatented process; a Merlin
Richards mystery.) [Architecture.]

Miles, Keith. *Saint's Rest.* New York: Walker, 1999. (During the
construction of a mansion in Oak Park, Illinois the body of a
murdered man is found in the wine cellar; a Merlin Richards
mystery.) [Architecture.]

Millar, Kenneth *see* Macdonald, Ross.

Mones, Nicole. *Lost in Translation.* New York: Delacorte, 1998.
(A search for the bones of Peking Man leads to romance in
China.) [Antiquities.]

Moore, Viviane. *Blue Blood.* London: Gollancz, 2000. (The
Chevalier Galeran investigates murders during the 1134
rebuilding of Chartres cathedral, burnt during a fire a decade
before.) [Architecture.]

Morgan, Speer. *The Freshour Chronicles.* Denver: MacMurray & Beck,
1998. (Set along the Arkansas/Oklahoma border in 1934 and
focusing on the excavations of the Spiro Mound, metaphors and

artifacts of a pre-Columbian Indian civilization are woven into a tale involving human greed and elements of self-preservation.) [Antiquities.]

Morrell, David. *Double Image*. New York: Warner, 1998. (A photographer becomes obsessed with a 1930's photograph and meets a contemporary lass with an uncanny resemblance.) [Antiquities; Architecture.]

Morrell, David. *Burnt Sienna*. New York: Warner, 2000. (Painter Chase Malone, an ex-marine, goes up against an arms dealer who cannot stand imperfections in his women, though their portraits preserve them.) [Art.]

Morrah, Dermot. *The Mummy Case Mystery*. London: Harper & Brothers Publishers, 1933. (An academic romp at Oxford's 'Beaufort' College begins with the murder of 'the supreme authority on the mortuary customs of the ancient Egyptians.') [Antiquities.]

Muller, Marcia. *The Tree of Death*. New York: Walker & Company, 1983. (The Santa Barbara Museum's Curator of Mexican Arts Elena Oliverez's boss turns up murdered and the weapon is a work of art.) [Art.]

Muller, Marcia. *The Legend of the Slain Soldiers*. New York: Walker, 1985. (The murder of an historian researching the Depression-era slaughter of Chicano farm workers has museum curator Elena Oliverez studying paintings for clues during Santa Barbara's Fiesta.) [Art.]

Muller, Marcia and Pronzini, Bill. *Beyond the Grave*. New York: Walker, 1986. (A treasure chest buried in 1846 figures in a crime that bridges 1894 and 1986 San Francisco; an Elena Oliverez mystery.) [Art.]

Muller, Marcia. *Cavalier in White*. New York: St. Martin's Press, 1986. (San Francisco's Joanna Stark, a former art security expert, pursues an elegant art thief across three books. It starts at an elegant art museum show.) [Art.]

Muller, Marcia. *Dark Star*. New York: St. Martin's Press, 1986. (Joanna Stark fears her expert art thief former lover is after a valuable Van Gogh; the chase laps around a California winery.) [Art.]

Muller, Marcia. *There Hangs the Knife*. New York: St. Martin's Press, 1988. (The final chapter settles personal as well as professional matters for Joanna Stark.) [Art.]

Murray, Donna Houston. *Lie Like a Rug*. New York: St. Martin's Press, 2001. (A Philadelphia prep headmaster's wife, Ginger Barnes, gives herself a crash course in domestic decorative arts to solve a murder.) [Art.]

Myers, Tamar. The Abigail Timberlake series. (Murder and high jinks dodge an antiques dealer.) [Antiquities.]

> *Larceny and Old Lace*. New York: Avon, 1996.
> *Gilt by Association*. New York: Avon, 1996.
> *The Ming and I*. New York: Avon, 1997.
> *So Faux, So Good*. New York: Avon, 1998.
> *Baroque and Desperate*. New York: Avon, 1999.
> *Estate of Mind*. New York: Avon, 1999.
> *A Penny Urned*. New York: Avon, 2000.
> *Nightmare in Shining Armor*. New York: Avon, 2001.

Newman, Sharan. *The Wandering Arm*. New York: Tom Doherty Associates, 1995. (A lost reliquary and a nefarious murder threaten to destroy the fragile détente of Christians and Jews in medieval Paris; a Catherine LeVendeur mystery. [Antiquities.]

O'Connell, Carol. *Killing Critics*. New York: Putnam, 1996. (Wild child cop Mallory finds her third case in a gallery showcasing performing art that turns deadly real.) [Art.]

Oliver, Anthony. *The Pew Group*. London: Heinemann, 1981. (The first of a series set in Flaxfield, England and drawing on the antiques trade, this one revolving around "a small piece of white pottery...rudely but endearingly fashioned with three little figures sitting stiffly on a high-backed settle"; a Mrs. Thomas and ex-Detective Inspector John Webber mystery.) [Antiquities.]

Oliver, Anthony. *The Property of A Lady*. London: Heinemann, 1983. (Involving a likely psychopath, the action moves from Flaxfield to France, and climaxes in the salesroom; a Mrs. Thomas and ex-Detective Inspector John Webber mystery.) [Antiquities.]

Oliver, Anthony. *The Elberg Collection*. London: Heinemann, 1985. (Danger and murder lurk throughout an investigation connected with an eponymous collection of Staffordshire figures; a Mrs. Thomas and ex-Detective Inspector John Webber mystery.) [Antiquities.]

Oliver, Anthony. *Cover-Up*. London: Heinemann, 1987. (The action pivots on a painting, possibly an early Stanley Spencer; a

Mrs. Thomas and ex-Detective Inspector John Webber mystery.) [Antiquities.]

Orton, Thomas. *The Lost Glass Plates of Wilfred Eng.* New York: Counterpoint, 1999. (A needy gallery owner is seduced by a trove of glass negatives from the 19th Century Chinese photographer that seem to suggest he had an unlikely mistress. With his ethics already in question, will Robert risk all?) [Art.]

Outland, Orland. *Death Wore a Smart Little Outfit.* New York: Berkeley, 1997. (A drag queen investigates a series of murders of artists in San Francisco,) [Art.]

Page, Jake. *Stolen Gods.* New York: Ballantine Books, 1993. (Blind Santa Fe sculptor Mo Bowdre sees through the recovery of Hopi sacred relics from unscrupulous thieves.) [Antiquities; Art.]

Page, Katherine Hall. *The Body in the Bookcase.* New York: Morrow, 1998. (Faith Fairchild is robbed and tracks the thieves relentlessly across New England by scouring antique shops.) [Antiquities.]

Page, Martin. *The Man Who Stole the Mona Lisa.* New York Pantheon Books, 1984. (Annotation unavailable.) [Art; Forgeries.]

Pamuk, Orhan. *My Name Is Red.* US: New York: Knopf, 2001. (Under Sultan Murat II 1578-90, Islamic artists are commissioned to illustrate a great book in the Frankish miniaturist style despite Islam's edict against representational art.) [Art.]

Pargeter, Edith *see* Peters, Ellis.

Paul, Elliot. *Hugger-Mugger in the Louvre.* New York: Random House, 1940. (When a famous painting is stolen from the Paris museum, the city is agog and the police are baffled, but not Homer Evans, who sees his way past the dark recesses of the Louvre, the lairs of the underworld, and the shady dens of shadier art dealers.) [Art.]

Pears, Iain. *The Raphael Affair.* London: Victor Gollancz, 1990. (The hunt for a hidden Raphael takes Jonathan Argyll and Flavia di Stefano into the murky corners of a Roman Church). [Art.]

Pears, Iain. *The Titan Committee.* London: Victor Gollanez, 1991. (An international art committee conference on Titan is disrupted by murder entangling Jonathan Argyll and Flavia di Stefano.) [Art.]

Pears, Iain. *The Bernini Bust.* London: V. Gollancz, 1992. (The sale of a minor Titan embroils Jonathan Argyll in another international art intrigue; a Flavia di Stefano mystery.) [Art.]

Pears, Iain. *The Last Judgment*. London: V. Gollancz, 1993. (Slightly seedy art expert Jonathan Argyll and his love, the Italian Art Squad's Flavia di Stefano, become entangled in artistic threads running back to World War II France.) [Art.]

Pears, Iain. *Giotto's Hand*. London: HarperCollins, 1994. (A string of art thefts sends Jonathan Argyll and Flavia di Stefano in hot pursuit.) [Art.]

Pears, Iain. *Death and Restoration*. London: HarperCollins, 1996. (Features slightly seedy art expert Jonathan Argyll and his love, the Italian Art Squad's Flavia di Stefano who become involved with a monastery and a purported Caravaggio.) [Art.]

Pears, Iain. *The Immaculate Deception*. London: HarperCollins, 2001. (Jonathan Argyll and his pregnant wife Flavia di Stefano, now head of the Art Squad, face a kidnapped Claude Lorraine masterpiece and an old adversary.) [Art.]

Pérez-Reverte, Arturo. *The Flanders Panel*. London: Harvill, 1994. [Original Spanish title: *Tabla de Flandes*.] (Young art restorer uncovers a cryptic message on an old painting: Who killed the Knight? Eventually, she finds out.) [Art.]

Peters, Elizabeth (Barbara Mertz). *The Jackal's Head*. New York: Meredith, 1968. (Althea Tomlinson returns to Egypt to clear her father's name if she isn't killed for a secret, one as ancient as Nefertiti.) [Antiquities.]

Peters, Elizabeth (Barbara Mertz). *The Camelot Caper*. New York: Meredith, 1969. (Jessica Tregath is pursued by various villains through Cornwall apparently in search o an antique heirloom and an Arthurian treasure.) [Antiquities.]

Peters, Elizabeth (Barbara Mertz). *The Dead Sea Cipher*. New York: Dodd Mead, 1970. (Dinah Van der Lyn embarks on an odyssey of terror through fabled ancient cities Sidon, Damascus, and Tyre.) [Antiquities.]

Peters, Elizabeth (Barbara Mertz). *The Seventh Sinner*. New York: Dodd Mead, 1972. (Jean Suttman's fellowship to study in Rome is a dream until she visits an ancient temple to Mithra.) [Antiquities.]

Peters, Elizabeth (Barbara Mertz). *Borrower of the Night*. New York: Dodd Mead, 1973. (Introducing art historian Vicky Bliss whose adventures in Mexico City link her to a career in a German museum.) [Art.]

Peters, Elizabeth (Barbara Mertz). *Crocodile on the Sandbank*. New York: Dodd Mead, 1975. (Introduces Amelia Peabody, a heiress with a passion for Egyptology, and Radcliffe Emerson, an Egyptologist, who find themselves stalked by a mummy while excavating.) [Antiquities.]

Peters, Elizabeth (Barbara Mertz). *Legend in Green Velvet*. New York: Dodd Mead, 1976. (A young woman goes on an archaeological dig in the Scottish Highlands....) [Antiquities.]

Peters, Elizabeth (Barbara Mertz). *Street of the Five Moons*. New York: Dodd Mead, 1978. (A note with hieroglyphs and a reproduction of the Charlemagne talisman lead to intrigue in Rome; a Vicky Bliss mystery.) [Art.]

Peters, Elizabeth (Barbara Mertz). *The Curse of the Pharaohs*. New York: Dodd Mead, 1981. (Clearly an act of sabotage, a curse is blamed for the mysterious deaths at the excavation of a recently discovered tomb; an Amelia Peabody mystery.) [Antiquities.]

Peters, Elizabeth (Barbara Mertz). *Silhouette in Scarlet*. New York: Congdon and Weed, 1983. (A one-way ticket to Stockholm leads to a hunt for a long lost Nordic treasure; a Vicky Bliss mystery.) [Art.]

Peters, Elizabeth (Barbara Mertz). *The Mummy Case*. New York: Congdon and Weed, 1985. (Particularly good on Ancient Egyptian pyramids; an Amelia Peabody mystery.) [Antiquities.]

Peters, Elizabeth (Barbara Mertz). *Lion in the Valley*. New York: Atheneum, 1986. (A criminal investigation while excavating her own site lands Amelia Peabody in murder, mystery and mayhem.) [Antiquities.]

Peters, Elizabeth (Barbara Mertz). *Trojan Gold*. New York: Atheneum, 1987. (A Christmas crime involves Heinrich Schliemann and the Trojan treasure hoard; a Vicky Bliss mystery.) [Antiquities; Art; Forgeries.]

Peters, Elizabeth (Barbara Mertz). *The Deeds of the Disturber*. New York: Atheneum, 1988. (Returning to England, Amelia Peabody investigates the murder of a night watchman found sprawled in the shadow of a mummy case.) [Antiquities.]

Peters, Elizabeth (Barbara Mertz). *The Last Camel Died at Noon*. New York: Warner Books, 1991. (Mystery and intrigue accompany the exploration of a lost Nubian city, relic of an ancient civilization; an Amelia Peabody mystery.) [Antiquities.]

Peters, Elizabeth (Barbara Mertz). *The Snake, the Crocodile, and the Dog*. New York: Warner, 1992. (A return to Amarna embroils Amelia Peabody in another caper featuring Egyptology.) [Antiquities.]

Peters, Elizabeth (Barbara Mertz). *Night Train to Memphis*. New York: Warner Books, 1994. (Art expert Vicky Bliss cruises down the Nile to foil the pirating of Ancient Egyptian art and discovers the prime suspect to be her on-again-off-again lover, Sir John.) [Antiquities; Art.]

Peters, Elizabeth (Barbara Mertz). *The Hippopotamus Pool*. New York: Warner, 1996. (A trip to Thebes to find the hidden tomb of Queen Tetisheri results in encounters with murders, grave robberies, kidnappings, and ancient Egyptian curses; an Amelia Peabody mystery.) [Antiquities.]

Peters, Elizabeth (Barbara Mertz). *Seeing a Large Cat*. New York: Warner, 1997. (In turn-of-the-century Cairo, a dream of a large cat and the excavation of tomb Twenty A are components of a macabre puzzle of murder, passion and cruel deceit; an Amelia Peabody mystery.) [Antiquities.]

Peters, Elizabeth (Barbara Mertz). *The Ape Who Guards the Balance*. New York: Avon, 1998. (The acquisition of mint-condition papyrus the *Book of the Dead* leads to the unraveling of a tangle of stolen treasures and ruthless murder in 1907 Cairo; an Amelia Peabody mystery.) [Antiquities.]

Peters, Elizabeth (Barbara Mertz). *The Falcon at the Portal*. New York: Avon, 1999. (It is 1911 and David Todros, married to Amelia's niece, is suspected of fabricating antiquities; an Amelia Peabody mystery.) [Antiquities.]

Peters, Elizabeth (Barbara Mertz). *He Shall Thunder in the Sky*. New York: Morrow, 2000. (As the Peabody's dig in for the winter, Ramses seems to have gone over to the dark side.) [Antiquities.]

Peters, Elizabeth (Barbara Mertz). *Lord of the Silent*. New York: Morrow, 2001. (By 1915, there is no escaping the effect of the war on modern Egypt nor the trials continually plaguing archaeologists.) [Antiquities.]

Peters, Ellis *see* Edith Pargeter.

Peters, Ellis (Edith Pargeter). *Death Mask*. London: Collins, 1959. (A young English boy stumbles upon a cache of Ancient Greek treasures.) [Antiquities.]

Peters, Ellis (Edith Pargeter). *City of Gold and Shadows*. London: Macmillan, 1973. (More is buried in an ancient Roman city in Wales than mere ruins.) [Antiquities.]

Peters, Ellis (Edith Pargeter). *Flight of a Witch*. London: Macmillan, 1964. (The Hallowmount, a mysterious hill on the border of Wales, holds associations with witchcraft, Druids, and ancient Christianity, and can help even a modern witch cast spells; a George Felse mystery.) [Antiquities.]

Peters, Ellis (Edith Pargeter). *Black Is the Colour of My True Love's Heart*. London: Macmillan, 1967. (The residential college housing the mystery is far more bizarre than the classical grandeur of Shropshire's Attingham Park and its gardens, the author's inspiration.) [Architecture.]

Peters, Ellis (Edith Pargeter). *The Knocker on Death's Door*. London: Macmillan, 1970. (A photographer takes an undue interest in the carved oak door on the local church, which prises out a body buried beneath the flagstones of the local gentry's historic home at Mottisham Abbey; a George Felse mystery.) [Antiquities.]

Peters, Ellis (Edith Pargeter). *A Morbid Taste for Bones*. London: Macmillan, 1977. (The history, customs, and antiquities of Shropshire resound through the *Cadfael Chronicles*, of which this is the first. 12th century Benedictine monk Brother Cadfael travels from Wales to bring Shrewsbury the bones of St. Winifred, to be enshrined and serve as a focal point for pilgrims. But is he successful? Nineteen further adventures continue Cadfael's work.) [Antiquities.]

Peters, Ellis (writing as Edith Pargeter). *The Heaven Tree Trilogy*. New York: Warner Books, 1993. [Individual titles originally published: *The Heaven Tree*. London: Heinemann, 1960; *The Green Branch*. London: Heinemann, 1962; *The Scarlet Seed*. London: Heinemann, 1963.] (Generations of medieval cathedral builders wage love and war.) [Architecture.]

Preston, Douglas with Lincoln Child. *Riptide*. New York: Warner, 1998. (An island off New England lures a crew to build a coffer dam to recover pirate treasure.) [Antiquities; Architecture.]

Preston, Douglas with Lincoln Child. *Thunderhead*. New York: Warner, 1999. (An archaeologist's daughter sets off to find a missing Anasazi ruin in Utah's canyonlands.) [Antiquities.]

Price, Anthony. *Colonel Butler's Wolf.* London: Gollancz, 1972.
(An espionage adventure set in Northumberland around
Hadrian's Wall that reflects on the military life back to the
Roman Empire; a Dr. David Audley thriller.) [Antiquities.]

Price, Anthony. *Our Man in Camelot.* London: Gollancz, 1975.
(Drawing on the author's archaeological interests, a novel
combining theorizing about ancient Britain with a monster KGB
plot; a Dr. David Audley thriller.) [Antiquities.]

Pronzini, Bill *see* Muller, Marcia.

Ramus, David. *The Thief of Light.* New York: HarperCollins, 1995.
(A corrupt Manhattan dealer with a cocaine habit, a fake Monet
deal, and murder darken the picture.) [Art.]

Ramus, David. *Gravity of Shadows.* New York: Harper, 1998. (A
vault of priceless art work and a scandalous Palm Beach secret
ignite a political bombshell.) [Art.]

Ramus, David. *On Ice.* New York: Pocket, 2000. (Ben Hemmings
builds barns for Atlanta's horse breeding elite until he's framed
for money laundering and builds a revenge plot.) [Architecture.]

Reed, Mary and Eric Mayer. *Three for a Letter.* Scottsdale: Poisoned Pen Press, 2001. (One twin, Ostrogoth heir to Rome's
throne, is murdered inside a mechanical whale. More automatons figure into a byzantine plot unknotted by Justinian's Lord
Chamberlain, John.) [Antiquities.]

Reuben, Shelly. *Spent Matches.* New York: Scribner, 1996. (Arson
in a private Manhattan museum locked-room incinerates
modern masterpieces, but the real art lies in finding the
connections between the Pre-Raphaelites and a young man of
Arthurian yearnings.) [Art.]

Richman, Alyson. *The Mask Carver's Son.* New York: Bloomsbury,
2000. (Suspense lies not in any crime but in how the son of a
Noh Theater mask carver can give rein to his passion for
painting. He moves to *fin-de-siècle* Paris but eventually returns
home to wrestle with cross-cultural demons.) [Art.]

Roberts, Carey. *Touch a Cold Door.* New York: Pageant, 1989.
(D.C. Detective Anne Fitzhugh is assigned the murder of
wealthy art patron Theo DeLisle, who's left a last desperate
message pointing to the murderer....) [Art.]

Robinson, Lynda S. *Murder in the Place of Anubis.* New York:
Walker, 1994. (The discovery of an extra body in the embalming

shelter alerts "The Eyes and Ears of Pharaoh" to a case melding ancient Egyptian religious beliefs and practices with sensational court intrigue surrounding King Tutankhamun; a Lord Meren mystery.) [Antiquities.]

Robinson, Lynda S. *Murder at the God's Gate.* New York: Walker, 1995. (The priests of Amun are yet bitter over the years under the heretic Akhenaten so Lord Meren keeps a spy at the temple in Thebes…who hideously dies.) [Antiquities.]

Robinson, Lynda S. *Murder at the Feast of Rejoicing.* New York: Walker, 1996. (This third entry in an excellent King Tut-era series finds Lord Meren at his estate entertaining a host of relatives while supervising construction of the Pharaoh's tomb. Both activities are interrupted by the murder of his beautiful cousin-in-law, creating an old-fashioned country-house puzzle for the minister to solve. An interesting take on Egyptian home life adds even more depth to the charismatic series protagonist.) [Antiquities.]

Robinson, Lynda. S. *Eater of Souls.* New York: Walker, 1997. (Lord Meren's investigation into the death of Queen Nefertiti is sidetracked by deaths attributed to the fearsome Devourer, the Eater of Souls.) [Antiquities.]

Robinson, Lynda S. *Drinker of Blood.* New York: Mysterious Press, 1998. (Lord Meren continues his search into the possible murder of Nefertiti.) [Antiquities.]

Robinson, Lynda S. *Slayer of Gods.* (New York: Mysterious Press, 2001. (Lord Meren learns what hand lay behind Nefertiti's murder.) [Antiquities.]

Rosenbaum, David. *Sasha's Trick.* New York: Mysterious Press, 1995. (An enterprising Russian con-man and an old-lag from the Gulag scheme over stolen art.) [Art.]

Ross, Robert. *A French Finish.* New York: Putnam, 1977. (With marvelous details, this novel concerns counterfeiting a Louis XIV desk to sell.) [Antiquities; Forgeries.]

Rowe, Rosemary. *The Germanicus Mosaic.* London: Headline, 1999. (Mosaic maker Libertus, a freedman in 2nd Century A.D. Glevum [Roman Gloucester], solves the murder of a man burned in his bath house hypocaust.) [Antiquities; Art.]

Rowe, Rosemary. *Pattern of Blood.* London: Headline, 2000.

Rowe, Rosemary. *Murder in the Forum.* London: Headline, 2001.

Rowe, Rosemary. *The Chariots of Calyx.* London: Headline, 2002.

Rowlands, Betty. *Finishing Touch*. London: Hodder, 1991. (While teaching a writing course for a college, mystery writer Melissa Craig encounters murder in the art department.) [Art.]

Rozan, S.J. *China Trade*. New York: St. Martin's, 1994. (NY Chinatown's Lydia Chin and her PI partner Bill Smith are drawn into a case in which rare Chinese porcelains shine.) [Antiquities.]

Rozan, S.J. *No Colder Place*. New York: St. Martin's Press, 1997. (An investigation lands PI Bill Smith an undercover job as a bricklayer on a 40-story residential building. Something's not kosher: equipment goes missing, materials are sub-par, a worker is discovered murdered in the elevator pit; a mafioso may be mixing with the mortar. Lydia Chin plays backup in the construction company office.) [Architecture.]

Russell, Jack. *Yellow Jack*. New York: W.W. Norton, 1999. (An apprentice to Louis Daguerre brings the new art to New Orleans where he photographs the victims of yellow fever....) [Art.]

Sanders, Lawrence. *The Second Deadly Sin*. New York: (Coming out of retirement, former Chief of Detectives Edward X. Delaney investigates the fatal stabbing of hated artist Victor Maitland.) [Art.]

Satterthwait, Walter. *Wall of Glass*. New York: St. Martin's Press, 1988. (Santa Fe PI Joshua Croft wonders if feathered kachinas are really worth dying for.) [Art.]

Sayers, Dorothy L. *The Five Red Herrings*. London: Gollancz, 1931. (An intricately plotted puzzle set in a Scottish artists colony that makes heavy use of railway timetables.) [Art.]

Saylor, Steven. *Catilina's Riddle*. New York: St. Martin's, 1993. (Gordianus the Finder inherits a country estate but in the end opts for urban Rome.) [Antiquities.]

Saylor, Steven. *Last Seen in Massilia*. New York: St. Martin's Press, 2000. (Gordianus and his son-in-law penetrate a city under siege. Its construction, fortifications, and traditions are formidable.) [Antiquities; Architecture.]

Shuman, Malcolm. *Burial Ground*. New York: Avon, 1998. (An oil baron hires archaeologist Alan Graham to check out a Tunica burial site on the mogul's new Louisiana plantation.) [Antiquities.]

Shuman, Malcolm. *The Meriwether Murder*. New York: Avon, 1998. (While exploring Desiree Plantation, Alan Graham comes across a tombstone labelled "Louis' that prods him to ask more of the fate of the explorer.) [Antiquities.]

Shuman, Malcolm. *Assassin's Blood.* New York: Avon, 1999. (While working a tract of Louisiana land slated to go under a dam, Alan Graham learns more of Lee Harvey Oswald.) [Antiquities.]

Shuman, Malcolm. *Past Dying.* New York: Avon, 2000. (Contract archaeologist Alan Graham investigates a Louisiana librarian's claim about UFOs but finds a rare coin and legends of local-boy Jim Bowie.) [Antiquities.]

Shuman, Malcolm. *The Last Mayan.* New York: Avon, 2001. (Alan Graham works the Yucatan where evidence suggests Columbus was not the first European to reach the New World. But why are two men now dead?) [Antiquities.]

Simpson, Marcia. *Crow in Stolen Colors.* Scottsdale: Poisoned Pen Press, 2000. (The skipper of a freighter in Southeastern Alaskan waters is nearly swamped in an attempt to hijack tribal totems.) [Antiquities].

Sipherd, Ray. *The Audubon Quartet.* New York: St. Martin's Press, 1998. (Four newly discovered Audubon paintings are declared to be fakes by art critic Abe Lasher; Lasher is then strangled; any connection?) [Art.]

Skeggs, Douglas. *The Estuary Pilgrim.* London: Macmillan, 1989. (An excellent batch of books focusing on the history of masterpieces and their recovery; this one focusing on a Nazi hoard of paintings that was supposedly destroyed in the Normandy invasion.) [Art.]

Skeggs, Douglas. *The Talinin Madonna.* London: Macmillan, 1991. (Murder and intrigue accompany the discovery of a treasure from the Hermitage in a London art gallery.) [Art.]

Skeggs, Douglas. *The Triumph of Bacchus.* London: Macmillan, 1993. (A Titian masterpiece is stolen from London's Royal Academy and held for ransom. The stolen Bacchus becomes the obsession of a forger, an inquisitive reporter, and its Lloyd's insurer.) [Art.]

Skeggs, Douglas. *The Phoenix of Prague.* London: Little Brown, 1996. (Set in Prague, an art collection formerly belonging to a Rumanian dictator becomes a focus of death and intrigue.) [Art.]

Skeggs, Douglas. *The Claimant.* London: Little Brown, 1998. (Revenge, power and passion in contemporary Hungary expose past treacheries and deceits, Nazi and Russian, as heirs to Festivis Palace squabble.) [Art.]

Slater, Susan. *Yellow Lies.* Philadelphia: Intrigue Press, 2000. (New Mexico Pueblo artist Sal Zuni produces superb carvings in amber he sells for big bucks. But....) [Art; Forgeries.]

Smith, Bridget A. *Death of an Alaskan Princess.* New York: St. Martin's, 1988. (The Juno gallery scene and Tlingit art are a fascinating backdrop to murder.) [Antiquities; Art.]

Smith, Sarah. *The Knowledge of Water.* New York: Ballantine Books, 1996. (The Mona Lisa is stolen from the Louvre in a Belle Époque mystery.) [Art.]

Smith, Wilbur. *River God.* London: Macmillan, 1993. (The first volume in a trilogy about modern archaeologists unearthing the story of Pharaonic adviser Taita and ancient Thebes.) [Antiquities.]

Smith, Wilbur. *The Seventh Scroll.* London: Macmillan, 1995. (A modern team of archaeologists search for a Pharaoh's unplundered tomb; Volume Two). [Antiquities.]

Smith, Wilbur. *Warlock.* London: Macmillan, 2001. (Since his beloved Queen Lostris' death, Taita has studied to become a warlock and ends using his skills to save her dynasty; Volume Three). [Antiquities.]

Sprague, Gretchen. *Maquette for Murder.* New York: St. Martin's Press, 2000. (Retired attorney Martha Patterson finds herself advising sculptor Hannah Gold when her celebrated new maquette, a model of a larger scale work, is one victim of a break in.) [Art.]

Stabenow, Dana. *A Cold Blooded Business.* New York: Berkley Prime Crime, 1994. (Inuit investigator Kate Shugak finds the theft of ancient Alaskan artifacts runs hand in hand with plunder on the modern pipeline.) [Antiquities.]

Stefanie, James R. *The Charters Affair.* IUniverse, 2001. (A superior Holmes *pastiche* where he and Watson uncover what's at stake in Little Stoke, home of a Neolithic burial site where in 1537 an Abbot disappeared along with his abbey's rich treasures.) [Antiquities.]

Stein, Triss. *Digging up Death: a Kay Engels Mystery.* New York: Walker, 1998. (A mysterious body of recent origin is discovered at the site of a burnt out 17th century tavern during construction in lower Manhattan.) [Antiquities.]

Steward, Samuel. *The Caravaggio Shawl*. Boston: Alyson, 1989. (A gay trio—author, Gertrude Stein, and Alice B. Toklas—pursue French fraudsters.) [Art.]

Stewart, J.I.M. *see* Innes, Michael.

Stone, Zachary *see* Follett, Ken.

Swan, Thomas. *The Da Vinci Deception*. New York: Bantam Books, 1990. (The first case for Scotland Yard's art expert, DCI Jack Oxby involves lost Leonardo drawings and manuscripts.) [Art; Forgeries.]

Swan, Thomas. *The Cézanne Chase*. New York: Newmarket Press, 1997. (As he searches for clues to the shocking defacing of 26 extant Cézanne self portraits and a mysterious death that occurs just outside London, DCI Jack Oxby knows that these senseless losses are not isolated incidents. More masterpieces—and men—must be targeted for destruction.) [Art.]

Swan, Thomas. *The Final Fabergé*. New York: Newmarket, 1999. (Jack Oxby finds himself pitted against a cadre of bloodthirsty Russian thieves in the hunt for a priceless Fabergé egg commissioned by Rasputin.) [Antiquities.]

Takagi, Akimitsu. *The Tattoo Murder Case*. Japan: 1948. US ed.: New York: Soho Press, 1997. (In prewar Japan, the full body tattoo was a work of art. In 1947, someone is flaying victims to preserve these masterpieces.) [Art.]

Thomas, Ross *see* Bleeck, Oliver.

Tidmarsh, Neil. *Fear of the Dog*. London: Penguin Books, 1997. (A London art dealer clocks up success after success. So why does painter Nicholas Todd hate him so? Hate him enough to wish him dead … A debut set in the darkest depths of London's art world.) [Art.]

Tiffin, George. *Mercy Alexander*. London: Macmillan, 2001. (A former model who's moved into self portraits turns PI when her friend, a high class stripper, is, literally, killed for kicks….) [Art.]

Thurston, Carol. *The Eye of Horus*. New York: Morrow, 2000. (An Ancient Egyptian backstory follows medical illustrator Kate McKinnon's efforts to find the story in the mummy's bones. Sadly the author died in 2001.) [Antiquities.]

Tolliver, Hal and Mary. *Done in Blood Red Ochre*. Raleigh: Pentland, 2000. (A retiree gradually paints a picture of a killer after a well-known art dealer is murdered in his Oregon home.) [Art.]

Tremayne, Peter. *The Monk Who Vanished*. London: Headline, 1998). (Sister Fidelma and Saxon monk Eadulf investigate the disappearance of an aged monk along with a set of priceless holy relics of Ailbe, the saint who brought Christianity to the Irish kingdom of Muman.) [Antiquities.]

Ulmer, Mari. *Cart of Death (Carreta de la Muerte)*. Scottsdale: Poisoned Pen Press, 2001. (A gallery worker is kidnapped, someone is stealing priceless art from New Mexico's churches, and Taos's Christina Garcia y Grant wonders what's up with a local museum?) [Art.]

Valentine, Deborah. *A Collector of Photographs*. New York: Bantam Books, 1989. (San Francisco artist Roxanne Gautier's startling paintings of male prostitutes set off shock waves throughout the art world and her inner world, causing her husband to hire Kevin Bryce to probe Roxanne's life.) [Art.]

Valentine, Deborah. *Unorthodox Methods*. New York: Avon, 1991. (Sculptress Katharine Craig seldom gets to Lake Tahoe, but she arrives just in time to be swept into a whirl of parties, a series of art thefts, and the murder of a local collector found impaled upon a sculpture.) [Art.]

Van Adler, T. C. *St. Agatha's Breast*. New York: St. Martin's Press, 1999. (The theft of six of seven paintings of martyrs from an Italian monastery leads to murder and deceit; the seventh painting is discovered to have been signed by Nicolas Poussin.) [Art.]

Vreeland, Susan. *Girl in Hyacinth Blue*. Denver: MacMurray & Beck, 1999. (The history of a Vermeer painting unfolds backwards into time until the detection reaches the artist himself.). [Art.]

Vreeland, Susan. *The Passion of Artemesia*. New York: Viking, 2002. (Renaissance painter Artemesia Gentileschi accuses her mentor of rape, undergoes trial and torment and the clash of femininity with genius.) [Art.]

Wadley, Margot. *The Gripping Beast*. New York: St. Martin's Press, 2001. (American Isabel Garth visits her ancestor's Orkney Islands home where trouble awaits among local archaeological sites and a rumored Viking treasure.) [Antiquities.}

Watkins, Paul. *The Forger*. London: Faber, 1999. (An American Art student in 1939 Europe, in trouble after a dealer has passed off his works as Old Masters, is asked by the Resistance to forge some great paintings to pass off on Nazi looters.) [Art; Forgeries.]

Warga, Wade. *Fatal Impressions*. New York: Arbor House, 1989. (When fine lithographs are replaced with virtually indistinguishable reproductions, those plundered learn that forgery is not necessarily a bloodless crime; a Jeffrey Dean detection.) [Art.]

Waterhouse, Jane. *Graven Images*. New York: Putnam, 1995. (True crime writer Garner Quinn wrestles with the story of a famous sculptor and his unusual images). [Art.]

Watson, Clarissa. *The Fourth Stage of Gainsborough Brown*. New York: Atheneum, 1979. (The murder of an egoistic artist produces a plethora of suspects.) [Art.] See also *The Bishop in the Back Seat*. New York: Atheneum, 1980. [Art.]

Watson, Peter. *Crusade*. London: Hutchinson, 1990. (To raise money for a crusade against poverty and injustice, the Pope commissions a famous auction house to sell spectacular treasures of the Vatican....) [Art.]

Watson, Peter. *Landscape of Lies*. London: Hutchinson, 1989. (Tracing a Tudor treasure through symbolism in a painting.) [Art.]

Watson, Peter. *Stones of Treason*. London: Hutchinson, 1990. (The Curator of the Queen's Pictures mixes in forgery, theft, and espionage in a story taken in part from the Cambridge Five.) [Art.]

Watson, Peter. *The Stalin Picasso*. London: 1998. (Communists and cubists in artful combination.). [Art.]

Webb, Betty. *Desert Noir*. Scottsdale: Poisoned Pen Press, 2001. (The murder of an art gallery owner casts suspicion upon, among others, an Apache artist; not an art mystery *per se* but relevant.) [Art.]

Weber, Katharine. *The Music Lesson*. New York: Crown, 1999. (More of a psychological thriller than a mystery, this tale involves the heist of a Vermeer masterpiece.) [Art.]

West, Christopher. *Death of a Blue Lantern*. London: Harper Collins, 1994. (A Chinese policeman copes with the smuggling of valuable artifacts.) [Antiquities.]

Westlake, Donald. *Dancing Aztecs*. New York: Evans, 1976. (UK title: *A New York Dance*.) (A romp through ancient Mexico.) [Antiquities.]

White, Randy Wayne. *Ten Thousand Islands*. New York: Putnam, 2000. (Sanibel Island biologist Doc Ford is caught up in a storm surrounding an ancient amulet of the Calusa Indians which proves to have unusual attributes.) [Antiquities.]

Wiese, Jan. *Naked Madonna*. London: Harvill 1995. [Translated from Norwegian; original title: *Kvinnen som kledte seg naken for sin elskede*.] (A literary novel, not a mystery, recounts a tale of lust and superstition as a peaceful librarian murderer attributes his presence in his cell to the power of a Madonna and Child altarpiece from Perugia. Events of 1989 repeat a much earlier history, preserved in papers at the Vatican Library.) [Art.]

Willeford, Charles. *The Burnt Orange Heresy*. New York: Crown, 1971. (An art critic is commissioned to steal a example of the work of a reclusive artist.) [Art.]

Williams, David. *Treasure Preserved*. London: Collins, 1983; New York: St. Martin's, 1983. (The famous Round House standing in decrepit magnificence in a south coast seaside town will be flattened by a developer unless Lady Brassett intervenes. Alas she meets with a fatal accident. A Banker Mark Treasure mystery.) [Architecture.] See also *Treasure in Roubles* (London: Macmillan, 1986); *Treasure in Oxford* (London: Macmillan, 1988).

Williams, Jay *see* Delving, Michael.

Wilson, Derek. *The Triarchs*. London: Headline, 1994. (An art security expert gets his start tracing a Rubens while on a parallel track the history of the painting is examined; a Tim Lacy art world mystery.) [Art; Forgeries.]

Wilson, Derek. *The Dresden Text*. London: Headline, 1994. (Museum security is foiled by thieves of a valuable medieval ms.; a Tim Lacy art world mystery.) [Antiquities.]

Wilson, Derek. *The Camargue Brotherhood*. London: Headline, 1995. (A crusty Impressionist of the Camargue leaves a killer legacy for modern art experts; a Tim Lacy art world mystery.) [Art.]

Wilson, Derek. *The Borgia Chalice*. London: Headline, 1996. (About a poisonous legacy from the dog days of the Renaissance papacy; a Tim Lacy art world mystery.) [Antiquities.]

Wilson, Derek. *Cumberland's Cradle*. London: Headline, 1996. (Rocks you with instruments of torture; a Tim Lacy art world mystery.) [Antiquities.]

Wilson, James Norman. *The Dark Clue*. London: Faber & Faber, 2001. (A Victorian drama mixing up some characters from *The Woman in White* with the artist Turner.) [Art.]

Wishart, David. *The Lydian Baker*. London: Hodder & Stoughton, 1998. (When a 6th Century B.C. solid gold statue of The Baker appears for sale in the Athenian black market the Roman sleuth, Marcus Corvinus, finds himself embroiled in organized crime and a pawn among unscrupulous, rapacious collectors.) [Antiquities.]

(For reader-sleuths who are interested in investigating the nonfictional aspects of art crimes we have appended the following small section of suggested titles. We would like to thank Professor Larry Silver of Northwestern University and now of The University of Pennsylvania for his recommended readings on forgeries.)

Ashmole, Bernard. *Forgeries of Ancient Sculptures: Creation and Detection*. [Oxford]: Holywell Press, 1961.

Chesnoff, Richard Z. *Pack of Thieves: How Hitler and Europe Plundered the Jews and Committed the Greatest Theft in History*. Garden City, N.Y.: Doubleday. 1999.

Fake?: the Art of Deception [Catalog of an Exhibition at the British Museum] (edited by Mark Jones with Paul Craddock and Nicolas Barker). Berkeley: University of California Press, 1990.

Fakes and Forgeries: [Catalogue of an Exhibition] the Minneapolis Institute of Arts, July 11-September 29, 1973. [Minneapolis]: The Institute, c1973.

Feliciano, Hector. *The Lost Museum: the Nazi Conspiracy to Steal the World's Greatest Works of Art*. New York: Basic Books, 1997.

Fleming, Stuart J. *Authenticity in Art: the Scientific Detection of Forgery*. New York: Crane, Russack, 1976.

The Forger's Art: Forgery and the Philosophy of Art (edited by Denis Dutton). Berkeley: University of California Press, 1983.

Hebborn, Erci. *The Art Forger's Handbook*. New York: Overlook, 1997.

Honan, William H. *Treasure Hunt: a New York Times Reporter Tracks the Quedlinburg Hoard*. New York: Fromm International, 1997.

Hoving, Thomas. *False Impressions: the Hunt for Big-Time Art Fakes.* New York: Simon and Schuster, 1994.

Hoving, Thomas. *Making the Mummies Dance.* New York, Simon and Schuster, 1992.

Kurz, Otto. *Fakes.* New York: Dover, 1967.

Rendell, Kenneth W. *Forging History, the Detection of Fakes.* Norman: University of Oklahoma, 1994.

Savage, George. *Forgeries, Fakes and Reproductions: a Handbook for the Collector.* London: Barrie and Rockliff, 1963.

Sox, David. *Unmasking the Forger: the Dossena Deception.* New York: Universe Books, 1988.

Von Bothmer, Dietrich and Noble, Joseph. *An Inquiry into the Forgery of Etruscan Terracotta Warriors at the Metropolitan Museum of Art.* New York: Metropolitan Museum of Art, 1961.

Watson, Peter. *The Caravaggio Conspiracy: How Five Art Dealers, Four Policemen, Three Picture Restorers, Two Auction Houses, and a Journalist Plotted to Recover Some of the World's Most Beautiful Stolen Paintings.* Garden City, N.Y.: Doubleday. 1984. (UK title: *Double-Dealer.*)

Watson, Peter. *Sotheby's: The Inside Story.* London: Bloomsbury, 1997.

Louis Silverstein

1938-2001

Biography

Endowed with a love of books, especially mysteries, since earliest childhood, Louis H. Silverstein served as a librarian at Yale University for 33 years in various technical services and special collections positions. His last position was as Curator of Yale's Arts of the Book Collection where he had a particular interest in the modern book arts, working with various artists and their agents. He has served as a consultant to the Phoenix Public Library, helping to build a collection of artists' books there. He has done editing, indexing, and co-authored "Lincoln Kirstein: The Published Writings, 1922-1927: A First Bibliography" (1978).

He also considered himself to be a literary anthropologist specializing in H.D. (Hilda Doolittle) and her circle and had published articles on H.D., several of which are available through the World Wide Web. Louis' life is memorialized at www.louishenrysilverstein.com.

To receive a free catalog of other Poisoned Pen Press titles, please contact us in one of the following ways:

Phone: 1-800-421-3976
Facsimile: 1-480-949-1707
Email: info@poisonedpenpress.com
Website: www.poisonedpenpress.com

Poisoned Pen Press
6962 E. First Ave. Ste 103
Scottsdale, AZ 85251

Printed in the United States
3387